Love-40

KU-171-814

Also by Anna Cheska

Moving to the Country
Drop Dead Gorgeous

00 2122833 X 5E

2

16
'012

Love-40

Anna Cheska

SEFTON LIBRARY SERVICES	
002122833	
H J	09/04/2002
F	£18.99
F	

PIATKUS

Visit the Piatkus website!

Piatkus publishes a wide range of exciting fiction and non-fiction, including books on health, mind body & spirit, sex, self-help, cookery, biography and the paranormal. If you want to:

- read descriptions of our popular titles
- buy our books over the Internet
- take advantage of our special offers
- enter our monthly competition
- learn more about your favourite Piatkus authors

visit our website at:

www.piatkus.co.uk

All the characters in this book are fictitious and any resemblance to real persons, living or dead, is entirely coincidental.

Copyright © 2002 by Anna Cheska

First published in Great Britain in 2002 by
Judy Piatkus (Publishers) Ltd of
5 Windmill Street, London W1T 2JA
email: info@piatkus.co.uk

The moral right of the author has been asserted

A catalogue record for this book is available from the British Library

ISBN 0 7499 0606 5

Typeset in Bembo by Palimpsest Book Production Limited,
Polmont, Stirlingshire
Printed and bound in Great Britain by
Mackays of Chatham Ltd, Chatham, Kent

For Rob

As always, thanks to my family for being there. To my Mum and Dad for their support, to Luke for helping to make me computer literate, and to my beautiful daughters Alexa and Anna.

Thanks also to all those who helped me write this book – though you might not have known it at the time! In particular, Jeannette, Peter and David for the original tennis inspiration and the American tournament. And to the Friday night tennis group at Davison – coach Graham, Gill, Pat, Sue et al for making me an honorary 'offshoot' of your group. I shall never forget *chip and charge*, though doubt whether I shall ever do it . . . Thanks also to Graham Baughan at West Worthing Tennis Club for information about tennis clubs – and I would like to stress at this point that the club in *Love-40* bears no relation whatever to West Worthing (apart from the beautiful blue courts!).

Special thanks must go to the marvellously successful John Otway, for agreeing to give away elements of his stage act to Michael in *Love-40*. Without Otway, Michael would never have been born. And here's hoping that he gets the hit he wants for his 50th birthday.

And to Rob Simons for all his help and support – not least his advice on aspects of musical performance and the music business.

Finally, I should like to thank Teresa Chris for being a wonderful agent and Judy, Gillian, Jana, Russell and all at Piatkus Books for being such a pleasure to work with.

Be wise with speed;
A fool at forty is a fool indeed.

Edward Young 1683–1765: *The Love of Fame.*

Love is a smoke made with the fume of sighs,
Being purged, a fire sparkling in lovers' eyes,
Being vexed, a sea nourished with lovers' tears.
What is it else? A madness most discreet,
A choking gall and a preserving sweet.

William Shakespeare 1564–1616: *Romeo and Juliet*

Anyone for tennis?

A typical line in a drawing room comedy

Chapter 1

Liam was scowling and so Suzi knew something was up. Even before her brother buried a simple backhand volley into the net.

Something . . . But how big a something?

Uh huh. She winced as he let rip his first serve to the woman who was supposed to be the love of his life. A big something.

Estelle dodged neatly. Her light toss of the head and deprecatory shrug as she got back into position, spoke volumes.

Uh huh. Suzi sighed. A big something closely connected to Estelle.

'Shit,' Liam breathed, thrashing the second serve into the tram lines.

'Love fifteen,' chirped Michael, Estelle's tennis partner for the afternoon and Suzi's lover for rather longer than that.

'Fuck it,' said Liam, glowering across the net at him.

Mixed doubles, Suzi reflected, never used to be such a dangerous game. She felt a bit of sunshine being taken out of her day. It wasn't fair, damn it. And she wasn't sure if she felt safer being on Liam's side or not. Safer still probably, to be in Chestnut Grove's utterly gorgeous, though somewhat battered conservatory, sipping

1

a well-earned G & T. And a heck of a lot more relaxing. Where had she gone wrong?

She let her gaze wander past the men's doubles being played on the next court, towards the clubhouse beyond; a building made of large honey-coloured bricks – Purbeck stone. The glass conservatory attached to the front of the building looked particularly inviting.

And after the G & T? Would she be expected to sort out Liam and Estelle's latest humdinger from hell? She wasn't sure she could face it. Because maybe she was fed up with being stuck in the middle of these two. Maybe it was time to duck out.

In the meanwhile, it was more a matter of ducking in order to avoid the firing line. Help. Suzi glanced a warning at Michael, who was very sweet but probably had no idea what was going on, poor lamb.

Michael winked back at her. Ignorance is bliss, Suzi thought, even when you're forty years old and should know better. But then, Michael hadn't had the dubious benefit of growing up with Liam, she reminded herself. He imagined this was just a jolly game of tennis amongst friends. The man knew nothing.

Still, the fierceness of the next serve took even Suzi by surprise. She blinked into the sun as the ball screamed past her. While Michael – all sticky-out arms and long, pale legs, in baggy white shorts and Elvis Costello T-shirt – swung a wild forehand and missed the ball completely. Though he'd willingly made up the four since becoming a regular weekend visitor to Pridehaven, Michael and tennis courts weren't a match made in heaven. Suzi watched him sweep the fingers of his free hand through his thinning fair hair in a gesture of defeat.

'Serve,' he conceded graciously. 'Didn't even see it.'

Estelle twirled her racket wearily. 'I'm not surprised.'

'Well played!' Suzi went for enthusiasm. She was beginning to feel desperate. This was their first game for several weeks, since a grey January and February had drifted into March, and it had seemed almost impossible to coincide the free time of all four of them with the infrequent breaking of murky cloud cover. But today – apart from being a Sunday, so the antique shop Suzi ran with Estelle was closed, Liam was not teaching and Michael had not yet returned to Fareham – there had been a definite promise of spring in the blue and white lunchtime sky. Heat, even.

And the courts of Chestnut Grove Tennis Club – four grass and four green hard courts – seemed to beckon. Spring, Suzi thought, was summed up by the gently dappled sunlight that crept through the leaves of the ancient horse-chestnut trees bordering the driveway that had given the club its name. Spring was the first time you got to play on the bouncy grass turf, though it was unusual, she knew, for the courts to be ready this early in the season. They had to be fertilised, rolled, marked out and the weather had to be kind. Suzi loved this place with a fierce passion. She turned her face upwards to the sun, felt the warmth, smelled the fragrance of freshly mown grass, heard the thwack of racket strings on slightly damp yellow tennis balls.

But spring, it seemed, had not brought any warmth to the relationship of her brother and Estelle. It had brought heat of a very different kind.

'Fifteen all,' Liam said in a crisp tone, eyeing Estelle with hostility. 'Ready?'

'And waiting,' Estelle called back, smoothing one hand along the length of her lycra shorts and bending to rub a grass stain from her white trainers. 'Do your worst.'

This time at least Liam's serve dipped in, producing a sweeping forehand drive from Estelle that Suzi managed to reach with an athletic leap to her left and a slightly scary skid across the grass in the tram lines. She hobbled back into position, reminding herself to do an extra ten minutes of yoga tonight.

She wasn't exactly in the first hot flush of youth (the big four oh was looming round the corner and would belong to her body and soul before Christmas) so maybe her days of skidding across grass tennis courts were numbered. She didn't want to have hip replacement surgery at her age.

Meanwhile, the G & T in the sunny conservatory became an even pleasanter prospect. But she felt somehow, that Liam was depending on her. And how could she let him down?

Michael just got to the next serve, but Suzi intercepted and put it past him. That was the great thing about grass. The serve/volleyer would always win through in the end.

'Good girl, Suze.' Liam grinned as he squinted into the sun to serve. 'Now we've got 'em.'

And some people thought tennis was a game? Suzi pulled in her pelvic floor and raced to retrieve what Estelle had probably assumed to be an outright winner of a return, slamming it across court with her two-handed backhand. Being small, she needed such techniques to match the power of the others. But had anyone ever proved that strenuous exercise was actually good for you, she wondered. Didn't it have side effects like exhaustion, strokes and heart attacks?

The shot was well placed, the ball hardly seemed to bounce at all and Estelle didn't even bother to run for it. 'Game,' she said in a bored voice. 'As per.'

'And set, I think,' Liam said, shooting her one of his hyena-smiles. 'Change partners?'

Here we go, thought Suzi. Trouble.

'Maybe . . .' Estelle began, as they gathered by the net, '. . . we need some *new* partners.' She adjusted the strap of her black vest-top and began rubbing suntan oil into her pale skin. It might be only

March, but Estelle was always prepared and she wouldn't burn for anyone. 'Completely new partners,' she reiterated.

Liam's plastic bottle of mineral water bounced on to the grass, Michael said, 'whoopsie, mate,' as he scooped it back up for him, and Suzi went on red alert. 'How d'you mean?'

'New blood,' Estelle elaborated. 'From the club.' With a wave towards CG's clubhouse, she proceeded to untie her pony tail and shake out the mass of dark red hair, before smoothing it from forehead to nape with one hand. This gesture held what was perhaps an unconscious sensuality, but Suzi saw Liam look sharply away, focusing his attention on the grip of his racket, which was worn and beginning to fray.

'But we're a foursome,' Suzi said, just as Liam chimed in with, 'Why the hell not? Suits me.'

Michael looked from one to another of them, blissfully unaware. 'What's the big deal?' he asked.

Estelle made a little pout. 'These two have won every match so far,' she said. 'It was a challenge to start with, but . . .' she fixed Liam with an accusing eye '. . . it gets boring after a while.'

To what degree, Suzi wondered, was Estelle referring to tennis? There were plenty of other club players, and some of the courts were also used by Chestnut Grove Youth Club, which had existed even before the tennis club had grown up by its side. It was the youth club, many of them felt, that stopped the tennis club from becoming too elitist. For tradition was all very well, but any club that didn't accept change, youth and evolution was likely, Suzi thought, to die. The youth club kept the tennis club on its toes; prevented the old-school blazer brigade from taking over and elbowing them out.

But if they were to change partners, who out of their foursome, Suzi asked herself, would be left out? And surely Estelle wouldn't *leave* Liam – not after all this time?

'Suze and I play well together,' Liam said, flinging a protective arm around her as if Estelle's criticism had been directed at her alone. 'We've got complementary games. We understand each other.'

Estelle pulled a face, but Suzi knew it was true. Brothers and sisters shared a special understanding, she supposed. And with their background none more so than they. But it wasn't easy looking out for Liam's interests when his girlfriend happened to be Suzi's business partner. And Suzi couldn't escape the feeling that this wasn't one of Liam and Estelle's regular sort of barneys. There was a bleakness in Liam's green eyes that worried her. And an indifference in Estelle that was striking warning chords in Suzi's heart.

For they belonged together, didn't they? Not just Liam and Estelle but Suzi too. A threesome begun when they were only nine and ten years old. She glanced across at Michael and gave her lover a reassuring smile. But it was a threesome that would always make it hard to admit another.

In the clubhouse afterwards, Suzi, Estelle and Liam made for the conservatory, while Michael went to the bar. Various club members had been drawn out of hibernation, Suzi observed, by the unusual combination of weekend and sunshine, and were dotted around the bar, clubhouse and conservatory, dressed mostly in shorts and sports shirts, rackets and kit bags at their feet, though a few hadn't yet taken off their tracksuits to bare winter-white legs to the world. The place was alive and buzzing with conversation, with the promise of months of tennis ahead, of cool beers after long evening games, of virtuous thirty-, forty-, fifty- and sixty-somethings saying to their doctors – *yes, I get plenty of exercise. Tennis, you know.*

Suzi spotted Erica Raddle and her sidekick Deirdre Piston sitting head to head at a far table by the bar. Deirdre was looking flustered

– making notes with one hand, patting another stray and rebellious fluffy hair back into her perm with the other. Whilst Erica was laying down her law, her own crowning glory cut into a short, no-nonsense style that wouldn't dare to rebel.

As she threw down her sports bag and lowered herself gingerly into one of Chestnut Grove's battered wicker chairs – whose faded floral cushion bore the imprint of many other behinds – Suzi wondered idly what great plan they were hatching. For Erica had what she called *ambitions* for CG's. And they were likely to be controversial ones.

Suzi had to admit, though, that the place could do with some tarting up. In the clubhouse itself, the Formica counter and lurid fluorescent lighting were about as intimate as a DHSS office. But the conservatory was something else again – a wonderful place to relax in. Even after this afternoon's fiasco, five minutes in here restored that elusive equilibrium, gave Suzi a sense of blissful tranquillity.

Probably an illusion, she thought, trying not to look at Liam or Estelle, stretching out instead in her creaky wicker chair, surveying the view. And it was one of the best – the grass tennis courts alongside, squared off by yew hedges that could, admittedly, do with a trim; green hard courts beyond and down a few steps, and beyond that, as the hill dipped, the village of Pridehaven, the river Pride itself which wound past her own little cottage, and eventually the sandstone cliffs and the sea. But it was an illusion that she'd enjoy for now. And a perfect place to get a drink at the end of play – or in this case, battle.

She surveyed the main contestants. Estelle was staring out of the window towards the grass courts where two women of indeterminate age were slogging it out. Liam was staring in the opposite direction, towards the bar. Silence.

Suzi decided on jolly. 'What about this grand opening tomorrow, then?'

More silence.

Estelle absent-mindedly stroked a waxy leaf of the small lemon tree in the corner behind her. Suzi had never actually seen a lemon on it and as far as she knew, she was the only person who ever watered the plant. But she liked the fact that it – along with the asparagus fern, broad-leaved palm and variegated ficus – was here. And she liked to imagine the scent of lemon too, adding a Mediterranean feel to the place.

'What d'you reckon it'll be?'

Even more silence.

'A convenience store? Toys? A pound shop?' New tenants had moved in next door to Secrets In The Attic, Estelle and Suzi's antique shop, but so far they'd refused to reveal the nature of their trade. It was driving Suzi and Estelle mad with curiosity. Throughout February, lorries had unloaded mysterious contents under the cover of late afternoon winter darkness, and the front window had remained curtained and black.

Estelle had tried a variety of tactics, such as loitering in their own shop doorway during delivery times, engaging the owners, Stan and Terry, in deceptively desultory conversations, even making a pot of tea and whipping up a chocolate sponge in an effort to gain entry and information. But they had no more idea now, the day before the opening, just what the mystery was all about.

'A hairdresser's?' Suzi said desperately, glancing down at the blue and white tiled floor for inspiration. Someone had thrown a raffle ticket under the glass-topped table. 'A bookie's?'

The silence was so palpable, Suzi almost felt she could gather it in her arms, take it home for a quick spin through the tumbledryer and give it back to them as freshly laundered conversation. 'A sex shop?' she said.

'Sounds good to me.' Michael returned with the drinks, Suzi was aware of the revolving door doing its thing, and then the atmosphere in the clubhouse changed radically as Amanda Lake walked in.

The dial moved to cold for most of the women and hot for all of the men. Amanda Lake, tall, blonde and willowy in golden tan and immaculate tennis whites. Suzi groaned. Amanda Lake, envied by women, lusted after by men. Amanda was all they needed now to turn a bad afternoon into disaster. She grabbed her G & T, closed her eyes, made a wish.

'Amanda! Coo-eee! How lovely to see you!' Erica rose from her chair and hot-footed it to the bar counter as fast as her large bosom would allow. 'And how is that *delectable* father of yours?'

Wish not granted. Amanda was still standing there.

Liam tore his hands through his dark curls, making them wilder than ever. 'Parasites,' he muttered.

'Amanda or her father?' Estelle enquired sweetly. 'At least her father has an estate to run. What does Amanda do to justify a place in the world?'

'Used to be a model, didn't she?' Michael leaned forward confidingly. 'Wonder why she chucked it in.'

Estelle raised an eyebrow. 'When a woman gets to a certain age . . .' She let the words hang.

Miaow. Suzi grinned. In fact, Estelle, at thirty-nine, was the older of the two, and it was unlike her to get her claws out. But who could resist bitching about someone so rich, gorgeous and upper class? And Suzi had to admit that Amanda deserved it, being the babe who had everything – with knobs on. They were all staring at her through the open double doors. But Liam's mouth was practically gaping open. Suzi glared at him. How could he be so *obvious*?

'Ping pong,' Erica was saying, waving red-varnished fingernails

9

towards the games room of the youth club next door. Her chest heaved within the white Aertex tennis shirt she wore. 'What do you think, Amanda . . . of a restaurant?'

'A restaurant?' Amanda's tone – always lazy, rarely expressive – indicated precisely how she felt. Bored. She flicked a strand of fine blonde hair from her face and gave Erica a cool once-over.

'An exclusive one, of course,' Erica elaborated, lips twitching to reveal a brief flash of horsy teeth, complete with smear of crimson lipstick. 'Sushi perhaps?'

'What the bloody hell's sushi?' Liam yelled, jumping to his feet and standing in the doorway like a man possessed.

It was at times like these, Suzi thought, as she tried to cringe away out of sight, that her brother revealed their Irish ancestry. Their mother had loved their father to distraction – had lived in her own kind of lost world when he died. But by God, she'd had a temper the few times Suzi had seen her let rip. And she'd passed it on to her son, who tended to make use of it rather more often.

'And where would the kids play table tennis?' Liam went on. 'And pool?'

'Liam . . .' Erica, who had clearly forgotten Liam's role as youth club co-ordinator, not to mention his Socialist principles, blinked her sparse eyelashes. 'It's only at the ideas stage. It would have to go to committee –'

'Outside, on the *barbecue* area perhaps?' His voice dripped sarcasm.

Suzi exchanged a glance with Michael, who shrugged and drained his glass in response. But what did she expect? Liam's excesses, Liam's views and the propensity with which he aired them, were not Michael's problem, any more than they should be Suzi's. Though they were. They always had been and probably always would be. Because whatever his faults, Suzi thought, clenching both knuckles tight, at least he wouldn't allow the tennis club to elbow the youth club out of existence. At least he still cared enough to get angry.

'Of course not, Liam.' Erica adopted a patronising tone. 'The barbecue *patio* would be most inappropriate. Fire risk, you know.'

'You take the games room away from the kids over my dead body,' said Liam, crashing his fist down on the bar counter.

Amanda laid a hand on his arm. 'Liam's absolutely right,' she said, with the authority of a woman who has always got her own way. 'It's a crap idea, Erica. CG's belongs to the kids too. It always has.'

Liam looked like a cat who'd won a mouse a day for the next six months. Suzi hoped Estelle hadn't noticed, but thought it unlikely.

Erica sniffed. 'We'll see what the committee thinks,' she muttered darkly.

'I know what *Daddy* will think.' Amanda's hand slipped down to cover Liam's. 'And presumably it would be his money that would be paying for it.'

Take it away, thought Suzi. C'mon, Liam. Think daddy's money. Just take your hand away.

'Not at all. I wouldn't dream . . .' Erica spluttered, looking as if nightmares would be nearer the mark, '. . . other ways of raising money,' she continued unintelligibly, her colour rising beneath the rose-pink of her foundation. 'Higher subscription fees,' she concluded.

'If you think we'll agree to higher fees,' Liam began, 'then . . . then . . .'

Amanda appeared to be absent-mindedly stroking Liam's thumb with her forefinger. Suzi downed the remainder of her gin and tonic and wondered how she could create a diversion. A quick river dance on the table top? Grab Michael's hand and fake an orgasm?

'Daddy won't support a restaurant,' Amanda informed them. 'Not at the expense of the games room. Daddy . . .' she squeezed Liam's hand '. . . is pro youth.'

'Good old daddy.' Estelle rose from her chair. 'So much for parasites, eh, Suzi?'

'Where are you going?' Suzi couldn't believe that Liam was just standing there. Just standing there, gazing at Amanda like a lovesick teenager. What was the matter with him? She looked helplessly at Estelle.

'Home. You can tell Liam I'll see him there.' Estelle grabbed her multi-coloured rucksack. 'Although to tell you the truth, Suzi,' she went on, 'I'm not altogether sure it'll be home much longer.'

Chapter 2

Not looking where she was going as she spun through the revolving doors of CGs, and with her mind muttering, *I should have left him years ago*, Estelle bumped slap-crash into Nick Rossi.

'Hey!' The tennis balls he was carrying spilled to the ground, promptly sprang out of their neat, plastic packaging and began skipping, bumpity-bump down the steps.

'Sorry.' Estelle blushed and quickly bent to retrieve the nearest one. 'I was miles away.'

'Anywhere interesting?' Nick Rossi smiled that easy, sensual smile of his and put a hand on her shoulder.

'Not really.' Like Amanda Lake, Estelle thought grimly, feeling the warmth and oh-so-slight pressure of it. He seemed to think a beautiful body and female admiration entitled him to intimate contact with whomever, wherever, whenever. Like an advert for Martini, Estelle thought.

'Let me,' he said, still smiling.

Let him what? Estelle knew herself to be at a disadvantage but found herself smiling back anyway. Well honestly, who could resist? Nick was in his early thirties, unmarried, tall, dark blond and hunky. He was also the best player CG's had to offer. Estelle wondered why he came here. Because the club was so traditionally English? Because he liked playing on grass? Because he liked playing with Amanda Lake? They weren't exactly an item, but you'd have to be insensitive as stone not to catch that chemistry zinging between them. But for some reason, it had apparently gone no further than chemistry.

'Playing today?' she asked. Stupid. Why else would he and his tennis gear be here? She straightened up and noticed with relief that his eyes were set just a little too close together. Thank heavens for imperfections. She'd have to take a closer look at Amanda next time their paths crossed.

He nodded, his hand staying right where it was. 'Mixed. Got to keep in practice for the American tournament.' Those eyes were hazel with green and orange circles around the iris, she registered, the close proximity making her nervous. 'Are you entering?'

Estelle repressed a shiver. 'I certainly am,' she decided on the spot, though she had told Liam earlier today that he and the American tournament could go and fornicate with themselves.

Nick smiled again – soft, like a caress. 'Then perhaps we'll be playing together once or twice.' He made the proposition sound erotic. 'That would be fun, don't you think?'

Better than playing with Liam at any rate, Estelle thought. With Liam, win or lose, she'd be beaten into a mental and emotional pulp. 'Terrific fun,' she purred back, indicating with a slight raise of one eyebrow that she knew what game he was playing (and it wasn't tennis) that she could play too, and that her heart would not be bruised by the casual flirting of Nick Rossi. He was several years younger than she. And unspeakably sexy. So she was flattered – but not convinced.

He acknowledged all this with a flicker of respect in those gorgeous hazel eyes and let his hand slip from her shoulder at last. 'Ciao,' he murmured.

'Ciao,' she tossed back at him, turning away with a graceful sweep of the shoulders, a flounce of her dark red hair and, damn it, a stumble as she tripped over one of the tennis balls.

'I should have left him years ago.' And this time she said it out loud as she ran down the steps and into the late afternoon sunshine. Just think what fun she could have had with all the Nick Rossis of this world.

Michael watched Suzi watching Liam and wondered when he should tell her his news. Would she be pleased? He examined the gamine face for clues. Imagined himself sliding a finger against the soft hollow of her cheek, down, down, into the cleft of the narrow chin. He hoped she'd be pleased, though he couldn't be sure. He'd known Suzi Nichols for over a year, been seeing her regularly for twelve months, staying weekends for most of that time. And yet, he didn't know her – not in any way that would make her remotely predictable. Perhaps that was what made her, he thought, so hard to resist.

'Another?' he asked her, waggling his empty glass to get her attention.

She debated this, head on one side, eyes flicking towards Liam and Amanda Lake. Wondering if her services would be required, he guessed, also wondering how much he minded. It was a bit like loving a woman already married to another man, he thought. Knowing there was part of her that would always be attached elsewhere. Worse, since she and Liam were unlikely to ever divorce. Trying to catch hold of what was tantalisingly out of reach could make a guy blind to limitations. Did they have limitations? He caught Suzi's eye. Whatever, it was bloody frustrating – feeling you were second best.

'What time have you got to get back to Fareham?' Suzi asked, instead of answering the question. 'Do you want to eat first?'

He captured her small hand in his. 'I'd like to take a shower first,' he said meaningfully. 'And then eat.'

Suzi's answering squeeze told him he had her undivided attention for the first time that afternoon. 'And then . . . ?' she teased.

He might tell her his news . . . 'I'll go back to Fareham.' He released her hand again and pushed his glass aside. 'So shall we hit the road?'

Once again, Suzi's glance shifted to the Formica bar. Michael watched Nick Rossi stride in, place himself firmly between Liam and Amanda, plant a kiss on each of her golden cheeks.

Suzi seemed to come to a decision. 'Let's,' she agreed. 'Will you miss me next week, Michael?'

'So much, that . . .' Michael almost told her. It was on the tip of his tongue, but he bit it back at her look of surprise. *Will you miss me*, was his cue to say, *you bet*, followed by her, *how much*, then, *this much*, a dialogue of foreplay that invariably led to making love. Suzi, he sensed, was unsettled by his unfinished variation on their theme.

So, 'I'll show you how much,' he whispered into her cropped dark hair, as he leaned forward to get to his feet. She smelled of tennis after-glow, her Suzi-smell, for she never bothered with perfume, and the scent of something vaguely animal that probably lived at her riverbank cottage along with the rest of the menagerie. It was a comforting fragrance. Comforting and familiar.

Yes, he'd miss her and he'd miss Pridehaven. The truth was, that Michael had never much liked Fareham, and neither did he enjoy working as a pharmaceutical assistant in a factory that belched out fumes unconvincingly declared harmless to the atmosphere.

His fault, he knew. When he'd made the decision ten years ago, to turn his hobby of building and repairing sound systems into an up and running business, he had failed to research the project thoroughly enough. Suffused with energy – Michael always was – he had created ambitious plans, advertised everywhere he could think of, ignored his budget, re-mortgaged his house, launched himself into the business without so much as a look over his shoulder.

Michael frowned his perplexed frown. He still wasn't sure how it had happened. It might have been the outlay – of business premises, brochures, advertising. It might have been the perfectionism and Michael's seeming inability to quote the correct price for a job. He knew his faults. But whatever it was, he had lost virtually the lot, lucky, he supposed, that he had not got further into debt, that he had escaped relatively unscathed from a venture that had left him living in a rented furnished flat in Fareham, working in a factory that he loathed.

What Michael really wanted was very different. He wanted to be a musician – a successful musician, the kind who received critical acclaim rather than hero worship (at forty he felt too old for hero worship, pleasant though it might be in small doses). And so, during every white-coated, nine to five day that led inexorably into another just the same, he dreamed of himself on stage. Sometimes in a modest venue, but more often playing Earls Court, where he had once seen the Rolling Stones. The image of Mick Jagger swinging on a rope down from a platform suspended high in the air on to centre stage, was one of his treasured memories.

And when he wasn't enjoying this pleasant fantasy, for Michael could swing on a rope as easily as the next man, he was waiting for Friday nights and thinking of Suzi Nichols.

He waved goodbye to Liam and followed her out of CG's club-house. Suzi Nichols dressed not in blue joggers and sweatshirt, but in a power suit with the kind of short black skirt Suzi never wore, in black stockings and suspenders that would probably compromise all her feminist principles, with pouting lips that whispered sweet nothings – not to Liam, but only and always for Michael alone.

★　　★　　★

Estelle's feet were hot in her trainers, so when she got to the riverbank, she tugged them off, digging deep into her multi-coloured rucksack for her flat strappy leather sandals. At the same time, she pulled out an indigo wrap-around skirt and wound it round her waist, conscious of her pale legs in lycra shorts – OK on the tennis court, but not so appropriate to Pridehaven on a late Sunday afternoon in March. And it was getting chilly . . . She pulled on her sweater and observed the clouds, gathering quickly, as though suddenly realising it was not summer, no, not even spring, and that they should never have left the sky alone in the first place because people would assume too much.

Estelle leaned on the parapet of the blue bridge over the River Pride. She loved this narrow river that wound its way from the Dorset hills in the north, through the town itself, past Suzi's riverbank cottage to the south and down to the tiny harbour with its sheltered, shingle bay and sandstone rocks not quite imposing enough or pretty enough to attract hordes of tourists to Pridehaven in the summer. Thank God, Estelle thought. She loved the river, despite – or maybe because of – what it had done to her.

To stare into the water was a therapy, she told herself, since water, and especially moving water, water that dragged along bits of twigs, reed and bulrushes, the seeds and dying flowers from wilting plants of the riverbank, made her remember too much. It would be easier, of course, not to recall events from thirty-five years ago, if that were possible. Memory played tricks – one could never be sure how experiences had been trimmed or frilled by time and other people's voices. But some internal spectator told her, *to be strong you must remember, deal with, resolve.* And so Estelle would often stand here at the bridge, gripping this blue parapet with white knuckles, staring down at the River Pride. Like a madwoman, she thought.

She was almost forty. At least half her life had gone and what did she have? A career that had only just stuttered into being. No children, maybe no man, certainly no mother. Perhaps she was wrong to come here to the bridge. Perhaps she should have moved away years ago. Why hadn't she?

The water was hypnotic and Estelle swayed slightly. Liam, she thought. Liam was the answer to that, just as he was the answer to most things. Except contentment, she reminded herself, watching a family of sleek, caramel and green ducks as they scooted along the surface of the water, each staring straight ahead, as focused on their journey as Estelle herself was not.

How could you be contented, living with a man who at any moment might move on to . . . she frowned, to something more interesting? A man you could never feel secure with.

Estelle released her hold of the parapet, flexing her fingers with some surprise at their stiffness. She and Liam had always fought. They pitted their strengths against each other rather than combining them; it was one of the things, she knew, that had kept them together so long. That and . . . she trailed her hand along the railing . . . the fact that they had always seemed to belong together. That there had never been – for either of them – another.

Apart, of course, from Suzi, Estelle thought wryly as she gathered up her rucksack and finally crossed to the other side of the river. Suzi was always there, had always been there, had been there even before Liam, when they had first become friends.

Estelle's steps quickened as she thought of those days, a tentative friendship begun by a teacher at her new school. 'Suzi will look after you. She's very kind.' The sympathy in the teacher's eyes, in all their eyes.

'You can come back to my house for tea,' Suzi had told her that first day. 'If your auntie will let you.'

And Estelle had shrugged, knowing that Auntie Mo, immersed

in the romantic short stories she wrote for women's magazines, kind but never in a million years maternal, would probably not even notice she'd gone. 'Won't your mum mind?' she had asked Suzi.

'Course not.' Suzi was clear on this point. 'We do what we want, Liam and me. Mum never minds.'

And it had been easy, Estelle reflected now, to slip into the routine that was so far from what she had always understood to be routine, at the Nichols'. Liam and Suzi's father had died years before, which gave them some common ground, and their mother – though clearly loving her children with intensity – still seemed somewhat lost without him.

Liam and Suzi, Estelle soon realised, had taken advantage of this fact, taken advantage of the independence their mother had inadvertently offered them. Liam, though (who had seemed to Estelle at the time to be scarily sure of himself), had taken a while to accept her. Only Suzi's stubborn insistence that Estelle be included in every game, every outing, every treat and as time went by, every secret, had made him tolerate her.

They had fought even then, she recalled, as she opened the church gate and slipped through to the graveyard. Once Estelle had found her feet. Fought and then loved and fought some more.

Once, near their beginning, they had planned to move away from here – away from the ties of childhood, teenage secrets, Estelle's vague memory of her mother's death. And yes . . . she passed by the flint walls of the church, glancing up at the stained-glass window depicting Jesus and the twelve disciples. Away even from Suzi too.

But they never had. Slowly, she left the graveyard behind, crossed North Street and headed for the house she loosely called home. Liam said Suzi would never leave Pridehaven, but sometimes Estelle wondered if it was Liam who was attached by some invisible umbilical cord, to the town of his childhood. For here he was, now teaching in the very school he had attended himself, the school his father too had once taught in, running the youth club where he had once played table tennis, taking Sunday afternoon hikes in the woods to the west of the river Pride, where all three of them had once played, and where she and Liam had first . . . she closed her eyes. First touched one another's naked bodies.

Oh yes, she thought, as she slotted her key in the lock of the huge Victorian building that housed three flats, including the one right at the top that Liam had first fallen in love with as a student, there were a hell of a lot of memories in those woods.

She took the stairs in twos; the first carpeted flight gave way to bare floorboard by the time she reached the garret, as Liam affectionately referred to it. He had rented it as soon as he left college and returned to Pridehaven to live, bought it as soon as his salary allowed him to. Estelle – who had stayed in Pridehaven while he did his teacher training, toyed with various career opportunities, ended up working as a clerical officer with the local water authority, where she'd progressed (though she sometimes wondered if that was the right word) into the customer complaints department – had moved in very soon after.

She used her second key to let herself in.

But it had remained Liam's garret, she reminded herself as she dumped her rucksack in the hall and went through to the galley kitchen. It had always been his choice.

There was some white wine in the fridge, a half-decent Bordeaux, so she poured herself a generous glass, wandered into the living room and surveyed its contents as if seeing it for the first time. If she left, she wanted it inscribed on her memory, just as it was at this moment.

To one side was a chair in front of a pine table, whose surface was hidden by the papers, books, exercise jotters and pens of Liam

Nichols, teacher and amateur poet. And if you swung the chair to the right, you would be facing a computer screen and keyboard; pencils, rubbers, elastic bands and Tippex spilling out of desk tidies – or un-tidies in Liam's case. Above were bookshelves stacked with poetry, books on education, Socialist essays, child psychology, you name it . . .

But Liam's influence didn't stop there. Estelle's critical gaze roved on, committing it to memory. On the floor by an armchair was a tray containing the remains of his breakfast, the dregs of a strong Italian coffee in a brown mug, the flaky crumbs of a croissant and a dollop of strawberry jam. His videos were piled haphazardly by the TV, his cassettes and CDs dominated the shelf space above the hi-fi, a pair of his jeans sprawled across the sofa, waiting to be ironed. And most disturbing of all, a Fauve print on the far wall seemed to watch Estelle's every move.

This wasn't home, Estelle thought to herself. This was Liam's home. Why, she wondered, had she brought so little of herself to this place in so many years? Had she known, all the time, that she wouldn't stay?

Out of the window she could see the car park at the back, her own racing-green Mini Mayfair snug in the far corner. Liam had taken them to CG's in his car. Estelle didn't care – she had relished the walk home, needed the thinking time.

CG's . . . She took a few paces further into the room and sipped the Bordeaux. It wasn't Amanda Lake she minded – the flirting, the deep intensity which Liam could so effortlessly turn on for anyone, from a child who'd written a beautiful poem to a socialite at the tennis club whom he really should despise. No, it was the childishness of it, Estelle thought, looking round the room from her new vantage point, feeling the coolness of the wine in her throat. The unquestionably self-centred aspect of Liam was what got to her. It was always *his* needs, and she, like Suzi, had always pandered to them.

She drained her glass and placed it purposefully on Liam's discarded breakfast tray. Always, she thought, but not any more.

Chapter 3

At 8.30 on the following cloudy but mild Monday morning as Suzi pulled her keys out of her bag to open up Secrets In The Attic, she glanced towards the mystery shop next door. The window was still covered with a dark blind and the lettering above was indecipherable, thanks to the tarpaulin tacked haphazardly over it. Kitchen gadgets? Candles and pot-pourri? Never mind, come nine o'clock, all would be revealed.

Although she switched on the lights as she went in, the contents of their own shop continued to look dark and cryptic, a Victorian chest competing for space with a wash-stand and an ebony vanity unit; a tall bookcase; Suzi's favourite grandfather clock.

'The dark allure of the past,' Estelle had said, in mock-Gothic tones, when they'd chosen a Victorian burgundy and cream paint for the interior of the shop. 'That's what we're selling.'

But now, as she re-arranged the window display to fill the gap created by Saturday's shock sale of a black and white 60s dinner service that was, according to Estelle, just 'developing its value', Suzi wondered if they'd got it right. Did people still want to buy-in to the past? Wouldn't most of them rather tour Habitat or Ikea for a taste of today?

'No sign of life from next door then?' Estelle flipped the 'open' sign as she came in. She and Liam lived only a few minutes' walk away, but she looked exhausted, her auburn hair tied into a long plait that fell forward over one shoulder, her pale face devoid of both make-up and smile.

Oh dear. No high spots on the horizon in the relationship department then. 'Not a flicker,' Suzi told her.

'Any post?'

'I'm avoiding opening it.' Suzi had spotted the familiar longhand scrawl favoured by their landlord. There was also however, a typewritten window envelope that looked boring enough to be instantly binnable.

Not so. 'Oh God.' It was from the council, suggesting that arrangements be made to pay the next Council Tax bill by ten instalments – starting next month. Helpfully, it provided the figure required, along with a direct debit mandate to complete.

At the sight of this figure – three figures, to be precise – Suzi repressed the gnaw of anxiety that she was experiencing far too often these days. Think good karma, her yoga instructor had once told her. But sometimes all she could think was bills.

They did a swap, Suzi holding their landlord's letter gingerly between forefinger and thumb (bad karma might be contagious). The tone was firm rather than unfriendly, she felt, though he too had taken it upon himself to suggest payments by instalments. Large payments.

'We need customers,' Estelle pronounced.

She wasn't joking. Suzi looked around the shop once more. Dingy as Pridehaven's fishing museum – and nobody was queuing to get in there. Secrets In The Attic might have the allure of the past, but it clearly wasn't alluring enough. 'It needs a face-lift,' she said.

Estelle nodded. 'It needs a make-over.'

'It needs a total transformation.' Good grief, when she'd sold that dinner service the other day she'd been tempted to crack open a bottle of bubbly to celebrate. She'd held her breath as the customer ummmed and aahed, mmmd and errrd, not relaxing until the cash was safely tucked in the till and the customer out of the door.

Something had to change, and it had to change quickly. They'd only just begun, so surely it wasn't too late for the shop to be saved? But what had to change? Suzi wondered. And how?

Liam had been invited into the headmaster's study for a brief chat before morning assembly. This was not an occasion for joy.

As Tony Andrews hit rambling monotone, Liam tried not to switch off. He had wanted a window of half an hour for classroom preparations; the requirements of literacy and numeracy and all the rest of the – crap, thought Liam, privately – curriculum now dictated by governmental busybodies, meant that every minute counted in school.

It bugged him that there was no time any more for re-arranging classroom furniture for a spot of drama, devising an off the cuff spontaneous word-play exercise just for the hell of it, or batting on about what Roger McGough and Brian Patten had done for poetry, and why the hell weren't they better appreciated?

Though Liam still did these things. He couldn't help it. He glanced across at the head's tidy in-tray, clear desk, comfortable squishy leather chair. Yeah, well. He hated to be dictated to, wouldn't be dictated to, he thought now, looking down at the floor and realising that one sock was black, the other royal blue.

Teaching was an art, in his view, a vocation that he had entered because it seemed important to communicate knowledge, to encourage self-growth. Some might call that a precious attitude, (would Estelle? He realised with a dart of shock that he wasn't sure) but those things mattered. What seemed far less important . . . he nodded vaguely at whatever point the headmaster might be making . . . was reaching certain goalposts at certain times, denying his pupils' individuality in favour of the right NCT results, foregoing games, poetry and drama because they were (according to that governmental busybody anyway) less crucial to his kids' development.

Crap, thought Liam again, watching Tony Andrews' mouth. The head had a hairy, unattractive moustache that twitched as he spoke, sharp bristles clinging to the moist, pink lips.

'So what do you think, Liam?' Tony asked. 'Will you do it?'

More demands, Liam thought, groping desperately for whatever words had passed him by. He looked out of the window as though the view of the children's wild area – getting wilder year by year as thistles and nettles swamped the meadow flowers and the pond scummed over – might remind him. He loved this school – with its small playground complete with hopscotch squares and netball posts and even smaller field. Its look was old-fashioned – diamond-paned windows like that of the head's study, wooden panelling, magnolia walls. But all that was part of what made it a tradition.

'Knowing your feelings for drama,' the head said helpfully.

'A play?' Liam tried to make this into a kind of I'm-considering-the-matter question.

Tony Andrews nodded with enthusiasm. 'The play is a crucial event on the school calendar.' He twiddled the hairs on his moustache and Liam looked away. 'Shakespeare perhaps?'

Liam made a quick calculation. 'End of summer term?' he asked.

'Exactly.' The moist lips stretched into a grin that revealed stained teeth and a piece of cereal lodged between two of them. Liam wondered what Tony's wife was like. He'd spoken to her at school functions, but she was one of those women who could very easily put any kind of intimacy on hold. 'Parents expect it, as you know,' the head went on.

'All rehearsals out of school hours, I suppose?' Liam was trying to sound unenthusiastic, certain he should milk this request and get something out of it for himself, other than applause and recognition if it turned out successful. But he'd already warmed to the theme. Shakespeare? An open air production – all the rage. Though perhaps a bit dodgy in this climate. But *Romeo and Juliet* was as relevant today as it had ever been. And it could be cut, simplified and adapted sufficiently for the kids to make a stab at it. Why the hell not? If Baz Luhrmann could make a film with Leonardo di Caprio as a Romeo guaranteed to cause a flutter amongst the hormones of every female adolescent in the land, then he could do something for the eleven- and twelve-year-old pre-pubescents. They'd be facing the Bard soon enough in secondary school – do them good to get a foretaste of what they were in for.

'No other way, old chap.' The head looked pointedly at his watch. 'And, as I've already said, no one else could make a half-decent job of it.'

Liam knew it was flattery of the most manipulative kind, but as he had with Amanda Lake yesterday, he enjoyed it anyway. 'I'll do my best,' he said, jumping to his feet and moving quickly from the room. Did he have any spare socks in his desk drawer, he wondered.

Estelle wouldn't like the idea of the play. She would say, *less time for us*, and her beautiful brown eyes would grow big and sad . . . Damn it. Liam pushed her from his mind. She should understand. There was more to life than love. He had a career, he had commitments. He didn't for one moment believe that she would leave him, though she had told him yesterday morning and again in the evening that she planned to.

Liam negotiated the narrow corridor decorated with Impressionist prints that provided an inkling to the passing stranger of certain aspects of the middle school syllabus. She wouldn't leave him because they were a couple, intertwined, interdependent, tied one to the other.

But still doing their own thing. Liam practically bounded up the stairs as he thought of the play. That was what kept a relationship healthy, wasn't it? Dependence and independence in equal doses. Well, roughly equal anyway.

Quite where Suzi or Amanda Lake entered the equation, Liam didn't have time to consider at this point. There was a classroom to re-arrange, a register to be done and a motley crowd of kids to be supervised during morning assembly. The rest could wait.

Estelle was restless. Suzi watched her pick up a water pitcher, trace the willow pattern on its side with a fingertip, put it back on the table. She frowned, paced the shop, went to put the kettle on.

At a quarter to nine she took a deep breath, said she was going upstairs to sort out some stock. She returned almost immediately. 'I want to move in,' she said, folding her arms.

'Move in?' Suzi was putting a hopefully generous float of change into their till – acquired from an old sweet shop and still possessing its original *pinggg*. She paused. 'In where?'

'Upstairs.' Estelle's pale face was flushed, but otherwise she seemed calm. 'As soon as I can clear it out.'

Suzi's mind switched gears. Things had never gone this far before. 'Liam?' she asked.

'Just me.'

'Right.' That wasn't quite what she'd meant, but Suzi shut the till, not wanting to think about it, and especially not right now at just before 9 am on a Monday morning. Already there were enough people outside the shop next door to be called a crowd. Balloons had appeared, as if they'd magically floated from the sky, tables and chairs had been placed on the pavement in a forlorn attempt to create a café atmosphere, Suzi supposed, and Terry was perched like an overweight budgerigar on a ladder, taking the tarpaulin down, belly resting on one of the rungs.

All this attention had to be good for business, Suzi thought. And any moment they'd find out what their neighbours would be selling. Sexy lingerie? (Terry looked the type). Pet food? She turned reluctantly back to Estelle. 'What happened yesterday?' she asked.

Estelle let out a huge sigh. 'I needed my car to go to that antique fair – you know?'

Suzi knew, though yesterday, she'd clean forgotten. They'd agreed to take turns scouting around, researching the competition, looking for bargains, and Estelle had been allocated the fair in Dorchester. She nodded.

'Liam decides to get up early, takes his car keys and *my car* out with him.' She paused for dramatic effect. 'And doesn't come back.'

Suzi shook her head in sympathy. 'So where'd he go?'

'Into school.' It seemed as if Estelle could hardly get the words out. 'To watch a CRICKET MATCH.' She flung her hands in the air. 'Mobile switched off, wouldn't you know. It was a miracle he managed to make it back in time for tennis. Although . . .' Her eyes narrowed. 'He bloody well would, wouldn't he?'

'Right, OK, I see.' She had a strong case, but Suzi still found herself looking for an escape route. 'Why'd he take your car?'

'His was out of petrol.'

Ah. A different tack was needed. 'But he adores you. You know he does.'

'That's not enough.'

Suzi didn't agree. It would be enough, she thought, for *her*, though she'd more or less given up on love – let alone adoration – having almost reached forty without falling into either of those states of heart and mind. 'I know he's infuriating,' she agreed. 'But

Liam's . . . well, Liam. He just can't help throwing himself into every project one hundred per cent. He forgets things. He –'

'He forgets who's waiting for him at home.'

'But if you love him . . .' Suzi had sympathy – up to a point – but it was the picture of her brother's hooded, dark eyes at the tennis club yesterday, that filled her mind. Not to mention the vision of a dilapidated Liam arriving on her doorstep sometime in the very near future looking for food, drink and t.l.c.

She watched Terry rip at the tarpaulin. Some joker started a slow hand-clap and one of their neighbours' wives (she hadn't yet worked out which was which) appeared in the doorway wearing a crimson-lipsticked smile and clutching a tray of wilting vol-au-vents.

'What about being happy?' Estelle demanded.

Suzi thought of Michael. Were they happy? They had fun, though yesterday he'd seemed a little uptight. Most of the time she enjoyed Michael, a bit like she enjoyed her animals and her plants and even the antique shop. But happy? 'I dunno.' She hadn't really given it much thought. But was that a good sign – or a bad one?

The two of them watched as the blind was slowly drawn from the window of the shop next door.

'Bloody hell,' Estelle said.

'Stan and Terry's Bargain Basement?' Suzi peered to look at the sign-writing. 'Fabulous old furniture, silly prices?' Under this lettering was scrawled, HOUSE CLEARANCES WANTED, EVERYTHING VALUED, COME AND VISIT THE FAIREST DEALERS IN TOWN. And a phone number. Fairest dealers in town? Good God. Suzi clutched Estelle's arm. The shop next door was selling second-hand furniture. Stan and Terry were not rather sweet or rather odd. They were rivals.

'And I made them a bloody chocolate cake,' Estelle breathed.

As they watched, Terry, big, bluff and a bit too friendly for Suzi's taste, opened the door and waved the small crowd of people inside. He was wearing an open-necked shirt and even from this distance, Suzi could see his gold medallion nestling in a forest of white chest hair. Yuck. Stan was there too – thin, dark and undeniably rat-like in appearance – handing out glasses of wine. It wasn't hard for Suzi to imagine a long tail whipping . . .

'At nine o'clock in the morning?' she muttered.

'I wouldn't mind a glass.' Estelle stepped on to the pavement. 'You hold the fort, Suzi.' She looked kind of angry and Suzi felt a twinge of anxiety. 'I'm going to take a dekko.'

Chapter 4

Michael Ashby felt pretty darn good as he swung his battered Ford Granada on to the main road and headed for Dorchester. He'd sent the letter. Another week nearer . . . Michael's shoulders tensed. OK, maybe he should have talked things over with Suzi first, but there had never seemed a right time. And he'd always believed in acting on impulse. That way you got to be the guy giving the girl the flowers. OK, he had to admit that acting on impulse had caused him problems in the past – his failed business was evidence enough of that. But what the hell, Michael was a firm believer in grabbing the moment, obeying your instincts, believing that something was right.

He accelerated, pushed a tape into the deck – some of the old stuff, soft and easy, The Eagles, nice mix, nice melody . . . And felt himself relax again. He liked this time of day, early evening, the air fresh but still, the sky pale grey and waiting for night-time velvet. On the road.

And no wonder there hadn't seemed a right time. Last weekend he'd barely had a look-in with all that hoo-hah about Liam and Estelle. Michael frowned as a white BMW overtook the Granada, gliding past with hardly a murmur. One day, he told himself.

He shook his head, hummed a few bars of 'Lyin' Eyes', one of the songs in his repertoire. Always went down well with women that one, something in the lyrics, he supposed. Yeah – if he had his way, Suzi's darling brother and the gorgeous Estelle would sort out their own problems, not expect Suzi to act as referee, counsellor, mediator and the rest.

'Lyin' Eyes' slid into 'James Dean'. Michael liked this one. You could do a fair bit of leaping around with it and he enjoyed a bit of leaping around when he was performing. Got the blood pumping, helped his nerves and the audience thought they were getting more for their money.

Michael speeded up at the dual carriageway. The BMW was out of sight – it would be. But what did he care? So long as he got to Suzi eventually. They hadn't talked much on the phone during the week – they never did, as if the geographical distance produced an emotional one too. But this weekend would be different.

Michael slowed to take the roundabout. He had it all planned. Tonight they'd go out for a beer, discuss how he was feeling about Saturday's gig. Not nervous exactly, but apprehensive.

He drummed his fingernails on the steering wheel as The Eagles hit the intro of 'Peaceful, Easy Feeling'. Who wouldn't be? It had been a while since his brief romance with pub singing, and he'd never sung in Suzi's home territory. He hadn't even planned it – he'd just happened to mention to the landlord at the Bear and Bottle that he sang and played the guitar, that he used to do gigs, and the next thing was, the guy had asked him for a tape.

The following weekend, *he* had approached Michael (Michael was pleased about that – he didn't want to look desperate for the work) and asked him to do a couple of sets in the pub. The date had been fixed and Bingo . . . 'Peaceful, Easy Feeling'. Michael sang. The date was tomorrow night.

It felt good. It felt like a turning point. It was never too late, he decided, for a change of direction, for a taste of success. And after the gig, Michael promised himself, easing into the outside lane, when he was flushed with the high of performance adrenalin and when Suzi was proud of him and smiling and – hopefully – eager to get him into bed (Michael knew only too well what a turn-on it was for women to be going home with a musician at the end of a performance. Otherwise – why would there be groupies?) he would tell Suzi about the letter, tell her what he'd decided.

It made him excited just thinking of it, and he realised he'd almost hit the ton. Reluctantly, he eased his foot from the accelerator. Him and Suzi, what a great combination. What a great girl.

What would she be wearing tonight? Michael allowed himself a moment of weakness, considering this. Something slinky and sexy perhaps? A black silky dress that would cling to her small slender body? Or a red skirt with side slits that . . .

Whoa. He stopped himself right there. Thoughts like that were for the weekdays when Suzi wasn't around. He'd be seeing her in an hour. And whatever she was wearing, he just knew this weekend was going to be hot.

Tenderly, Suzi watered the seedlings in her greenhouse. Tomorrow she'd pot them on, two to each peat container. She brushed soil from her fingers. She knew from experience that the seeds would take off, especially with all this unexpected March sunshine. Though it was late afternoon, it was still warm in the greenhouse, protected as it was from the sea breeze that she knew would bare its teeth at her as soon as she slid open the door.

Suzi inspected the seedlings with a critical eye. 'Don't forget to grow,' she warned them. She was aiming for a bumper crop this summer – tomatoes, aubergines, courgettes, peppers; she'd be freezing ratatouille by the bucketful with any luck.

In the corner, tabby cat Treacle stretched out in the bag of straw destined to lift the strawberries away from the earth in a few months' time. Suzi rubbed his neck to make him purr, allowed him to nuzzle into her wrist. She glanced at her watch. At six-thirty, she promised herself, she would go inside, pour herself a glass of white wine, put some Bryan Ferry on the CD player. Mmmm. Chill out.

And tonight she wouldn't cook – she wasn't in domestic goddess mood, she was more *Ground Force* or maybe *Gardeners' Question Time*, since she was hardly a Charlie Dimmock. And she wouldn't dress up. Not that she did very often – she didn't have the wardrobe for it and she preferred to be comfortable, if she were honest. As for Michael – he never minded what she wore. She'd just wallow in a deep bath with a few drops of ginger oil and maybe another glass of wine to refresh the parts that needed it most. And then throw on whatever fell out of the wardrobe first when she opened the door. She chuckled. What the hell . . .

She'd wait for Michael to arrive and they'd order a take-away – Indian maybe. Chicken passanda. The aroma of cream, coconut, mild spices seemed to drift into the greenhouse to tease her.

Yes, a bit of a 'chill' was what they needed, Suzi decided, whisking a spiky strand of dark hair from her brow and kissing the tuft of fur just above Treacle's nose. Because it took Suzi an hour or two in Michael's company before she could unwind enough to feel close to him again. Not that she was complaining, she thought, re-filling her water spray and misting the next batch of cherry tomato seedlings. It was just the way things were.

Beyond the greenhouse she could see her small flock of buxom and matronly Buff Orpington hens, foraging in their run, looking for food. And Charles the randy cockerel strutting his stuff, encircling them, casual but confident, letting them know who was boss. Suzi smiled. She liked the chain that ran between her kitchen, her garden and the hens. The flock gobbled up her veggie waste, the vegetables in her kitchen garden thrived on chicken manure. And then there were those delicious eggs . . .

She stretched into a back bend that eased her aching muscles. The week had been even crazier than usual – what with Estelle cleaning and clearing the debris from the flat above, hardly even stopping to eat, looking more dusty and manic with each day that passed, and the revelation of Stan and Terry's Bargain Basement. She and Estelle had maintained a huffy superior silence on the subject, but she wasn't sure who they were fooling. Stan and Terry's place was full of customers, theirs empty. So what price superiority when you had a living to make?

Suzi arranged the seedlings on the slatted shelf of the greenhouse. In the event, she'd barely had the time to think of Michael, let alone miss him. She paused, seed tray in hand. And realised that she liked it that way. But wasn't that terrible? How was it that years of living alone had made her so independent, so selfish of her own time, her own space? Was she irredeemable? Was she a hopeless case? Was she destined to be a gardening spinster, her animals and her plants substitutes for a man, children; items of life that were supposed to be more desirable?

'Suze!' The voice was faint.

Suzi replaced the last tray, straightened up and watched Liam as he picked his way across the soggy lawn of her riverbank garden. At his feet were Samson and Delilah, the two rescue dogs that had hated each other on sight when Suzi had acquired them and who were now inseparable.

As Suzi watched, Liam bent to pet Samson, big, black and ugly but solid and dependable as a rock. Delilah, in contrast, was a tiny cream Jack Russell lookalike – though something indefinable had been added and the temper was missing. Delilah hadn't snapped at an ankle since Suzi had taken her in. But she was still running scared

– you could read it in her brown eyes and couldn't help but wonder about her past. Suzi watched her now, trotting along in Samson's shadow. Samson was a whole lot of dog to hide behind.

'I thought I'd find you out here,' Liam yelled through the greenhouse door. He must have come along the riverside path, she realised. He had a canvas bag slung across one shoulder, and in his free hand he held a bottle of wine, carried loosely by the neck. Two sure signs, Suzi knew, that he planned to stay awhile. She felt Bryan Ferry and her bath drifting sadly away from her.

She slid open the door. 'She's moved out then?' As predicted, the sea breeze almost blew her breath away. A gaggle of gulls flapped overhead, screeching and cawing to the wind.

'I know it's pathetic.' Liam was not a big man but he leaned so heavily against the side of the greenhouse that Suzi couldn't help feeling twitchy about the glass. 'I should go out and get drunk, or stay in alone, write a few poems and have a good bawl, I suppose.'

'Not necessarily.' Suzi braced herself for another mini-tornado – ah, she thought, the pleasures of living by the sea – stepped out of the greenhouse and pulled the door to, leaving a cat-sized gap for Treacle, should he eventually summon enough energy to move.

'But the flat seems so bloody empty . . .'

'That'll be the day.' Suzi pictured the organised chaos that characterised Liam's living space.

'I don't want to be alone,' Liam said sulkily. He had flung his bag down on the grass and it was proving to be of interest, not just to the two dogs, but also to Hester the goat, who had strained her leash just as far as it would go and had already managed a decent masticate on the strap. 'I need to talk to someone,' Liam went on. 'To you, Suze.'

Despite herself, Suzi remembered Estelle's words. It's always *his* needs, she had said. 'Perhaps you should be talking to Estelle,' she countered, kicking the bag out of Hester's reach.

Seemingly unaware of the wet strap, Liam picked it up and followed her as she made her way back inside the cottage. Hopeful of food, Samson and Delilah trotted alongside and by the back door they were joined by Castor the white cat, who jumped elegantly down from the fence to beat them all to it.

'She doesn't want to talk to me,' Liam grumbled. 'Not very adult of her, is it? She says she wants space, for God's sake. Space. I ask you.' He began rooting for a corkscrew. 'Anyway – how come you're on her side all of a sudden?'

'Am I?' Suzi considered this as she prepared food for the animals. Actually, she didn't want to take sides. She was in a difficult position and she'd far rather not get involved at all. She ladled food into bowls.

'So what d'you reckon she does want?' Liam grumbled.

Suzi considered this. What did most women want? Money? A good sex life? Security? Someone who wanted to cuddle them especially when they had their period? 'Maybe Estelle wants to get married,' she suggested.

Liam stared at her. 'Is that what she said?'

'No . . .' In fact Estelle had said nothing of the kind. But wasn't it about time? Wasn't that what people did?

Suzi warmed to her theme. 'Maybe she wants children,' she went on.

'Children?' Liam made them sound like an alien species. 'But . . .'

'People do.' Suzi put the bowls down for the dogs and cats. 'She's only thirty-nine. It's not too late.' She paused, thinking of the biological clock that women talked about, that she'd never even heard ticking. And she felt a sudden sadness. 'Is it?'

Liam seemed to have gone into shock. His eyes glazed, his eyebrows met in a frown and he pushed a hand through his dark curls. 'Marriage? Children?' Shaking his head, he managed to recover sufficiently to yank out the cork, pour himself a large glass and down it in one. 'I've asked her,' he said. 'I used to ask her quite often.'

'Oh.' Suzi was surprised; guilty, she supposed, of falling into the stereotypical way of thinking, that it was the guy who was unwilling to commit. 'And she refused you?' Part of her couldn't imagine any woman refusing Liam. But then again, not every woman saw Liam through rose-tinted sisterly spectacles.

'She said, weren't we fine as we were. Are. Were,' Liam told her. 'She said she wasn't sure.'

Of what, Suzi wondered. Or of whom? She had known Estelle for practically her whole life, and yet she could be so secretive. She had never, for example, discussed with Suzi how she felt about marrying her brother. How on earth had that subject got left out? 'And children?' she ventured.

'Need security,' Liam snapped. 'Or that's what she's always said. Although why she imagines –' He broke off abruptly, looked at Suzi. 'Do you want to marry Michael?' he demanded.

'Good grief, no.' Suzi was surprised he had to ask. Liam and Estelle had been together for ever, but it was still early days for herself and Michael. And she and Michael had never had the intensity Suzi associated with love. Not that she knew anything about it – having never been in it – but she could make an educated guess. She had dated various men, enjoyed their company, been to bed with one or two who had – like Michael – crept past her wariness, who had liked animals, not tried to dominate her, been kind, sweet, tender. And OK, those men were few and far between. She had to admit that the majority of her adult life had been spent living alone, her passions reserved for CG's, her animals, her cottage and the books she still consumed voraciously, although she no longer worked in Pridehaven library. But as for love . . .

Anyway, she bent to stroke Castor's sleek coat and received a head-butt in return. She had her animals, didn't she? She had no reason to feel sad. What did she need with love?

It was Saturday afternoon and Estelle paused mid-vacuuming to scan the local paper she'd picked up from the floor. She flicked the switch, the whine of the vacuum faded and the heavy throb of Pink Floyd's *Dark Side of the Moon* took over. Goodness knows how, but it energised her just to have it on in the background; she could hear the thrust of it deep in her senses, over and above everything else. Either that, or she was having an eighties reversion. She'd better be careful, if she went any further back she'd be needing therapy and wearing love-beads.

HOUSE CLEARANCES WANTED, the advertisement read. With a jokey illustration of a man bent double carrying a wardrobe – but still with a smile on his face. CLEAR THE DECKS . . . START ANEW . . . FAIREST DEALERS IN TOWN.

Estelle sat down heavily on Aunt Mo's old rocking chair, practically the only piece of furniture she owned, despite the shopful downstairs. The chair seemed more at home here than it had in Liam's garret, Estelle reflected, remembering the childhood evenings she'd spent curled up on the sofa, telly down low, faintly aware of Auntie Mo in the corner, scribbling on a notepad, rocking for all she was worth. 'Helps me think,' she used to say. Every now and then the steady rhythm of the creaks would change and she would come back to the real world, ask Estelle, 'Do you want anything, ducks?'

But Estelle would long ago have got hungry and helped herself. She shook her head at the memory. Such loneliness. It was easier all round when she started spending her time at Suzi and Liam's.

She rocked slowly, looking around the small living room that was at least hers – for a while. She might paint it, she thought, something decadent and seriously seductive like chocolate and cream, or fruity like tangerine and cranberry. Something that reminded her of youth and having fun. Only, who was she being seductive for? And was she over-reacting to the fact that she was nearly forty?

Though Auntie Mo had never been a bad parent substitute, Estelle reminded herself. She had taken her brother's child in without hesitation, given her as much time and love as she could spare – for a woman obsessed with the other world of the romantic fiction she created. And best of all, she had left what money she had – not a lot, writing fiction clearly not being as lucrative as one might have thought – to Estelle, when she eventually died. Not of a broken heart or something faintly romantic like leukaemia, but of a stroke that wiped her out quickly and cleanly, shortly after she'd written the words, THE END.

Sad though Estelle was to lose her, she was grateful on Auntie Mo's behalf for the timing (for imagine how distressed she would have been to leave her hero and heroine entrenched in misunderstanding) and certainly grateful for the small legacy that had enabled her to join forces with Suzi to create Secrets In The Attic. She was just getting to the point in the customer complaints department she worked in – customer services really, but complaints summed it up more accurately – when she was likely to lose her cool. Just about to reach that career point of no return, when she might adjust her headphones one day and say to some moaning old git, *look, why don't you just fuck off?* It wasn't easy working in a complaints department. After all, listening to abuse all day couldn't possibly improve one's self-esteem.

And when all was said and done, Estelle agreed with most of the customers who were complaining – they *were* being overcharged by a bureaucratic, autocratic monopoly of a company. And they still got lousy water when they turned on their taps. The River Pride still flooded and there was always a hosepipe ban come

August, even when it had rained all through July. So who could blame them for complaining?

What a relief then, to leave it all behind. To be, with Suzi, her own boss. And to be living next door to the fairest dealers in town.

Fairest dealers in town? Estelle folded the paper with a sigh. They'd be the only dealers in town at this rate. It was her turn to do the Saturday stint today and how many customers had she had all morning? Three – only one had bought anything, and that was an old Bunty annual priced at three quid that Suzi had paid £2.50 for at a car boot sale six months ago. So she hadn't felt a moment's guilt about shutting for lunch and coming up here instead. At least she could use her time constructively instead of staring into space and thinking about Liam. Liam – too much and not enough, that just about summed it up.

Someone, she realised, was banging on the door downstairs, shouting, 'Shop!'

Reluctantly she dragged herself to her feet. She should show willing, she supposed. She'd never forgive herself if it turned out to be the customer she'd been waiting for – the one who was desperate to take that disgusting Victorian mahogany tallboy off her hands, and who wouldn't say no to the inlaid writing desk while he was at it.

It wasn't, though – it was Stan from next door.

'Yes?' Estelle glared at him. His navy blazer was shiny at the cuffs and there was a brown stain just below the waistband of the fawn slacks – peculiar to men over sixty, Estelle thought. He looked seedy. He did not look like one half of the fairest dealers in town.

Stan grinned his ratty grin – a million miles away from *Wind In The Willows*, Estelle thought – revealing nicotine-coated teeth and receding gums. 'This isn't the way to run a business, now is it?'

he said, tapping the 'closed' sign with the stained forefinger of his right hand. 'We won't make any money by keeping the punters on the pavement, will we, eh?'

'I can't see it has anything to do with you,' Estelle snapped. 'What do you want anyway?' She ground her teeth and thought calming thoughts. Like how therapeutic it would be to dip this man's head in the River Pride on a winter's day. Like how surprising it was that outside the antique shop, there was life, people, colour and sunshine. 'Well?' She kept her voice level but drew the line at a smile.

'Any chance of a cuppa tea?'

He had to be joking. 'I'm busy,' she informed him tartly. 'So if you could get to the point?'

'The point . . .' He leaned on the doorway and Estelle reminded herself to give it a wipe down afterwards, '. . . is that me and Terry, we couldn't help noticing that you and your lady partner don't do a lot of trade.'

Estelle waited. She was damned if she was going to give him the satisfaction of a response.

'And Terry thought we should apologise, like.'

'What for?' Estelle shifted her weight to the other foot and glanced pointedly at her watch and then outside. Her green Mini Mayfair was sitting by the roadside – luckily, restricted parking hadn't yet hit Pridehaven.

'For muscling in. Though a spot of healthy competition might do you some good, love.' Stan waved at a customer coming out of the shop next door. 'That's what the punters want,' he said. 'A bit of a bargain. Good quality furniture at rock bottom prices.'

The last thing Estelle wanted to do right now was listen to the sales pitch of a man she despised. 'We're appealing to a different market,' she said, wishing she believed it.

'Not really a game for a woman though, is it?' Stan looked her up and down with his heavy-lidded gaze, not in any kind of sexual way, she decided, but as if he were assessing how many wardrobes she could hump down two flights of stairs at certain times of the month. What should she tell him? That with wings anything was possible?

'I don't see why not.'

'Oh, no hard feelings.' Stan grinned.

Bastard, she thought. She'd like to give him hard feelings of the painful variety, right where it hurt the most. 'None taken,' she assured him.

'But if you ever want to pack it in . . .'

'I beg your pardon?'

'We always wanted bigger premises, you see.' Stan peered over her shoulder, a look of the mental tape measure in his eyes.

'Then perhaps . . .' Estelle moved sideways to block his view. 'You should move on elsewhere.'

'We've only just got here.' Stan laughed at this, emitting a stench of tobacco and musty old rope.

Estelle recoiled. She wished, she really wished she'd never made that chocolate sponge. 'Sorry,' she snapped. 'Nothing doing.'

'Ah well, only asking.' Stan flicked back his cuff to reveal . . . yes, she could have guessed, a particularly ostentatious Rolex watch. Probably a fake, Estelle thought; it looked like one of those awful market jobs. 'Gotta go, gotta whole lot of jewellery to buy,' he added, rubbing his hands together.

'Jewellery?' Estelle's look around the bargain basement had revealed plenty of furniture, but no jewellery.

'We're branching out.' She could tell he was enjoying himself. She'd love to slam the door in his face, but she didn't want him to see he'd got her rattled.

'I'm buying a load from old ma Barnaby.' He grinned again, and Estelle just knew that Hilda Barnaby had told him that, yes, she'd already spoken to the ladies from Secrets In The Attic, before telling him exactly what price they had offered for the Victorian brooch, pearl ear-rings, necklace and amethyst ring that Mrs Barnaby wanted to sell. What was worse was that Estelle had spent hours listening to Hilda Barnaby's family history. *And* she had offered her a fair price, damn it. She had even felt sorry for the woman – having to sell what had been in the family for generations.

'We couldn't offer as much for the jewellery,' Stan confided now, watching her face intently. 'You went a bit over the top there, love, if you don't mind me saying – I mean we've all got to make a profit, right?'

If she stayed absolutely still, Estelle thought, she wouldn't scream and she wouldn't thump him one. Don't get angry, get even. The trouble was, anger was so cathartic, so cleansing, it gave you so much more satisfaction in the end.

'But I offered to clear some other stuff out for her, might sell it, might not, you know the sort of gear. Offered to take it off her hands, like.'

Estelle did know the sort of gear. It must be the furniture Hilda Barnaby kept in her spare room, the furniture Estelle had been shown but had not valued because Estelle hadn't known she wanted to sell it – the furniture that was worth at least a grand of anyone's money.

And in that moment Estelle realised something about Stan and Terry, the fairest dealers in town. They weren't just rivals, a couple of blokes trying to make a living. They were con men – the kind of low life who would rip off an old lady as soon as look at her.

'Heavy game for women,' Stan said. 'In more ways than one. Think about it, love.'

Estelle tensed. 'Is that a threat?'

'Nah.' Stan turned to go. 'Just a piece of advice.'

★   ★   ★

After he'd gone, Estelle didn't open up the shop as perhaps she should have. Neither did she go round to Suzi's as she was tempted to – Liam would be there, she just knew it, and the last person she wanted to see was Liam.

Instead, she thought for a moment, looked up a number in the phone book and made a call. Then she grabbed some money from petty cash, picked up her bag and headed for the door. Outside, to her right, Pridehaven's Saturday market was in full swing, stalls selling everything from cheese and chutneys to brightly printed sarongs like the one Estelle was wearing. In Pridehaven, women didn't restrict their wearing of sarongs to the beach. They wore them all through spring and summer – so long as there was a touch of sunshine. And today, the sky was clear, the sea breeze was fresh and Estelle had made up her mind. There were plenty of people around but the shop would have to stay closed.

She locked the door behind her. First things first. There were things she had to do.

Chapter 5

Liam got changed into his tennis kit and heaved himself into one of the wicker chairs in the clubhouse conservatory. As always, you felt you were sinking into a swamp to begin with, until the cushions moulded around you and you ended up so comfortable you weren't sure you'd ever be able to get up again.

He savoured the view; one he'd been enjoying for as long as he could remember, one he wanted to remain available for everyone – money and class notwithstanding. Took in, as he always did, the motley collection of building-tops – from the Gothic-style Victorian houses, like the one he himself lived in, to the Edwardian grandeur of the old Bull Hotel, to the red roofs of the new housing estates. And then there was Pride Square, the bridge and disused water mill by The Bull, and underneath, the river, swimming its way to Pride Harbour and the sea.

He could make out some of this vista, knew the rest of it by heart. It was, he supposed, in his blood.

It was a club afternoon, so any member could turn up to play – partnerships were random, gender immaterial. If life were like that, Liam reflected, it would be simpler to manage.

But for now the clubhouse was deserted, so after lingering

guiltily for a moment in the tranquillity of the place, Liam dug some paper out of his bag, found his battered copy of *Romeo and Juliet* and began scribbling some notes.

If a few key scenes could be condensed, he reasoned, and maybe a couple of song and dance routines added to the whole thing . . . (Kenneth Branagh had done it, hadn't he?) Shakespeare might become more accessible, rather than just men in tights making long, incomprehensible speeches before killing each other and then themselves.

Shakespeare 4 kidz. He could see it now. Liam grinned. He might even start a middle school trend.

'Are you here to play tennis?' A soft purr to his left stopped him mid-sentence. 'Or are you creating a lesson plan to die for?'

Liam grinned up at Amanda. The girl was drop dead gorgeous, and though he'd always believed man would grow bored with a pretty face, he wasn't sure of this with Amanda Lake. Class and perfection were a heady mix. 'I'm re-writing the Bard,' he told her, explaining about the school play, perhaps, he admitted privately, making it sound more important than it really was.

While he was talking, she'd taken the rickety chair next to his, drawn it closer and sat down. She smelled of expensive perfume along with what could have been a whiff of pot. He was faintly surprised at this. Amanda was a rich girl. If she was into drugs, he'd expect it to be the occasional line of coke or pills.

'Gosh.' She looked very impressed. 'Can anyone come along?'

'Oh, it's only a school thing.' Liam backtracked. He couldn't quite see Amanda seated on a hard wooden chair in the school hall with all the parents.

'But I'd love to come,' she breathed. 'Could you get me a ticket?'

Liam fidgeted. Thought of Tony Andrews licking his lips, *And who might this be?* Thought also of Estelle – how would she react

to Amanda in the audience? It didn't bear thinking about. But . . .
'Maybe,' he compromised. 'I'll let you know nearer the time.'

She got to her feet. She was wearing a turquoise and white
designer label tennis dress under a thin white fleece; white socks,
flashy tennis shoes. Her blonde hair was arranged in a chignon,
the golden nape of her neck bare but for a few delicate platinum
strands. Jesus . . . Liam wondered if he had the strength for this.

At CG's, most of the younger players didn't bother with tennis
whites, since they had been voted optional a few years ago – much
to the disgust of Erica and the blazers, as Liam referred to the Old
School of the club. It didn't encourage young blood, had been
the argument; kids hated to be told what to wear, the days of
tennis whites and wooden rackets were over. And if kids – of
all backgrounds, Liam always stressed – weren't encouraged into
the game, how much longer would English tennis fans have to
wait for a British winner at Wimbledon?

No, getting down to grass roots didn't include tennis whites
as far as Liam was concerned. And Nick could look a bit of a
prat since he always chose to wear them. But in Liam's opinion,
Amanda Lake always looked good – she couldn't not.

'Do you fancy a game?' he asked her.

Amanda glanced at her tiny gold watch. She frowned. 'Why
not? That's what we're here for.'

Liam got to his feet. 'Singles?' He wasn't bothered about playing
a woman, though it would be bloody difficult to keep his eye on
the ball. For a start he knew how good she was – she'd probably
wipe the floor with him.

'Singles,' she confirmed. 'Though I must say, Liam darling, I'd
be happy to play mixed doubles with you any time.'

They strolled through the door that led out of the conservatory and
on to the small patio outside. Erica had christened it the Barbecue

Patio, some money had been allocated for decorative cast iron chairs and circular tables and the building of a barbecue from fire-bricks. So when weather permitted, it was equally pleasant to sit outside the conservatory. Surprising almost, Liam thought, that anyone actually played tennis.

'Grass?' Amanda enquired.

For a moment, Liam recalled the fragrance of pot and thought she was offering him something quite different. Then he realised his mistake.

'It's dry enough,' she added.

'Why not?' There were certain rules to be adhered to when playing on grass – like the courts shouldn't be used before 10 am, that they must be checked by the groundsman or a committee member before play. But it was mild again today and it looked as if the light cloud might break at any time and surprise them with some sunshine.

Liam bent down to check. The court was dry and the grass springy. He flexed his muscles. He was feeling good.

'So you teach English?' Amanda murmured, touching his arm.

He felt himself grow taller. 'In middle schools you teach the lot.' As they piled their gear on to the wooden bench court-side, and sorted out rackets and balls, Liam found himself explaining some of the rudiments of the educational system to a captive audience. Estelle always looked bored when he sounded off about his job, but Amanda seemed riveted. Her baby-blue eyes hardly left his face and the questions she asked showed she'd been listening. But, what had she meant about the mixed doubles, he wondered.

'I didn't realise it was so complicated,' she murmured, as she spun her racket. 'Rough or smooth?'

'Rough,' Liam said, suddenly not caring about the game. He'd much rather sit down with her and go on talking. Though come to think of it, maybe they could do a bit of that after this blasted

committee meeting tonight. Erica Raddle always chose the time
to suit Erica Raddle; seven o'clock on a Saturday evening was
hardly ideal for Liam, but on the other hand a friendly drink
with Amanda afterwards could make it worthwhile. Not in
any sexual way, of course. He had Estelle – in theory at least.
He was in love with Estelle, and he would get her back. He
had no worries on that score; it was only a matter of time.
Amanda wasn't his type, but she was so . . . obliging. And
sexy. She made a guy feel good, and right now Liam wanted
to feel good.

'Rough,' she confirmed. 'You'll serve, I take it?'

They had a warm-up first, then launched into the first game.
It was a perfect playing day – not too hot and with no breeze to
speak of. Liam served a couple of aces and took the game easily.
He began to feel better still.

'What's your favourite subject to teach?' Amanda asked him
at the end change. Her perfume mingled with the scent of the
grass. Decadent and delicious.

'Poetry.' And Liam couldn't help himself – off he went
with the verbals again. An end change was supposed to be
a break of three minutes max but there was so much to
say – especially about contemporary poetry, which was his
particular bag – that it was almost ten minutes before they
restarted.

But, hell, Amanda didn't seem to mind. She nodded and smiled,
head to one side, eyes fixed on his face. 'So driven,' she said.
'So dedicated.' Smoothly, she collected the balls and prepared
to serve.

If Estelle had said that, Liam reflected, trying not to swagger
as he moved into the receiving court and flexed his playing arm
again, he would think she was taking the piss. She *would* have
been taking the piss . . .

He flinched at the thought, but re-directed himself by watching Amanda's graceful service action as she stood in her virginal whites, framed by the grass courts; in the background, the honey-coloured stone and glass of Chestnut Grove's clubhouse. What a picture she presented. And, God, that woman could toss a ball.

Unfortunately, it caught the net tape and didn't drop over. She served the next one wide.

'Bad luck!' Liam called, moving over to the other court. She hadn't got into her stride yet, that much was obvious. And where Estelle was cynical, Liam found himself thinking, Amanda Lake was clearly as sincere as they came. Bit of a surprise that, and it just showed that you couldn't make assumptions about people – even the rich kind.

They had a couple of good rallys, then Amanda hit a forehand wide, and before Liam had quite grasped the fact, he'd taken the game and was about to serve again. It was easier to serve when you were seven foot tall. Once again, he managed two aces (he was sure one of them was long but Amanda said not and like the good sport she was, declined to re-take the point) and there he was, leading three love. Wowee – he hadn't realised he was so good.

'It's ages since we played together,' Amanda said archly at the next end change. 'You've really improved.' The sun had come out and Liam was really warming up. Amanda slipped off the fleece. The tennis dress had narrow shoulder straps that crossed over at the back.

'Do you think so?' Liam tried not to look either too pleased or at her breasts. She was sweating ever so slightly – only on Amanda it was more of a delicate glow – and her nipples were clearly outlined under the white fabric. He glanced away. Over at the clubhouse he thought he glimpsed a tall figure standing just inside the glass conservatory watching them, and then it was gone, moving back into the shadows beyond.

'Absolutely,' said Amanda, smoothing back her hair and throwing him an intimate smile.

Another four had come on to the adjacent grass court to play doubles, and a couple of guys were on their way over from the clubhouse. Liam squinted towards the conservatory, but whoever it was had not re-appeared. Just someone watching the action, he told himself.

Things had been going so well that he was disappointed when Amanda took her next service game, though she did say, 'God, darling, I thought you were going to give me a whitewash there,' which was quite sweet.

But he kept his serve again to lead 4–1 when they changed.

'I thought about teaching once,' Amanda confided, sipping her barley water.

Liam was gob-smacked. 'But you were a model.' Maybe it was a dumb thing to say, but he couldn't see Amanda at teacher's training college to save his life. The women there were lovely – often dedicated, usually full of enthusiasm and sometimes good-looking too. But there weren't many Amandas.

She shrugged, an elegant movement of the slim brown shoulders. 'That was then.' She eyed Liam with what seemed like admiration. 'I'm looking for a new career path.'

'Yeah?'

She laughed. 'Oh, I know what you're thinking . . .' the golden brown hand rested on his arm again.

God, the woman couldn't stop touching him. Liam wondered how old she was – late twenties maybe? Well, they said that younger women couldn't resist the older, more powerful man. Liam wasn't sure he was more powerful, but he was certainly older, and at forty, men had a certain panache, he'd heard. As

Estelle had once said, complaining about the unfairness of it, a bit of grey around the temples made a woman look old, a man more distinguished.

The blue eyes gazed into his. 'You're thinking I'm just some blonde bimbo with more money than sense.'

'Of course not,' said Liam, who had been thinking precisely that. He tried in vain to think of a career path compatible with Amanda and failed miserably. He could imagine her shopping, having breakfast or lunch with friends called Sorrell and Saffron, even partying all night. But a career path . . . ?

Amanda's eyes became almost steely as she took the next game, and Liam really struggled with his following service. All of a sudden Amanda seemed to be finding his serve relatively easy to cope with; the returns came back fast, fluid and with maximum topspin, making him race panting from one side of the grass court to the other. As if she were playing with him . . . And he wasn't talking tennis. But at deuce, she flashed him a radiant smile and hit the return into the net. Liam put everything into the next serve, it flashed past her, and it was 5–2.

At the end change, Liam became aware of Nick Rossi, standing on the patio, outside the clubhouse, arms folded, watching them. It had been him watching before, Liam was certain. Hardly a surprise since he and Amanda often played together – two of a kind, he supposed. 'Rossi doesn't look too happy,' he remarked, since she didn't seem to have noticed him.

She towelled her face and neck and didn't look round. 'That's his problem.'

'Had the two of you arranged a game?' Liam didn't much like Rossi (he worked, but was too social-strata-A for Liam's taste) but he had no wish to tread on anyone's toes.

'Mentioned but not confirmed.' Once again, Amanda put her hand on his arm. 'You don't have to worry, Liam. Nick and I aren't an item.' She smiled, leaned closer. 'It's just a game.'

And it was only when Amanda hit a double fault, allowing Liam to take that game and the set, that Liam began to wonder what on earth she might mean.

'We should play together more often,' Amanda said as they made their way back to the clubhouse. There was no sign of Nick Rossi now, but Amanda seemed neither to notice nor care.

'I'd like that.' And Liam thought of the American tournament. Next time he played with Amanda, he decided, he'd rather like them to be on the same side.

After a game of doubles and a quick shower in the changing rooms, it was 7 pm and the committee were assembling in the clubhouse. Liam saw that Suzi hadn't arrived yet, but Amanda, now wearing a scarlet mini-dress and black ankle boots, was smiling at him, beckoning and patting the seat next to her.

At the head of the table – or tables, because six had been pushed together for the meeting – sat Erica Raddle. Deirdre Piston was on her right, assembling paperwork and clearing her throat importantly from time to time. The remaining places were taken by other committee members – Margaret Quaife, one of Pridehaven's most upright pillars of the community and a town councillor; Beryl Rathbone, sporty and brisk; Diana Taylor, equally committed to tennis, bowls and the WI; and Simon Hanley, the manager of the club. Age-wise, Liam reflected, Old School and Blazers had the edge; class-wise ditto.

As Liam sat down next to Amanda, Erica turned to her. 'Is your father coming tonight, dear?'

'He's busy, I'm afraid,' Amanda said sweetly. 'But he sends his best.'

'His best what?' Liam hissed. 'Shouldn't he come? Wouldn't he be on our side?'

'I'm not altogether sure,' she whispered back. 'Erica's been after Daddy for ages. And you know what men are like.'

Liam wasn't sure that he did. He looked across at Erica, and tried to imagine anyone fancying her. It was hopeless. 'What about her husband?' he asked. William Raddle preferred golf to tennis, but surely Erica could count herself fortunate to have anyone?

'Don't worry.' Amanda squeezed his hand. Worry? High anxiety was nearer the mark. 'We'll show Erica what's what, and I'll work on Daddy later.'

Despite his disapproval of the means she might employ, and though Liam would have preferred the workers to be uniting against the idle rich, he was still glad to have her on his side. There was a lot at stake here – not for him, but for the kids at Chestnut Grove youth club. As youth club co-ordinator, he automatically got a place on committee in order to protect their interests. And it was Liam who had fought for Suzi's inclusion, well aware that he needed all the help he could get. Amanda had got on because her father's father had been instrumental in the original creation of Chestnut Grove and Nick Rossi . . . Well, Liam didn't know how the hell he'd got there.

He decided – following the promising hand squeeze – to try his luck with the lady by his side. 'Do you fancy a drink after this fiasco?' he asked her. 'We may need one.'

Amanda pulled a disappointed face. 'Love to, darling, but I've got a party. Fenella Trenton-Smythe – it's a 30s bash, and I promised I'd be there.'

Apart from re-crossing her long, tanned legs, she barely acknowledged the fact that Nick Rossi had entered the room. He sat down opposite her.

'Another time, though?'

'Another time,' Liam confirmed, feeling that rejection could seem surprisingly close to victory.

'But what's happened to your girlfriend?' Amanda went on. 'Have you come to a parting of the ways?'

Liam hesitated. Part of him wanted to make some throwaway comment, to dismiss the fact of him and Estelle. But another part of him couldn't do it. 'Sort of,' he compromised. Which was sort of true. She had, after all, left him.

Amanda leaned closer. The faint scent of pot had disappeared, but she had clearly given herself another dousing with the expensive perfume. 'So you're free and available then?' she asked. 'Sort of?'

Liam rather liked the sound of that. He noticed the flicker of irritation on the dark face of Nick Rossi, but what was that to him? Amanda was a free agent, Liam was a free agent. Estelle had walked out. And wouldn't it serve her right if Liam took the opportunity to have a little fun? He looked into Amanda's inviting blue eyes and for the life of him couldn't think of a good reason why not. 'I am indeed,' he said.

In the Bear and Bottle, Michael launched into the Beatles, 'I saw her standing there.' 'She was just seventeen . . .' He liked to use it as his first number – it was a bit of a rocker and set the tone. Sometimes he worried that he should bring his set into the new millennium, but what decent music had appeared in the last decade? It was mostly cover stuff in the charts anyway, so why bother?

Instead of, 'how could I dance with another', he sang, 'how could I dance with her mother . . . when I saw her standing there?' It got a cheap laugh, which was the best you could hope for when your audience was an untested one.

He had been slightly worried, he had to admit, when he'd

seen the blackboard outside advertising tonight's gig. 'The Ashby Phenomenon', they'd called him, and Michael had never seen himself as a phenomenon somehow. However, there were enough people in the pub when he got there to put him at ease (too many or too few and he might have walked out again). The atmosphere was friendly, someone had given him a pint of Best, people were smiling and Michael was warming up.

As he sang – and bounced, because Michael liked to bounce – he tried to think of a way to fix the mic on to his body, so he could bounce right round the pub if necessary. And he kept one eye on the door in the far corner. She had said she was coming. She had said she wouldn't be late. She had said she wouldn't miss it for the world. So where the hell was she?

He slowed right down for 'Yesterday', the second of his Beatles' medley and as the notes died away, launched straight into 'Twist and Shout'. On a really good night they'd get up and boogie for that, but there wasn't much room in the Bear and Bottle, so Michael did a spot of twisting himself, being careful to avoid the lead to his electric guitar. A bit of fancy footwork earned him a wolf-whistle or two (Michael always took care to show he wasn't taking himself too seriously) which allowed him to play to the crowd.

At the end of the song he tried a couple of jokes. Not bad. A few were laughing, there were even more smiles and he'd gained lots of eye contact. Most important of all, more people had come in and no one had left. He wondered if he could bend a wire coathanger and stick it round his neck or something – that would be an original mic stand, for sure. Or would he just look like a pillock?

There was, he sensed, an air of expectancy in the pub, but Michael was going for melody now, so he tried a bit of Simon and Garfunkel, speeded up for The Eagles (mellow or what?) and finished the set with a bit of 70s boppy stuff to get them moving in their chairs if not on the floor. That would be a bit dodgy for the amps and stuff anyway.

Michael grinned and bounced and slung the guitar behind his back. He had a brief fantasy of some record company guy wandering into the pub. *Hey, this guy is really cool. And is that a coathanger round his neck? What a fashion item. What a trend setter. What couldn't we do with him . . . ?*

Yeah, well. It was going OK. But where the hell was Suzi?

Chapter 6

'Item number ten,' boomed Erica, shifting her bosom. 'The question of subscriptions.' There was a telling pause. 'Of course we shall have to raise them.'

Suzi groaned inwardly and tried to think subscriptions rather than the feat being performed by Erica's brassière. She was already late, and this looked like another thorny time-consumer. Sure enough . . .

'Why do we?' Liam demanded. He shook the papers he was holding. 'The accounts look healthy enough to me.'

'We can't rely on benefactors alone. We are a private members club. And we need to raise more money.' Erica looked as if any second she might pat Liam on the head. If she did, Suzi thought, she didn't think much of her chances. 'For our *improvements*,' Erica added.

'Improvements,' echoed Deirdre, nodding frantically.

'Like turning the youth club's games room into some up-market restaurant, for example?' Liam threw down accounts and agenda.

Here we go, thought Suzi. Though Erica had a point about improvements. The clubhouse was shabby – they could usefully spend some money on a paint job and some new furniture. Though she couldn't bear the thought of new furniture in the conservatory, it was so timeless and such a perfect fit. But the games room was another matter . . .

Liam jumped out of his particular rickety chair and Suzi winced. 'Christ! What's the matter with you people?' He tore his hand through his dark curls.

'Calm down, old chap. Nothing's been decided yet – unless I missed it in all the excitement, of course.' Nick Rossi, Suzi noted, was playing Mr Supersmooth tonight. He looked as hunky as always – Suzi could almost see those shoulder muscles rippling under the cool and silky white shirt that had just enough buttons undone to reveal a brown neck and dark blond chest hair, and yet not enough to be *obvious* . . . He was also, she noted, getting to Liam.

Liam turned on him. 'Somebody's got to think about the youth club,' he snapped. 'The youth club was here first, don't forget. The aim of CG's is meant to be to bring kids into the game and provide a venue for them to let off a bit of steam. Not to take away their social room because some poncy gits want to experience a bit of cordon bleu.' He fixed Erica with an accusing glare. 'And we're apparently willing to sell our principles in order to do it,' he concluded, sitting down again.

Erica raised her gavel. Suzi tensed, but instead of attacking Liam for calling her a poncy git, she brought it down on the table in three sharp raps. 'Let's discuss this rationally,' she said, eyeing Liam as if he'd just escaped from an asylum. She sucked in her cheeks, inadvertently making herself look more horsy than ever.

'Good idea,' said Margaret Quaife, moving her chair infinitesimally further from Liam's.

Suzi sighed. Rational discussion? How long would that take?

'Over some refreshments perhaps?' Erica turned to Deirdre, all sweetness and girlie pow wow.

'Refreshments,' Deirdre confirmed. She patted a fluffy curl

back into place with one plump white hand. 'Yes, of course, refreshments.'

Suzi had heard that Deirdre had once won a county medal and sported a killer of a forehand, but this was hard to equate with the Deirdre of today, quite aside from the fact that Erica kept her too busy with tea-making and admin for her ever to have time for tennis. But every committee, Suzi supposed, needed a Deirdre Piston, and at least everyone who took advantage of her good nature also, apparently, loved her to bits. Even now, Diana was patting her hand and calling her a sweetie, and Simon was treating her to one of his curt nods of approval. Committee meetings without refreshments were like cars without wheels.

Suzi fidgeted in her seat. She hadn't, actually, ever wanted to be on this committee, but had allowed Liam to persuade her, just as he'd persuaded the rest of the committee to invite her on, with phrases like 'young blood' and 'new ideas'. Suzi didn't feel that her blood was in the slightest bit young and she hadn't voiced an idea since she'd been here. But at least, she supposed, she could be on Liam's team when needed.

She tried to catch his eye but – surprise, surprise – he was totally preoccupied with Amanda Lake. Liam, seemingly, had an agenda of his own.

It had not, she thought, been a productive weekend so far. Michael had got a strop on – just because she'd insisted on keeping her promise to come here before seeing him perform at the pub. And now . . . she glanced at her watch, he was going to be in a worse one. He hadn't liked Liam hanging around last night either – but that was tough luck, because if you couldn't turn to family in a crisis, then who could you turn to? There was no way she could have turfed Liam out into the night.

So although her brother was behaving like an idiot . . . she watched Amanda cooing and simpering at him as if he was the best thing since fake suntan oil, and Liam lapping it up as if the poor fool believed every look and every word . . . Suzi would always be there for him. Solidarity. She and Liam went back for ever. He had her support. For Suzi, there was never any question.

In the interval, Michael accepted a pint from the landlord and a top-up fifteen minutes later from an enthusiastic blonde sitting near the amp. She was alone, he noted and quite sexy. She was dressed in a black top and short skirt showing more than half-decent (and possibly stockinged?) legs. But she was not, unfortunately, Suzi.

What was Suzi playing at? It had been bad enough last night, dreaming of the evening ahead all through that drive to Dorchester, only to find her and Liam ensconced on the sofa with an empty bottle of wine, into one of their old times scenes that Michael could live without. And now this.

No, Suzi had said, when Michael arrived at the cottage, she didn't want to go out because she wasn't in the mood and anyway, she couldn't be bothered to get changed. And yes, Michael had already noted the patched-up dungarees and faded T-shirt, but that was his problem. When you indulged in fantasies you were heading for disappointment. Would Michael mind if they all stayed in and ordered a take-away, she'd said. Well, Michael would mind actually, but that was neither here nor there because before you could say vegetable biriany, the menu for the Indian was being waved in front of his face and any chance of a drink down the pub (Michael hated wine) let alone some time with Suzi alone, had – like himself – slunk into the depths of Suzi's old sofa.

'You've got a great voice.' Michael had not noticed the blonde approaching his space again. 'Dead smooth.' She smiled. 'Like clotted cream.'

Michael gulped. Where was Suzi? 'Cheers,' he said. Her voice was husky and he'd never heard so much sexual innuendo packed into one sentence before.

'Would you sing something for me?' she continued.

'If I know it.' Michael drank his beer too quickly and almost choked. At the bar the landlord gave him a nod and he glanced down at his watch.

'"Lay lady lay",' she whispered, close to his ear. 'That song is such a turn-on.'

'Right, er, OK.' Michael grabbed his guitar. He knew the chords but usually avoided Dylan songs – he could never resist drawling them out in parody. And did he want to turn on the blonde? Probably not. If she turned on any more he'd never make it back to Suzi's alive.

'Fresh air!' Estelle declared, throwing open the door of the shop. It was getting very dark outside, but what the heck . . . fresh, moody night-time air was even better. She sniffed. She was drowning in . . . not the scent of the past or the salty sea air – but the thick, heady aroma of new paint.

She picked her way back through the pieces of furniture shrouded in dust sheets that she'd pushed into the centre of the shop floor. Climbed over the Chesterfield – in order to reach the paint pot in the corner.

She surveyed the freshly painted walls. 'New beginnings,' she said, raising her glass in a toast, only to find that it was empty. Now, where was that damned bottle of Australian chardonnay? She found it on top of the bookcase. Also empty.

'I've had enough,' she told the face of the grandfather clock, peeping from between the creases of its sheet shawl. But the question remained – of what?

Upstairs, her microwaved lasagne sat on the table where Estelle had left it. A candle flickered on the shelf where she'd already arranged her collection of green glassware – as if, she thought ruefully, this flat could so easily become a home . . .

She thought of Stan's stained smile – the smugness of it, the conviction that he held all the cards, that she and Suzi would fold under the slightest pressure. Not a game for women, indeed. What a bloody, bloody nerve the man had.

Sod him. Estelle pushed the lasagne to one side. She wouldn't give in so easily. Starting up this business had meant more than a new method of earning a living because she was fed up with customer complaints. It had meant independence – a way of shouting from the rooftops, to Liam and anyone else who'd listen . . . This is mine and it's important. This is my new pathway and I'm going to make it work. It wasn't too late, she thought, to be able to make it alone.

Slowly, Estelle got to her feet, switched on the kettle for coffee. She'd chosen antiques, because she'd always had a hankering for the past. And a fear of it too. Liam used to tease her about it – when they'd visited old churches or National Trust buildings on rare Sunday afternoons out. He'd catch her in a dream and say, 'Good vibes or bad vibes, Estelle? Who lived here? What did they get up to?'

And she'd laugh and stop wondering, but not for long.

History fascinated her, and it had been no hardship to teach herself enough about antiques and their value, what to look for in ceramics, glass and wood, until she knew enough to get by. She was still learning, of course, and learning that some parts of the business interested her more than others.

Suzi, she was aware, had joined her because Estelle needed a partner and some more money to sink into the venture and Suzi not only had some spare capital she wanted to invest, but had been thinking of leaving her job and doing something else anyway. Working in the library had been great, she'd told Estelle once, when she'd been able to spend half the working day reading voraciously. But times changed, new managers appeared with new concepts and vocabulary like creative time management, customer challenges and target borrowers. And Suzi had decided she too wanted a change.

But the important thing was that they trusted one another and Estelle had needed someone to trust, someone with whom she could share the responsibility of the business.

Liam . . . she smiled . . . had splurged his share of his mother's money on everything from poetry books to CG's tennis and youth club, from a state of the art computer to a host of good, or more likely, political causes. But Suzi was more cautious and Secrets In The Attic had benefited from that caution.

Estelle sighed. Whether or not Suzi had benefited was more open to doubt. Suzi . . .

Estelle sat bolt upright, suddenly sober. Christ. What would Suzi say when she saw what Estelle had done?

By the time Deirdre returned with a tray of bland, milky coffee, the arguments had grown more heated.

Erica and Margaret had staunchly maintained that their private members were and would always be the backbone of the club, that high subscriptions would enable CG's to maintain standards (though whether of facilities or members, Suzi wasn't sure) and that better facilities would, in a roundabout way, bring more young people – and the right young people – into the game. Liam had scoffed that the right young people were those whose parents could afford extortionate fees, that she was perpetuating the archaic idea of tennis as a game for the well-heeled and that kids were hardly likely to flock to CG's just because it boasted an upper-crust restaurant. Erica had reiterated that much depended on the *sort* of young people one wanted as part of the club, and Liam had replied with a set of expletives roughly grounded in his particular form of Socialism. It looked, to Suzi, like stalemate.

'Bring in *those* type of youths,' Erica said, her large face flushed with emotion, 'And you get *language*.'

'Oh, yes. Language,' Deirdre repeated.

'Language?' drawled Amanda. 'Is that a disadvantage or a plus point?'

'Language that offends our neighbours,' Erica elaborated. Her eyes were blue and flinty, bordered by sparse gingery lashes. Suzi wondered if William Raddle ever looked into them and whispered sweet nothings. It wasn't an image she wanted to dwell on. 'Their gardens back on to the tennis courts, remember,' Erica added. And it was true that the far hard courts were separated only by a fence from three or four of Pridehaven's more desirable properties up on the hill.

'Language?' Liam jeered. 'What sort of a bigoted, elitist view is that? Swearing belongs to the real world at least.'

Erica wagged a knobbly index finger. 'Ah, but do we want to be part of that world?'

'It's the one we bloody well live in.' Once again, he thrust his hand through his hair, creating a look that was growing more demented by the second, Suzi observed. And on he went. 'We don't live in some upper-class protected bubble where *one* breathes clean air, takes tea at four in the afternoon, patronises anyone who earns less than £50,000 a year and is scared to say the word "shit".'

Although Liam might have been describing Amanda Lake's own background, Suzi couldn't help noticing the almost imperceptible touch of Amanda's hand on Liam's arm that apparently indicated her support. And Suzi would like to bet that Nick Rossi had noticed it too. Suzi didn't know what was going on between

Liam and Amanda, but she did know that Liam was playing with fire – when he should be getting his own life in order.

'And they damage the nets. Smash their rackets into the tape when they lose a point. In temper. I've seen them.' Erica accepted the coffee Deirdre offered her and took a cautious sip. 'They're always knocking balls over because they're so . . .' she shuddered, '*wild*, and they even bring their bicycles on to the court when there's really no need.'

'Yes.' Deirdre nodded with enthusiasm. 'They bring their *bicycles* on to the *courts*, you know. And there's no need.'

Erica glared at her.

Suzi decided she'd had enough. 'So shall we vote on raising fees?' she suggested brightly.

Liam scowled.

'Very well,' said their chairperson, with a brief and resentful baring of teeth. 'For? Against?'

The show of hands indicated a stalemate as Suzi had forecast. Liam, Suzi, Amanda and Beryl voting against Erica, Deirdre, Margaret, Diana and Nick. After a brief hesitation, Simon (always uncannily aware of the club's best financial interests), voted on Amanda's side.

'Why not put it to the club members?' Liam suggested. 'That's democratic.'

Erica did not look overjoyed at the prospect of democracy. 'At any rate,' she said, addressing Liam. 'Even you can't object to more tennis activities in the summer to raise money for the club.' She went on rapidly – as if concerned he might. 'Any ideas from the floor?'

'We've already got the open competition,' Suzi said, resisting the temptation to look at her watch.

'And the children's tournament.' Erica's expression softened. 'Christabel will be entering again this year.'

Erica's granddaughter Christabel, as Suzi recalled, had enhanced neither Erica's voice (too much shouting had meant she'd lost it) nor her reputation for fair play.

Deirdre put her hands together, but not in prayer. 'I do love the children's tournament,' she said wistfully. 'Such promise, such hope, such –'

'And the American tournament.' Erica consulted her notes. 'Plenty of names down for that one.'

'We're all interested,' said Nick, watching Amanda covertly, 'in mixed doubles.'

Well, well, well. The agenda, thought Suzi, was becoming more complex by the second.

Liam leaned forwards. 'How about an under-15s tournament that the kids from the middle and secondary school can enter,' he said.

Erica frowned. 'Most of them don't even know how to play properly,' she said. 'I really don't see why we should subject *our* young people to –'

'I disagree. They could knock spots off the club under-15s,' Liam said. 'These kids play on street corners and in the park. They've got a feel for the ball. It's in their blood.'

'Then they should prove it.' Nick Rossi was leaning back in his chair, regarding Liam cooly from hazel eyes. His gaze flickered to Amanda; Suzi saw her look away and caught the tension twanging between them. And there was Liam, horribly innocent, but somewhere in the middle of it all, she realised.

Liam though, had risen to the challenge. 'How could they do that?' he asked Nick.

'A competition of course. Chestnut Grove Tennis Club kids versus school kids.'

'Oh, I don't think –'

But what Erica thought was destined to remain a mystery, since

Liam slammed his hand down hard on the table. Cups and saucers shuddered and Deirdre let out a small gasp. 'Bloody good idea,' Liam said.

Suzi raised her eyebrows heavenward. She knew all that stuff about playing on street corners was a load of hogwash. It might be true of the Williams sisters, but in Pridehaven, kids played football, pool, talked and texted endlessly on their mobiles and went to the pub. Most of them were unfit and existed on junk food and half of them smoked – cigarettes, gear, whatever. The number of kids at Chestnut Grove Middle and Secondary schools who had ever picked up a tennis racket could probably be counted on the fingers of one hand. Liam knew that too, better than most. But Liam tended to get carried away by his own rhetoric. And Liam, she knew, could never resist a challenge.

'Vote?' Nick suggested.

It was passed – with Erica, Deirdre and Margaret abstaining.

As if she knew she was in danger of being ignored still further, Erica rose to her feet and waved her gavel. 'I declare this meeting closed,' she said, bringing it down on the table.

Everyone winced.

Suzi jumped to her feet and made her getaway.

Erica sighed as the clubhouse rapidly emptied. She couldn't help but feel that some of the younger contingent didn't take Chestnut Grove Tennis club and its concerns as seriously as they might. And she feared that the club was in danger of losing its precious exclusivity. To think that she had been planning this meeting for months. 'When ...' she asked Deirdre, 'does re-election come up? And where was Henry Lake tonight, when we needed him?'

He could have been the deciding vote, because Erica took Amanda's views on the subject with a pinch of the proverbial.

She sensed that she herself understood Henry Lake that little bit better than his daughter did.

She should never, she thought, have taken William's advice about not telephoning to remind Henry about the meeting. What did William know? Very little actually. In Erica's view it was quite understandable that a busy man like Henry could overlook Chestnut Grove's meeting. But a word from Erica and who knew – he could have been sitting beside her now inviting her up to the manor house to celebrate their small victory over the likes of Liam Nichols. She should indeed have telephoned. After all, she would never, as William had rather unfairly hinted, have been a nuisance.

'Re-election?' Deirdre frowned. 'Well, now . . .'

But Erica didn't wait to hear Deirdre's reply. Instead, she pushed the clubhouse key towards Deirdre and her tray of dirty cups and went to get her coat. She couldn't be expected to clear up, on top of everything else. It had been a trying day and Erica Raddle was exhausted with the effort of trying to keep it under control.

She would just make it for the start of his second set, Suzi realised, hot-footing it down the hill to North Street. She had never bothered to learn to drive and had got into the habit years ago of walking everywhere in Pridehaven. Liam had offered her a lift to the pub tonight, but she'd felt cross with him, not wanted an argument and so decided to walk it. Ten minutes and she'd be there. She was already late, but she'd make it up to Michael.

She pulled her jacket closer around her, for now that it was dark, the spring evening had grown chilly. He'd be fine. Michael didn't need her – not like Liam did. And he'd understand. Michael might be moody at times, but he was a pretty laid-back sort of person. There would be other gigs – other times when he really needed her support.

She turned into West Street and headed for Pride Square and the Bear and Bottle. Out of season, Pridehaven was fairly quiet, but this was Saturday night and the fish restaurant was full. Next door, the pub frequented by Pridehaven's youth contingent was pulsating with some of the mindless rap Suzi hated, and next door to that was The Bargain Basement. Suzi speeded up, passed Secrets In The Attic, did a double-take, spun back on her heels.

'Good grief!' Not only was the front door wide open . . . Burglars, she thought, all our valuable stock gone walkabout and we're bound to be under-insured. But . . . the lights were on and in the next millisecond she registered the sunflower-yellow walls, the windchimes singing in the breeze. What had she done? 'Estelle?'

She stepped inside. Nothing. No one. All the furniture was stacked in the middle of the shop, everything cocooned in dust sheets, the dust sheets splattered with sunflower-yellow paint. So was most of the window display. And was that a yellow footprint on the Chesterfield . . . ?

Suzi blinked and her voice rose. 'Estelle!' she shouted.

Chapter 7

Michael was singing The Animals' 'House of the Rising Sun' when Suzi entered the pub. It was crowded and smoky, and she stood at the back for a moment, staying out of sight, watching him give it some. He'd been working himself hard. She could see the faint film of sweat on his brow, the dampness of his fair hair. The sleeves of his denim shirt were rolled up and his eyes were closed in concentration. But not for long – they snapped open as someone got too close to one of his precious speakers. And stayed open as he reached the instrumental interlude, the part of the song where he started grinding his hips, raising suggestively the neck of the guitar.

She smiled. Living that beat, Michael called it.

It was hard to equate the Michael who had become her lover, who sat beside her on her tatty sofa in the riverbank cottage and held her hand, with this . . . performer. To watch him now you'd think he had an ego the size of a house. Suzi leaned against the pillar beside her. And she'd thought exactly that, hadn't she, when she'd first met him – during that weekend away with Liam and Estelle.

She tapped her feet, watching Michael's expression, the way he responded – so apparently sure of his audience. He'd been performing that night too in a crowded pub in the New Forest and Liam – being Liam – had got chatting to him afterwards. Suzi had kept out of the way, feeling only mildly irritated when Liam invited him back to their small hotel for a drink. She found Michael Ashby too full of himself, too crazy by half.

Then she was left alone with him for a few minutes and he'd leaned towards her, looked into her eyes and said, 'Why do you look so sad?'

'Do I?' Suzi had blinked at him, seeing him again, or perhaps for the first time.

'Yeah, you do.' He had touched her hand, his fingers stretching out towards hers, and she'd allowed her fingers to curl under his palm, just for a moment. That was the start. A small start, but Michael was a persistent man.

He invited her to Fareham, himself to Pridehaven, he phoned her, wooed her, charmed himself into her life, and until tonight, she had almost forgotten how they had begun. He had never, she realised now, been as sure of himself as he appeared. And equally, it had never even been her decision for them to become . . . well, whatever they'd become.

Suzi looked around the pub. The beams were decorated with dried flowers, the walls with brasses and gilt mirrors. The furniture was solid and the feel of the place rustic, traditional, comforting. And the clientele were loving Michael. He had all the charm of a little kid performing for the first time – the shy smile, the knees almost knocking together as he bent over his guitar in concentration. He had captured his audience. They were tapping their feet, rocking on their heels, keeping time, even singing along – some of them. Michael had done OK.

Last orders were called and Suzi pushed her way through to the bar to get a beer. Had she been sad when she'd met Michael? No more than now. She'd always thought of herself as contented. She enjoyed her life with her animals in the cottage, she enjoyed Secrets In The Attic, and she liked the change from routine that Michael brought when he came down on Friday nights. The feel of a man in her arms, someone kind to talk to, who was more responsive than Samson, even on a bad day. And if there was more . . . well, Suzi hadn't found it, and that was probably some failing in her.

Secrets In The Attic . . . She pulled a fiver out of the pocket of her jeans. What a night. A committee meeting from hell and then discovering that her partner had decided to get drunk and paint their shop and half its contents bright yellow. Secrets in the attic? It looked more like sunny afternoons in Provence.

Michael was still trying to extricate himself from the blonde – he knew he shouldn't have given in and done 'Lay Lady Lay', it was against all his better instincts – when he saw Suzi.

She waved. She was wearing figure-hugging jeans and a black T-shirt, no make-up, all short spiky hair and a big grin.

Michael's heart leaped, before he remembered how angry he was with her. And she made no effort to come close enough to see off the blonde, damn it. Was she so sure of him?

'Got to have a word with my girlfriend,' he told Blondie, who pouted the sort of dark red lips that might suck a man dry and murmured, 'See you again soon then, Michael. That's the best version I ever heard – apart from Dylan's, of course.'

Of course.

Michael squeezed his way through, touched the nape of Suzi's neck. 'Where were you?'

She rolled her eyes. 'You won't believe it when I tell you. First, the committee meeting went on for ever, then –'

'Couldn't you have left?'

'Left?' She blinked up at him, still smiling, not yet realising that this was going to be a row.

Michael didn't want to, but he couldn't help himself. 'Walked out. You know, told them, sorry, but there's somewhere you have to be. Someone you have to be with.'

'Oh, I see.' Suzi's eyes narrowed. She seemed to be re-appraising the situation. 'I had to stay there,' she said at last. 'Erica's doing her best to take over the youth club and turn CG's into something terribly exclusive and awful. We have to stop her. It's important.'

'And I'm not.' He knew it was childish, but the adrenalin had left him, his after-performance high ruined. He felt disappointed and yes, he felt childish.

'Of course you're important.' Suzi touched his arm. 'But I knew you'd do fine without me. And you have.'

Michael just gave her a long look and went off to get his leather jacket. That was hardly the point.

'I suppose Liam was there?' he said, when they pulled up in the yard by the riverside, which was as near as they could get to her place. What was wrong with him? Could he be jealous of her brother?

'Yep.' Suzi had gone all tight-lipped. Their journey back to the riverbank cottage in the battered Granada had been a silent one.

'Arguing with anyone who'd listen to him, no doubt.' Michael was aware of the sneer in his own voice. What was up with him? He didn't want this.

Suzi got out of the car, led the way down the path and into the cottage and petted the dogs who had come to greet them. 'At least Liam cares,' she said hotly. Briefly, she buried her face in Samson's fur. 'He believes in the future of CG's. He wants ordinary people to benefit. Our local kids, for example.'

Michael felt the exclusion of her words. The local kids were nothing to do with him. He didn't even live here. 'Up the workers,' he scoffed.

For a moment, he thought she was going to ask him to leave.

For a moment he felt the drop of panic in his groin. He had gone too far. Then she turned away. 'I don't want to argue. I'm going to bed.'

Michael followed her up the narrow staircase. It curled its way like a comma into an equally narrow landing which led to Suzi's bedroom. He ducked to enter. This wasn't how he'd meant it to be. It was supposed to be flushed and warm between them now – post-performance heat sparking them off into a session of sex to remember, Suzi looking up to him, wanting to please him, with, OK, just a hint of groupie adoration in her dark eyes. But it wasn't like that, not at all. Yeah – and whose fault was that?

She got undressed slowly – he tried not to watch, but his eyes were drawn back to her small, slim figure as she stripped off her jeans and T-shirt, as she pulled back the patchwork quilt, switched on the bedside light, shrouded within its fringed navy linen shade. He knew it didn't matter to her that they might go to bed and not make love, that he might not hold her close, that he'd be lying beside her, staring up at her night-time ceiling, while she slept soundly on. Suzi was ace at pretending indifference.

Michael took off his shirt. Or *was* she indifferent?

'The landlord reckoned I could have the spot once a month,' he told her as she returned from the bathroom.

'Great.' Suzi climbed into the high bed. She plumped up her pillows and settled down.

Great. Meant nothing, did great. 'Fact is, I'm learning some new material, really getting into it again.' Michael stepped out of his jeans.

Suzi's eyes were closed. 'Great,' she said, more sleepily this time.

'The job's pissing me off,' he continued conversationally, going through to clean his teeth. The bathroom of the two-bedroomed cottage was tiny and Michael had to stoop to enter. He fixed his gaze on the multi-coloured copper unicorn Suzi had hung from a ceiling flocked with silver stars.

'So I've given in my notice,' he said, when he returned to the bedroom. He ducked under the eaves to deposit his watch on the pine dressing-table. That would shake her. And he wanted to shake her, wake her, make her look at him, for God's sake.

'You've done what?' She opened one eye.

Half a look was better than none, Michael told himself. 'I'm leaving work,' he said. 'Leaving the factory. Leaving Fareham.'

The other eye opened.

'In fact I was wondering – what do you reckon about me moving in here?'

It was two weeks later that Suzi got home from Secrets to find the narrow hallway of the cottage crammed with amplifiers, guitars and speakers.

'Are we opening up a music shop?' she said mildly. The last two weeks had been equally crammed – with guilt and bafflement mostly.

She had been baffled that Michael had given up his job in Fareham, even more baffled that he was expecting to move in with her.

In a way, she supposed, picking a route over one of the speakers, she had liked the fact that Michael lived in Fareham, and not Pridehaven, that he wouldn't encroach on her space or her weekdays, suddenly turn up and expect her to drop everything in order to do what he wanted her to do. It was selfish of her perhaps, but she was used to living alone.

And then there was the guilt. Guilt that she was too selfish to want him living here, guilt that she hadn't wanted their relationship to change, that permanence seemed a threat not a comfort. And guilt that she had inadvertently made him feel so unwanted, because when he'd dropped the bombshell and assessed her unguarded initial reaction, he'd looked so sad, she'd promptly taken him in her arms, hugged and hugged as if she could snatch that first horrified reaction away again. Oh, yes, Suzi was good at guilt. Weren't all women?

'Of course I want you,' she had said, wondering if she said it often enough, whether it would happen, whether she would feel it. 'Stay here for as long as you like.' Knowing she'd made it sound temporary, knowing that was the only way.

She was fond of Michael – of course she was. She enjoyed his company, enjoyed going to bed with him, was happy to help him out if she could. And she would even . . . she climbed over an amplifier, give his musical equipment a home. Though it was telling, wasn't it, that of all his possessions, there were more guitars, amps and speakers than all the rest put together.

But how the heck, she couldn't help wondering, had Michael ever come to the conclusion that she'd want to share her home with him? It was hardly a spur of the moment decision for any couple. In fact right now, to Suzi, it felt life-threatening more than anything else. How would she cope? What had she let herself in for? And more to the point – for how long was Michael thinking of staying?

Chapter 8

Michael wandered into the garden of the riverbank cottage and surveyed the lawn dispiritedly. In theory this was now his home, a home shared with Suzi. Only it didn't seem that way somehow. And how come goats were so stupid? Hester always walked to the full length of her leash before she started eating, sidestepped and ate, sidestepped and ate, oblivious of the greener grass close to her tethering post. The result? A crop circle.

But then . . . He moved closer and stroked Hester's white head. Who could blame the poor creature – never taken out like the dogs, not free to explore her territory like the cats. Even Suzi's flock of chickens had more freedom.

Hester stopped munching for a second to look up at him soulfully.

'I understand,' Michael told her, glancing rapidly behind him to make sure Suzi wasn't watching him out of the kitchen window. 'And just to prove it – I'll take you out.'

He went back inside, called to Suzi, 'OK if I take Hester out?'

'Out?' Suzi looked up from the novel she was reading and raised an eyebrow.

'For a walk,' he clarified, aware it sounded daft.

'Why?'

'Why not?'

Suzi shrugged. 'Don't lose her, then.'

'I won't.'

Michael returned to the garden, untied Hester, held on to the leash and attempted to open the back gate, usually a simple task that was hampered in this instance by the two dogs chasing each other between his legs and a surprisingly strong, lunging goat. Eventually he managed it.

'C'mon, girl.'

After ten metres the struggle was becoming a mammoth one.

After twenty, it was almost impossible. Hester (or maybe all goats? Michael wondered) did not like being taken out on her leash. Probably thought he was treating her like a damn dog.

After thirty metres, Michael was about to give up. Hester, the placid goat, had become a goat from hell, one minute refusing to move, the next charging this way and that, irrespective of path, direction or river. Michael's palms were sore, he was beginning to sweat and he had the uncomfortable feeling – remembering the expression on her face – that Suzi had known how it would be.

'Enough.' He decided to let Hester off the leash. She'd probably stand quietly, munching, give him the chance of a sit down. And Suzi would never know he'd not made it further than fifty metres . . .

He untied her. Hester promptly charged off down the path.

Michael stared at her retreating back. 'Er . . . Hester!' And with rising panic, 'Hester!' at full volume. But Hester was now out of sight.

'Shit.' Michael followed her, further down the path and then into the woodland beyond. 'Hester!' No sign. No sound. Only the gulls screeching in the near distance and the soft rush of the river, now just out of sight. The path grew more muddy as he hit the shade of the trees, made his way over the skeletal roots of beech and yew.

'Hester!'

For fifteen minutes he trailed the woodland path, shouting at Hester, swearing at Hester, pleading with Hester, and then imagining what Suzi would say. Christ! What would Suzi say?

'C'mon, Gazza!' Liam tore a hand through his hair. 'Switch that thing off!' Liam hated mobile phones. He despaired of the way they'd become indispensable, infiltrated themselves into everyday existence. He hated people talking into them with self-important voices. And he worried that today's youth spent most of its time punching out meaningless text messages or with the things permanently glued to their ears. God alone knew what damage they were doing to themselves and this fragile environment.

Meanwhile, fourteen-year-old Gareth Brown was haring to the net of the tennis court, all wild ginger hair and heavy black-framed glasses, making for his over-sized hooded sports jacket, casually thrown on the support post ten minutes ago. 'Might be important,' he gasped theatrically, as the third rendition of 'Old Macdonald had a farm', began.

Liam looked up at the grey sky and then into the middle distance that was Pridehaven. All he needed now was for the heavens to open, and they'd be off. Commitment wasn't big around here. 'Carry on, the rest of you,' he called to the others. 'Service practice.' There was a collective groan.

Gazza had thrown out half the contents of his jacket pockets, located the mobile, but seemed too out of breath to speak into the thing.

That didn't bode too well as far as his fitness was concerned. Liam eyed the black and silver pack of ten cheap brand cigarettes, assorted disposable lighters, packet of Rizlas with cardboard strips torn off, all lying on the asphalt, and sighed. Why was he bothering? He was trying to train a load of kids whose idea of sport was sitting around getting stoned. Gazza and the other twelve- to fourteen-year-olds plucked from the youth club might know what to do on a football pitch, but tennis was another ball game – literally. Maybe Erica Raddle was right. Maybe tennis was a class thing. Maybe this lot didn't care about the youth club they went to, the ethos of CG's, even the bloody view. Maybe he should just give up and let them do what they liked with the place.

'How's it hanging, babe?' Gareth managed to ask whoever was on the other end of the line. He glanced across at Liam. 'Can't stop. Gotta skedaddle. I'm in training.'

Well, that was something, Liam supposed, ducking as another ball flew purposefully in his direction. The lad sounded keen. And he had to admit there'd been no shortage of volunteers from the youth club when he'd told them about the tennis tournament. 'Those fat old tarts don't stand a chance,' and, 'yeah, let's show 'em a thing or two' had been the gist.

'It's cool,' Gazza was saying now, as he shoved lighters, fags and the rest back inside his jacket pocket. 'Take a trip. See ya later.' Liam raised his eyes heavenwards.

On court – fearful of the fate of the more delicate grass, Liam had taken them on to the hard courts instead – the others were still pounding the balls every which way, focusing on power at the cost of accuracy, in order to defeat the enemy. Liam had begun to wonder if he was that enemy, considering the number of tennis balls he'd had to avoid so far.

'Crap serve,' yelled Steven Hunt, also known as Stunt, not because he was vertically challenged (though he was) or because of his name, but because he regularly walked the plank across the River Pride down by the harbour. 'Out by a bloody mile.'

'Just long,' Liam confirmed to Tiger Rogers, the server in

question, tall and skinny and with the strangest service toss – more like a muscle spasm – that Liam had ever witnessed. It had started to drizzle with rain. So far the boys didn't appear to have noticed, but Liam knew it wouldn't be long.

'Yeah, bloody long way out,' said Stunt.

'Watch it.'

'Watch what? Your fat arse?'

'Here it comes. Number two.'

'Second serve.' Liam waited, close to despair. Perhaps this time, he'd taken on too much.

Tiger tossed the ball with a jerk of one bony wrist, sidestepped to the left, swung his body round and whacked it.

It shot past Steven Hunt, whether by luck or judgement, perfectly placed in the far corner of the service court.

Everyone stopped and stared – no one more surprised than Tiger himself. Except perhaps Liam.

'Bloody ace,' said Gazza.

He wasn't joking. Shit, Liam thought. He had their support. And they were trying their best. How could he even think about giving up now?

Michael spotted two women approaching from the other direction. Maybe they'd seen her? 'Hester!' he called weakly.

'Lost your dog?' The first woman clucked with sympathy. 'I had one like that once,' she confided. 'Never came when called. I had to bring a whole bag of dog biscuits to get him to come back to me.'

'What does she look like?' the other woman asked more helpfully.

'This tall.' Michael held up his hand. 'Coarse white coat.'

'Breed?'

'Goat.'

'Pardon?' The second woman, dressed in tweed jacket and brogues, took a step back.

'She's a goat. A pet goat.' What the hell was so strange about that?

'I haven't seen any goats,' said the first woman doubtfully, as woman number two took her arm and pulled her away.

It was beginning to rain. Michael walked on, rehearsing what he would say to Suzi. *She tore the leash out of my hand . . . I chased after her – for miles . . . She charged off, I hung on, she dragged me along the ground . . . I tried to stop her. What could I do?* Somehow, whatever he said, he didn't think Suzi would understand.

The light was getting dim by the time Liam and his six volunteers trooped back into the clubhouse. Liam half-wished CG's already boasted a restaurant, though not at the expense of the games room – he'd stand this lot a meal for what they'd achieved today. They might be rough but they were certainly ready, and a couple of them had showed real promise. Surprisingly – for the lifestyle they led wouldn't have suggested it – they had stamina, whilst years of messing around with a football in the park had given them bodily co-ordination and a good eye for the ball. Best of all, they wanted it.

The clubhouse was full of the usual cross-section of people. Liam nodded to Simon and Diana, frowned as he clocked Nick Rossi in the far corner of the conservatory, talking to Estelle. Her flame-red hair was a halo around her pale face, she was smiling and leaning slightly over the glass-topped table, towards Rossi, as if she couldn't quite hear or believe what he was saying. It was probably bullshit. But what bothered Liam the most was that neither was dressed for playing tennis. Rossi was in close-fitting designer jeans and one of his poncy sweaters and Estelle wore a long and close-fitting midnight-blue skirt and a silk top Liam had bought her on holiday in France last year.

For Christ's sake! Did the woman have no feelings? And if they weren't playing tennis . . . Liam strode up to the bar to buy drinks for the lads . . . then what the bloody hell were they here for?

'Will there be girls at the tournament then?' Gazza asked Liam as Liam handed him his coke. He eyed it dubiously – probably considering a quick top-up from the miniature tucked in his pocket, Liam thought.

'One-track mind,' jeered Stunt. 'Who'd be interested in you?'

Gareth peered back at him through his thick black-framed glasses. 'If there's girls on the other side, we need some too.' He spoke very slowly. 'Nerd brain.'

'Look who's –'

'Excellent point,' chimed in Liam, to whom trading insults signified a loss of team spirit. He turned his back on Estelle and Rossi without acknowledging them. What did he care? 'D'you know any girls who can play?' This was tricky. Far too many girls, in his experience, didn't take up sport until they wanted to lose weight or keep fit – and that often didn't happen till they were nearly forty.

'Diane Parker's a rocket,' said Tiger.

'Yeah, but does she play tennis?'

'She does it against the school wall.'

This time it was a chorus. 'Yeah, but does she play tennis?'

Liam waited for the laughter to die down. 'Ask her, will you?' He addressed this to Gareth. He was the natural leader – if anyone could sort it, Gazza could. 'And if she wants to play, get her to bring a friend or two.'

'Consider it done.'

At this point, Erica Raddle bustled into the clubhouse, doing a double-take and shooting Liam a look along the lines of – these rough specimens belong in the youth club if you please. She pointed to the door that led through to the other side of the bar and the social room. From here, Liam could see a load of kids clustered round the pool table, and another four pounding the table football machine.

And the toffee-nosed old cow wanted to take it all away from them. Liam pulled a face at her back as she peered over Deirdre's shoulder and started pontificating. Chairperson? You'd think she owned the place. Deirdre, he could see, was busily putting gold-coloured leaflets into envelopes. Deirdre was always busily doing something.

'We'll be next door,' Gazza said to Liam. 'Same time next week with girls?'

'And plenty of practice in between,' Liam confirmed. Because God, if they were going to beat what the tennis club had to offer, they'd have to go some, however much they wanted it.

As the kids dispersed, he looked over towards Estelle's table. It was empty. No Rossi. No Estelle. They must have made a pretty rapid departure once his back was turned.

Liam left his beer untouched on the counter and hot-footed it out of there. As he passed Deirdre and Erica he caught a snatch of conversation.

'I'd like to lose the "chestnut",' Erica was saying. 'Grove Lodge has a far more appropriate ring to it.'

Liam turned to stare at them, but they ignored him.

'Grove Lodge Tennis Club,' echoed Deirdre. 'What a marvellous idea.'

Michael turned to trudge wearily back to the cottage. It was getting dark. He'd never find her now.

At first he thought he was imagining the bleating behind him

– the imagination could play such cruel tricks. Then he heard it again and spun round.

'Hester!' He tried to grab her collar but she dodged, apparently content – now that he was travelling in a homeward direction – to trot along next to him.

When they got to the garden gate, she submitted to the leash, and he tied her up, the relief so overwhelming he almost kissed her.

Instead, he knelt down in front of her. 'I take you out,' he said, wagging an admonitory finger, 'and this is how you repay me.'

Hester bent her head back, Michael relented and chucked her under the chin and the next thing he knew was contact, a blast of pain, a sensation of spinning and the awareness that he'd been somersaulted backwards on to the lawn behind.

'Christ!' Michael glared at her, but Hester merely continued munching the lawn.

He staggered inside, clutching his head.

'You were a long time.' Suzi was in the kitchen. And eyeing him strangely. Her eyes were all kind of squinty and her mouth screwed up – almost as if she were trying not to laugh, or cry. 'Are you OK?' she added.

Michael let go of his head. 'Yeah, I gave her a good runaround.'

'Did you let her off the leash?' Suzi poured some wine into two glasses.

'Hmm? Yeah, mmm.' He took the glass she offered him and downed it in one.

Suzi was watching him closely. 'I bet you were dead worried when she didn't come back,' she said after a moment.

'What?' Had she seen them? No, impossible. Michael thought fast. 'No, I knew she wouldn't go far.' He tried to sound as if he knew what he was talking about. He hated Suzi thinking that he was a bungling idiot.

'Because of the herding instinct?' Suzi asked.

'The herding instinct. Yeah, right.' What the bloody hell was that when it was at home?

Suzi began chopping onions. 'Goats do like to go their own way,' she said. The knife sliced into the white flesh. 'And you are the herd, of course.'

'Of course,' Michael echoed. Chop, chop, went the knife. Oh, so he was the herd, he should have realised that.

'The herd often splits into smaller groups,' Suzi was saying. 'But when you turn around, back they come with you.' She swept the onion to one side of the chopping board with the knife.

Michael hated know-alls. 'And I suppose you thought I wasn't aware of that?' Without waiting for a reply, he shot her a baleful glare and walked out of the room.

'Are you sure you're OK?' he heard her call after him.

But it was only when he was out of sight that he clutched his head once more. Thank God she hadn't seen the head-butt, he thought. His credibility rating would have sunk down to zero.

Chapter 9

The man who had walked through the open door of Secrets In The Attic strode up to Suzi and placed a business card on the counter in front of her.

She looked up – way up, he was a giant of six feet and the rest – into grey-green eyes, registered a short fiery beard and shock of improbably copper-red hair and promptly looked down again.

JOSH WILLIS, ANTIQUE FURNITURE AND RESTORATION, she read. Suzi thought of Stan and Terry. LOWEST PRICES PAID, their latest advert in the local *Pridehaven Gazette* had read. THERE IS NO COMPETITION. What she did not need in the shop, Suzi thought, was another antique dealer, especially one that looked like Little John from Sherwood Forest.

'Yes?' She glanced up again, keeping her voice clipped and frosty, though the amused look in the grey-green eyes made her want to smile back at him. His hair, she realised, was actually the colour of the leaves of one of her acer trees in the back garden of the riverbank cottage, though his eyebrows were a much lighter copper – like sand. And he had a carefully crumpled look about him – he was wearing a linen shirt, trousers and jacket, not matching, but blending into an interesting three-tone effect. A very crumpled three-tone effect.

'An unusual place you've got here.' He looked around and Suzi followed his gaze as if seeing it for the first time. Yes, it was unusual – now.

They had built on the sunflower theme ('now that you've done it, we may as well go with it,' Suzi had said to Estelle, when they'd finally managed to clean all the yellow paint off the window display and the Chesterfield) by filling a couple of huge vases with bright, fresh flowers, and replacing the dingy Victorian prints that had hung on the walls, with Van Goghs and Cézannes. From the ceiling floated dream-catchers, crystals, and mobiles made of driftwood and seashells, shifting their hips in the breeze coming from the open door.

The antique furniture had been moved to the sides of the shop floor, leaving room for a purple, fluorescent green and orange rug that screamed alternative rather than tradition. And the antique jewellery was now displayed on modern carousels, with mirrors inset. More mirrors adorned the walls, of all shapes and sizes, some old, some new, reflecting the light and giving the shop a contemporary and airy feel that was, OK, totally out of keeping with an antique shop, as Suzi was aware.

The signwriter Estelle had apparently called whilst under the influence of alcohol – or possibly schizophrenia, Suzi thought privately – had re-vamped the outside of the shop. To the passing pedestrian, Secrets In The Attic might have been expected to sell flowers, kitchen equipment or trendy gifts. What daisies, sunflowers and bluebells dotted amongst the yellow lettering did not say, Suzi knew, was antiques. And to reinforce all this, the door was left open, the windchimes sang and there wasn't a speck of dust in sight. They'd gone further than feng shui. This was total overhaul.

'Antique shops don't have to be musty places,' Suzi said to the interloper.

'Oh, I'm not criticising.' He grinned again, a cat's grin that spread across his face. 'It's er . . . refreshing.'

And this time Suzi grinned back. Refreshing, hit the mark. She wouldn't give Estelle the satisfaction of knowing it, but she rather liked the new look herself. It was a lot more pleasant to work in, for a start. 'You've got a shop yourself, I take it?' she asked. Hopefully he wasn't about to take over the baker's on the other side of them. Sandwiched between The Bargain Basement and a man like this, they wouldn't stand a chance.

'No. I buy and sell as I go along. Mostly abroad,' he told her. 'That's what I wanted to talk to you about. I thought we might find some mutual benefit.'

'Oh?' Despite the fact that she knew she should be cautious – in the world in which Suzi and Estelle now moved, the word 'dealer' was often regarded as euphemism for 'crook' – and despite the fact that it wasn't so long since Michael had moved into the riverbank cottage, Suzi felt a flush of interest. Not yet excitement, but borderline, she admitted to herself, gripping the edge of the counter and feeling another twinge of the guilt that seemed to have become a dear old friend and companion. What exactly did 'mutual benefit' mean?

Oddly enough, she and Michael had hardly made love since he'd moved in, and Suzi was beginning to wonder if this was how it would be. She was also wondering – since he hadn't mentioned it – if he'd given any thought to the length of his stay. He had been no trouble, he had fallen over himself to fit in, though that in itself didn't seem as if it should be necessary, Suzi thought, feeling guilty again.

And maybe he was right, she'd told herself rather often lately, maybe their relationship had been due for a change. Maybe this was what they needed to bring a new depth to it. So why, she wondered, did it feel so wrong?

'Are you free for lunch?' Josh Willis asked.

Suzi had half thought about nipping back to the cottage, maybe taking Samson and Delilah out for a quick walk along the river. But Michael was there, she remembered with a further stab of . . . yes-there-it-was-again.

'I am as it happens.'

'Great. Shall I come back at one?' He pushed the card closer towards her. His hands – like the rest of him – were large, his fingernails clean and cut straight across, no rings, no frills.

'OK.'

He left with a nod and a wave and a step that was confident and knew exactly where it was going. Unlike me, Suzi thought. Unlike me.

She picked up the card. Josh Willis . . .

Estelle had crossed the River Pride and was walking in the woods to the west, tracing a familiar path that began with beech trees and grew darker as it wound away from the river, close to the brooding yews. Suzi was in the shop today, though Estelle would go in later, she decided, and tell her about her new idea. It was more difficult than she'd imagined, sharing a business partnership, even with a woman she respected and cared for, like Suzi. Estelle supposed she simply had this urge to move onwards, alone, just to see if she could do it.

But at least it gave her free time. And in that free time she so often found herself drawn here, as if she had a bungee rope tied round her waist and attached to the woods, she thought wryly. Too often, perhaps, she was drawn here.

She was flattered that Nick had sought her out, arranged to meet her for a drink at CG's and taken her to his mother's home, even if it was only to take a look at Shelagh Rossi's jewellery. He had been attentive, courteous and surprisingly fun to be with, she'd found. Best of all had been the moment when Liam had walked into the clubhouse — Estelle couldn't have manufactured it better if she'd tried. And didn't it serve him right? Amanda Lake — hah!

Shelagh Rossi was a lovely lady — she had shown Estelle round the house on the hill that she'd shared with her Italian husband, Nick's father, who had died five years before. And in the high-ceilinged bedroom with Italianate furnishings, she had laid all her jewellery out on the the calico bedspread of the canopied four-poster. There were some beautiful pieces, and much of it went beyond Estelle's knowledge of the subject, she realised. She'd have to do a bit more research if she was going to give a professional valuation.

'That's fine, my dear,' Shelagh Rossi replied, when she told her this. 'But unfortunately, it's not just a valuation I'm considering.'

Estelle couldn't fail to see the glance exchanged between mother and son. But they were living in a striking Gothic Victorian mansion set in five acres of landscaped grounds. Surely she didn't need to sell her jewellery?

A shrug from Nick seemed to persuade Shelagh to go on. 'I understand that an auction might be best for certain pieces,' she said, picking up a brooch — the ruby in the shape of a swan was set in gold filigree. 'I'm asking you to act as an agent, my dear. I like you. And I'm sure we can rely on total client confidentiality.'

Estelle had agreed, arranged to return three days later when she had done more research, with the view of taking some of the pieces to Sotheby's. And she had managed to stop herself asking questions. It wasn't any business of hers, she told herself, why Shelagh Rossi was selling. She should be grateful for the work, glad that Nick and his mother felt her sufficiently trustworthy and knowledgeable.

But it had made her think. She had gone back to the flat above

Secrets In The Attic and taken out the box that contained her own jewellery – the pearls left to her by Auntie Mo, and her mother's rings. One diamond solitaire – Estelle put it on the third finger of her left hand, turned her palm so that the light reflected from the stone. And one huge sapphire set in platinum. She placed this on her little finger. She loved this ring, loved the depth of blueness in the stone, the colour of her mother's eyes in the photograph Estelle kept by her bedside, the photograph taken – so Auntie Mo had told her – just before her mother's death. Her mother's smile was enigmatic, almost as if she had known. And on her finger this very ring.

Jewellery . . . Every woman loved jewellery – even Suzi, who tended to scorn anything girlie. A tantalising mix of the old and the new, a precious gift from generation to generation. A token of love.

Estelle had slipped her mother's rings from her fingers, compared her own band of jade and silver, the tiny moss agate she wore on her little finger. Antique and modern. And most women appreciated both. She couldn't help thinking that Secrets In The Attic was not taking full advantage.

At a quarter to one, Suzi peered into the mirror above the wash-basin in Secrets In The Attic's tiny loo. The mirror was old – it made *her* look like an antique, giving her reflection a brownish tinge more dirt than suntan, she thought, sucking in her cheeks and wishing she'd bothered with eye make-up this morning. She rarely did. Mornings were a rush of cleaning up the cottage – just enough so she could face it when she walked back in at the end of the day – feeding the animals, a slice of toast on the hoof, a quick wash and out into the world. How women found time for early morning eyeliner, liquid foundation and blow-drys, Suzi had no idea. Those women were obviously far more organised than she.

By five to one she had tidied the shop, put the cash away in the safe, turned the sign from 'open' to 'closed' and suddenly, there he was looming in the doorway, as crumpled and three-tone as before.

'Hi.' Suzi wouldn't have been surprised if he'd drawn a bow and arrow and gone for the bull's-eye of the nearest dream-catcher right there and then.

'Pub lunch do you?'

Finding her voice temporarily out of action, she nodded agreement and he led the way, striding along West Street towards the Bull Hotel, so that Suzi had to half-run every few paces to keep up with him. But she didn't mind. It was a lovely spring day, the breeze was warm on her cheeks and there seemed to be a scent of promise in the fresh sea air as they reached the grand old Bull Hotel, situated by the bridge and the old water mill of the River Pride.

They made their way inside. Suzi came here occasionally – the Bull was an anachronism really, boasting flocked wallpaper, pink and grey pastel carpeting and even an old-fashioned powder room complete with dressing-table, box of tissues, hand lotion and padded chair.

The bar, with its gleaming pumps, glasses and bottles stacked high against a backdrop of mirrors, looked as out of place as it would have in an Edwardian sitting room. Even odder, Suzi decided, looking at the blackboard menu, was the notion that The Bull Hotel would provide pasta, curry or surf 'n' turf. Beef and dumplings followed by a pudding of spotted dick would, she thought, have been more appropriate.

'In what way,' she asked him when her mushrooms in garlic sauce with ciabatta bread and Italian leaves had been placed in front of her, 'did you think we could benefit each other?'

Josh Willis attacked his steak as if he meant it. 'I could shift some of your more unsaleable items for you,' he said. 'There's a decent market in Germany for a lot of the stuff that's out of favour here right now.'

Suzi considered this. It sounded reasonable enough. 'So how does it work?' she asked. 'Do you take commission on what you sell?'

He shook his head. 'I can't afford to cart stuff over there and maybe back again for someone else's profit. I'd buy from you – whatever pieces I think I can get rid of.' He paused mid-munch and speared a piece of meat.

Suzi winced. The man was a hunter. The image flicked into her mind – Josh Willis, not in a three-tone crumpled linen suit, but in a loin-cloth, Tarzan-style. He was leaning forwards, dead focused, spear in hand, going for the kill . . . And he was a man to go all out for what he wanted – whatever he might be wearing at the time. She waved her napkin in front of her face, trying to ward off the inevitable blush. Wondering what would happen to anyone who stood in his way.

'At a low, knock-down price, of course.'

The words 'Bargain Basement' came to mind. Suzi narrowed her eyes and tried to decide whether or not this man reminded her of Stan or Terry. The flecks of gold and grey in the red beard offered no clues, and the warmth in his eyes didn't mean a thing. Of course, everyone was out for what they could get – this was a cut-throat business. But was he a crook? She found herself hoping not.

'How low?' she asked, sensing it would pay to be direct.

He considered. 'I'd have to check it out, but probably half your marked prices.'

'Hah!' He didn't react, so Suzi said it again. 'Hah! You are joking?'

'I don't joke about business.' He eyed her gravely. 'I could take a fair bit of your stock,' he said. 'If you need the money, it would release some of the capital you've got tied up in things you might never sell.'

About to snap that he had no reason to think that she needed the money, nor to suggest that her stock wouldn't sell, Suzi stopped as she remembered the mistakes they'd made in the first few months. Mistakes like the walnut writing bureau and mahogany bookcase that still sat, silently accusing, in Secrets In The Attic. 'How much profit d'you reckon on making?' she asked. 'What's the margin?'

He grinned the cat's grin. 'D'you expect me to tell you that?'

Suzi nodded. 'Why not?' If he was being straight with her . . .

'OK.' He put down his knife and fork. 'I'm looking to sell it on for the kind of asking price you have in mind right now.'

Big margin then, Suzi thought. Big profit for the hunter.

'Not as big as you think,' he said, as if she'd spoken out loud. 'I have to pay my expenses for going over there. I get stuck with things too. I'm not a rich guy. I make a decent living but not a great one.'

'Why do it then?' she asked, hoping to lure him into a few confidences. And what was wrong with trying to find out some personal details? There was such a thing as being too focused on business.

He met her gaze and didn't look away. 'I like the life.'

She waited for him to elaborate, but clearly that was as far as he was prepared to go. Personal information? Negative commitment. 'Fair enough,' she said, though it wasn't.

But despite this mixture of directness and evasion, there was something about Josh Willis that Suzi trusted. An honest vibe was coming through, and Suzi was big on vibes. Though come to think of it . . . she took a bite of the delicious olive ciabatta . . . her judgement could well be flawed by the large glass of white wine he'd bought her earlier. A cunning trick, and one she should have been ready for. A true business woman would have stuck to pineapple juice at this stage of the proceedings.

'What d'you reckon then?' He held out his large square hand. 'Do we have a deal?'

She took it, because it seemed churlish not to. The hair on the back of his hand was fine and, like his eyebrows, the colour of light sand. 'Come back to the shop after lunch and make me an offer or two,' she suggested, feeling quite proud of the way her business acumen was functioning under the circumstances. She'd made a few mistakes, but could hardly be called a pushover.

What she should do at this point, of course, was tell Estelle. Suzi considered this. For about a millisecond. She wouldn't have hesitated – had it not been for the niggle of resentment that remained. Had Estelle considered telling Suzi of her urge to paint the shop sunflower-yellow? She didn't think so. So why should she do the same? It might be petty of her – OK, so it was petty, definitely petty – but for now, at least, she wanted to keep the offers of this particular hunter to herself. She wasn't however, sufficiently into self-analysis to ask herself why.

'Then,' she said, feeling the warmth of his hand, knowing she'd held it for a few seconds too long, conscious suddenly of her vulnerability, 'we'll discuss whether or not we have a deal.'

The light was filtering through the pale leaves of the beech trees, gradually drying the earth into a mud-caked surface that was easy, Estelle found, to walk on. And once, it had been equally easy to lie on, she recalled, thinking of Liam as she kept thinking of him – young, vibrant and exciting. With an intensity in his green eyes that could relate to anything he cared passionately for – a poem, a child, justice, recognition; but most often Estelle herself. She could picture that burning in his eyes, even now, all these years later. That was the hardest thing.

She walked on, steps slowing now. Pictured his sinewy arms as he pulled her towards him. *Estelle, my love, Estelle.* She could taste his lips, the fresh, black Italian coffee he'd been drinking, touch the soft hair that curled over the collar of his shirt, smell the apple soap he'd washed with that morning, and the indefinable Liam-scent that clung to his dark chest hair, that she wanted to breathe in until she drowned in it.

Estelle let out a deep sigh, allowed her hand to trail across the bark of one of the beech trees that might, just might, have been the one they first made love under. Ah, that spring afternoon when Liam had said, 'are you sure it's OK?' and she had gently pressed the frown from his brow with her fingertip, until his wide mouth curved into its smile and yet his eyes still burned. Burned for her.

Almost of their own volition, her fingertips found a knot in the wood and caressed what might, to some, seem a small imperfection. That afternoon, they had undressed each other and made love naked, under the beech tree, with the sun warming her back, her knees digging into the mud-caked earth, the grass staining her bare shins, her hands around his lean waist, her face burying into his shoulder; soft skin, hard bone, the swell of muscle, breathing in the Liam-scent.

Estelle clung closer to the beech tree, resting her face against the coolness of its bark. What had happened to the lovers who had been one another's world? Those lovers that she had hoped could never be broken apart, simply because their fit was such a perfect one?

They had made love, staring into one another's eyes, touching one another's faces, linked with one another's fingers. And afterwards, Estelle recalled sadly, he had held her as if he would never let her go . . .

'So how's business?' Josh Willis asked Suzi as they walked back towards Secrets In The Attic. 'Quiet?'

Suzi found herself tempted to tell him about their financial problems, forgot for a moment herself and Estelle's vow of female independence, found herself thinking that a man like this might have some answers. But perhaps all that was due to the wine too, she told herself. 'Everything's quiet in Pridehaven,' she murmured, proud of her own discretion. She too could be a closed book, she decided.

And Pridehaven was quiet – it was one of the reasons she loved the place. Quiet, except of course for the gulls that flapped and shrieked at dawn, dusk and several of the hours in between. But never boring – it had a hardness to it, a slightly seedy, slightly Bohemian seaside edge. There was nothing smug or pretentious about Pridehaven. It could be basic and in the winter it could be bleak. But it remained beautiful and it had always brought Suzi a sense of peace.

'Bloody hellfire!' shrieked a female voice as Josh and Suzi drew near to The Bargain Basement. 'You wanna get your dates sorted, you do. And your head while you're at it!'

'Very quiet,' agreed Josh. 'A positive haven of tranquillity.'

The door to The Bargain Basement had sprung open to reveal two women sparring up to one another. Stan's wife, Lorraine, was wearing fake leather trousers and matching coat over a revealing white lycra top, her dyed blonde hair piled high on her head, her body language saying, 'drop dead, bitch'. Her companion, Terry's wife, Rita, was dark, almost Mediterranean in appearance. She wore red lipstick, lots of big costume jewellery and a yellow mini-dress with crimson poppies on it, teamed with a silver Puffa gilet and black, strappy sandals.

'The villa's booked,' said Rita. 'You can't un-book a villa.'

'And I can't switch flights,' snarled Lorraine.

'Fine, darlin'.' Rita flashed a smile at Suzi and Josh as they drew level. 'Then we'll close the place up for two weeks.'

Suzi and Josh exchanged a glance. It was almost, Suzi thought, as if this red-headed giant of a man knew exactly what problems she and Estelle were experiencing.

'Hi, Suzi, hi, Josh,' said Rita before spinning back to face Lorraine. 'Yeah, let's close the place up.' She waved silver-varnished fingernails in the other woman's face. 'We'll see what the boys make of that.'

'The boys won't like it one bit,' said Josh, as Suzi let them into the shop.

'Too right.' Though Suzi couldn't help thinking that for herself and Estelle, even two weeks without The Bargain Basement would be pure bliss.

While Suzi made coffee, Josh got to work with a notepad and pen. Turning everything they had, Suzi thought sadly, into a few squiggles on a piece of paper.

'We weren't doing too badly before they arrived next door,' Suzi said doubtfully.

He glanced across at her over the writing desk.

'At least not as badly as we are now,' she amended, the expression in the grey-green eyes forcing her into honesty. 'People used to drop by for valuations, we got the odd house clearance.' As she spoke, she tidied the desk in front of her, caught sight of the landlord's latest letter and shoved it behind the till.

'And how bad is it now?' He hardly paused, merely whipping out a tape measure from the depths of one of the crumpled linen pockets and making more notes.

Why bother to pretend? She couldn't be a closed book even if she Sellotaped together all of her pages. 'We'll be finished if we can't turn things around,' she admitted. She flicked disconsolately at the dream-catcher hanging just above her. And what would she do then? She couldn't face returning to the library – that's if they'd have her. She'd moved on.

But it seemed hopeless. True, the changes they'd made to the shop had helped draw people in. It was bright and it was welcoming. But those people were also, unfortunately, being drawn into the shop next door, only to be seduced by all their basement bargains – poor quality goods but at more affordable prices.

Josh Willis stopped writing. 'Then it sounds as if there's only one way to go,' he said. 'Now . . . these are the prices I'd be willing to pay.' He handed over the notepad.

Suzi frowned as she deciphered his writing. They were lower than she'd been expecting. She wasn't even sure they'd make a profit on some of it. And which way was he talking about, that was the only way to go? Shut up shop? Go bust? She didn't like to ask.

But it was only after she'd given a tentative agreement to his offers and arranged to call him the following day to confirm, only after he'd left her alone once more in the shop, that Suzi realised. *Hi Josh?* So how did Josh Willis, Pridehaven's answer to Little John, know Terry's wife Rita? And now that he was aware of exactly what she had in stock, how much she was asking for it, and how desperate they really were, what was he planning to do with that information?

Suzi groaned. She was a pushover after all. And Josh Willis was a hunter. She'd like to take that spear of his and stick it where it would really hurt, damn him.

Chapter 10

Liam couldn't help observing that the balcony scene was lacking in the one element normally associated with it. Romance. This could be due to the fact that Juliet (Jade Johnson) was chewing gum and showing by the distaste in her clear blue eyes that she did not and never would fancy her Romeo (Bradley Jacobs).

'Show some emotion, Jade,' Liam encouraged. 'Remember you're young and you're in love.'

There were the inevitable titters.

'And take out the gum, while you're at it.'

With a disdainful lift of the eyebrows, Jade did so, lodging it on to the back of the chair in front of her, currently masquerading as the railings of a famous balcony. She stuck out one hip at a raunchy un-Juliet-like angle. 'Romeo, Romeo,' she intoned, in a bored voice. 'Wherefore art thou, Romeo?'

Crystal Woods sniffed disparagingly.

Had the casting been a mistake, Liam wondered. Jade Johnson was a natural extrovert, and although three years younger than the original Juliet, certainly had the physical features of a girl of fourteen. She was up front in more ways than one, as Liam couldn't help noticing the first time he saw her out of school uniform in rehearsal, wearing tight jeans and a low-necked close-fitting T-shirt. But would she be prepared to swallow her principles and act?

'When do they get to snog?' enquired Marcus Weatherby, who had auditioned for the part of Romeo, but who, being six inches shorter than Jade, had produced a differential that could, Liam predicted, create problems of credibility.

'No thanks to snogging with that creep,' said Jade, flicking back her dyed blonde hair.

'Your loss, babe.' Bradley smiled his wicked un-Romeo-like smile and pushed back the greasy dark brown hair that continually flopped into his eyes.

Liam raised his hand. 'They're not going to snog,' he said. 'They're going to dance.'

'I only do Le Roc,' said Jade.

'You'll do what I –'

'I can do high kicks,' contributed Crystal Woods, Jade's main competitor for the part of Juliet. She might be able to do high kicks, Liam reflected, and her platinum blonde hair was probably natural, but Crystal's pale, insipid face, flat chest and skinny legs had not said Juliet Capulet to Liam. They had said undernourished eleven-year-old plagued with a permanent cold.

'And tap,' said Crystal. 'I got a certificate for tap at the festival. Third class.'

'Le Roc will do just fine,' said Liam, wondering what the hell it was. 'Perhaps you could help me choreograph, Jade? I was thinking of "Let's face the music and dance".'

The phone rang, but Suzi was reluctant to pick up. On the other side of the shop Estelle glanced across at her enquiringly.

With a sigh, Suzi reached for the receiver. 'Secrets In The Attic?'

'Suzi?'

'Yes.' She recognised his voice at once – deep and slightly growly.

'Are we still on for a deal? Only I'll be off in a couple of days' time and I've still got some space in the van.'

Oh yeah? Suzi stood up straighter. The hand holding the telephone receiver to her ear was stiff with dutch courage. 'I'm sorry,' she said. 'I've had second thoughts.'

There was a pause. She wondered what he was thinking. Did he suspect that she was on to him, that she'd realised he was chummy with Stan or Terry or both, that she was feeling a complete and utter idiot for opening up and telling him what a financial mess they'd got into at Secrets In The Attic? He was a competitor, for heaven's sake. And in cahoots with their other competition. He was a low-down rat. He was worse.

'Prices too low, were they?' he asked at last. 'I couldn't go much higher.'

'It's not that,' Suzi said quickly. She didn't want to enter into negotiations with him. Next thing, he'd be standing here on the threshold again and she didn't want that, didn't want to see him. She felt too much of a fool. The trouble was, that somehow the man had got to her.

'What then?'

'Well . . .' What was the matter with him? Couldn't he take no for an answer? Why didn't he give up now that he'd been sussed? She glanced across at Estelle and shuffled some papers from one side of the desk to the other. 'I've discussed this with my business partner,' she said.

Estelle looked up. 'Discussed what?'

'And?' asked Josh.

'And she doesn't want to sell the stuff,' Suzi said helplessly.

Josh Willis laughed, a big growl-laugh that rumbled along the telephone line and made Suzi feel more of a fool than ever. 'You're telling me it's got nothing to do with the prices I offered? But that your partner doesn't want to sell the stock you've got in the shop?' he said.

'Er, well, yes.' Suzi tried to sound forthright instead of mad.

'If that's the way you do business, it's no wonder you've got problems,' he said.

So typical of his gender, Suzi thought. Ready to criticise at the slightest opportunity. 'Any temporary problems we may be experiencing have nothing to do with you,' she snapped. Only, why was he making her talk to him like this? Why wouldn't he just go away and leave her to feel guilty alone?

Another pause. 'So I take it you'd rather I didn't visit you again?'

Suzi felt completely put on the spot. Of course she'd rather he didn't visit her again. How could she face him? She thought of the red beard, the bulky body, the grey-green eyes and cat's grin. She didn't want to be confronted by him. And yet . . . And yet . . .

'I really can't see the point,' she said.

'In that case,' he growled, with no hint of humour in his voice, 'neither can I.'

'Hold her,' Liam ordered Bradley. 'Hold her as if she's flesh and blood, not Dresden china.'

'You said, no snogging,' protested Jade as Bradley moved in.

'I'm not talking snogging, I'm talking close contact.' In despair, Liam pushed Bradley out of the way and took Jade into his arms. As he did so, he was aware of a creak indicative of the hall's swing door being pushed open. He relinquished Juliet and her cheap perfume.

'You are Romeo and Juliet,' he told them both. 'You're madly in love. Head over heels, truly, deeply, more in love than any other couple have ever been in the history of the world. Got it? You die for the love of one another. You're a frigging role model for the love stuff. If you can't pretend, we'll have to forget the whole thing.' His voice rang out and echoed round the school hall.

'Hi, Mum,' Jade said to the woman who had come in.

Liam turned to face her. Her hair was the same colour as her daughter's and equally unnatural, she was tall and had muscular well-toned legs and a figure she was not trying to hide. She looked very out of place in the school hall with its dark laminated floor, fluorescent lighting and magnolia walls decorated with child-art. Liam was just thinking that she seemed vaguely familiar and not just as the mirage that Jade would become in thirty years' time, when he realised who was now standing just behind her.

'Amanda?' He blinked.

She waggled her fingers, put them to her lips and indicated that she would wait at the back of the hall.

Bloody hell, thought Liam.

'I hope,' said Jade's mother, with a wiggle of the shoulders, 'that there won't be *too* much *close* contact.' She looked Liam up and down, and he was sure he could make out a suggestive glint in her eyes. 'If you know what I mean.' She winked. 'Jade's a big girl. But she's not even twelve yet, you know.'

'I know,' Liam said crisply. 'And I can assure you, Mrs Johnson, that you need have no concerns on that score.' What he did not need were accusations of sexual harrassment, or of encouraging tweenage boy/girl intimacy, come to that. They could manage that kind of thing without him. And he didn't need Amanda witnessing this sort of scene either. 'That's enough for today.' He clapped his hands in dismissal. 'See you all Tuesday after school.'

Liam waved away interruptions of, 'She sticks her bloody elbows into me, sir. When I try and get in close, I mean.' (Bradley). And,

'I could do it better, sir.' (Crystal). 'I like Bradley . . .' (at which point Bradley made a puking action behind her back). 'I started ballet when I was three and my mum says –'

'Tuesday,' Liam said firmly. 'And thank you all.'

As they began to disperse, he approached Amanda, who was smiling, her eyes wide and excited. 'Golly, a real rehearsal. With *lots* of drama too!'

'Drama I could live without.' Liam kissed the cool cheek she offered him, conscious at the same time of the rumours of approaching wedlock that would be circulating Chestnut Grove Middle School by lunchtime tomorrow.

'But the show must go on,' Amanda said obscurely. 'And it looked terribly exciting.' She was dressed in an almond-green suit, the skirt of which hovered just above her bare knees. It looked classy and expensive. She looked classy and expensive.

'What are you doing here anyway?' he asked her, aware how oafish that sounded.

'You didn't call me.' She pouted prettily. 'So I came to *you*.'

What for, he wondered. What would a girl like Amanda want with a man like him, a poor – and oafish – hung-over teacher (he'd been drinking too much since Estelle left) whose time was so taken up with coaxing the kids of the youth club into tennis and the school's year 7s into Shakespeare that he had no time left for Amanda. Or Estelle, he thought sadly.

'You did offer me a drink.' Amanda moved one step closer. 'So I thought, how about tonight?'

Liam smelt again that exclusive perfume, quite a contrast to Jade Johnson's. They should ban scent like Amanda's, he thought. Who needed aphrodisiac in a bottle when you were looking at Amanda Lake? 'Sure.' Liam was expansive, though he was so knackered, he'd rather get his head down – alone – in his garret flat. Things must be bad.

He was distracted by the approach of Jade's mother. All bony shoulders and tits, he found himself thinking.

'Call me Lorraine.' She thrust long, painted fingernails towards him. 'And if you need any help with . . .' She floundered.

'The set?' suggested Amanda.

'Yeah, the set. Or . . .'

'The lighting?'

'Yeah, or . . .'

'The costumes?'

Liam took the hand she was offering him, and the opportunity to pull her away from Amanda and her not so helpful comments. 'Thanks. I'll let you know,' he said.

'Good.' She looked him up and down once more. 'I like a man who knows what he wants.'

Was he one of those? He doubted it.

'But don't you let them boys get too close,' Lorraine reminded him as she ushered Jade out of the hall. 'She's only eleven, remember.'

How could he forget? Ye Gods. Liam thrust a hand through his hair. Where was Estelle when he needed protection?

'Isn't it wonderful how your life can change when you're free?' Amanda took his arm.

'Wonderful,' echoed Liam.

'Poor darling. She's after you, and who could blame her?' Amanda chuckled.

Liam frowned at her. 'I'm sure she's not. She's probably happily married and –'

'A compulsive man-hunter,' Amanda said. 'I know the type. But let's not talk about her.'

Fine by him. Liam watched the kids gradually dispersing from the hall and into the narrow corridor beyond. 'Why did you come here – really?' he asked her.

'Among other reasons . . .' A seductive smile. 'I wanted to know . . .' She led him gently back towards the stage. 'If you're umpiring for the under-9s tournament next weekend?'

Next weekend? Liam did some rapid calculations. What with the play and the tennis coaching on top of his other commitments, he was in danger of getting seriously overbooked. But he had promised . . . 'Yep,' he told her. 'Unfortunately.' The under-9s were the worst. He waved off the final stragglers, checked no one was left behind.

'So am I,' said Amanda, as together, they left the hall.

'Good.' Liam leaned back to switch off the lights. The only problem was that so, God damn it, was Estelle.

'Who was that?' Estelle demanded.

'Hmmm?'

'On the phone.'

Should she lie? Suzi decided not to bother. 'A dealer.' But she didn't mention she'd as good as promised to sell half their stock to him, didn't add how much she'd liked him. 'Not to be trusted,' she added, to convince herself.

'Men . . .' Estelle rolled her eyes.

Suzi grabbed the chance. 'And talking of men –'

'No.' Estelle smoothed a lock of dark red hair away from her face. 'I don't want to talk about Liam, Suzi, I really don't.'

Suzi wasn't going to let that stop her. She was fed up with both of them mooning around missing one another like two separate halves of the same circle. The trouble was that she loved them both. And it might sound ridiculous, but there was something wrong with her world when these two were apart. 'But you still care,' she reminded Estelle. 'You should talk to each other at least.'

'There's no point.'

Suzi sighed. Liam had his faults but he was hardly an out and out bastard. Or low-down hypocrite . . . like Josh Willis, for example.

'And a relationship needs more than two people caring,' Estelle added. She was sitting, head bent, cleaning some jewellery. 'It needs to be worked at, it needs to be cherished. Otherwise . . .' she squeezed more metal polish on to her cloth '. . . it withers and dies.'

Suzi thought of Michael. Had their relationship withered and died? Could it be revived with a dose of Grow-more and a snippet of mutual affection? She flipped open the till and began to count the takings. It didn't take long. And what happened when a relationship became suffocating, she found herself wondering. When there was no sunlight, no water? What happened when a pleasant Friday-night change of routine became an everyday thing? And you didn't like it, didn't want it, needed your me-time back?

Suzi shut the till again. It wasn't Michael's fault, and perhaps that was why it was so hard to remind him that theirs was supposed to be a temporary live-in arrangement. It would be like kicking out Samson or Delilah, she thought. Or Hester. She smiled as she recalled the expression on Michael's face that evening – when he'd finally got Hester back to the cottage, when he got up from the lawn where she'd head-butted him. Poor Michael. She'd had to stop herself from rushing out there to comfort him; she'd realised somehow that loss of face would be the worst injury Michael could suffer right now.

'Forget about me and Liam.' Estelle jumped up from her seat, red hair flying, as Suzi realised guiltily that she already had. 'And listen to my great idea.'

'Mmm?' Suzi wondered when Estelle would realise that she was the only one getting great ideas. That Suzi's plans (like the one concerning Josh Willis for example) had a habit of ending in disaster.

'How d'you fancy specialising in jewellery – antique and modern? Repairs, old and new, the whole bit?' Estelle paced the floor, expanding on her theme, showing Suzi first a garnet bracelet ('an antique any woman would want in her collection') then a modern jade and platinum choker ('they're both compatible with today's woman, today's lifestyle, don't you think?').

'Mmm.' Suzi was only half-listening, the other half still mulling it all around – Josh, Michael, Liam and Estelle.

'It makes sense, Suzi.'

'Hmm.' Talking of sense, she was a fine one to talk. Getting drunk and painting the shop sunflower-yellow were hardly the actions of a rational woman.

What Estelle needed . . . no, what Liam and Estelle needed, was a helping hand – her hand, Suzi decided. She simply had to get them in the same place at the same time. Should be easy enough.

She nodded as Estelle shoved a casket of ear-rings into her lap and continued to drone on. 'Mmm,' she said.

A concert perhaps? The music would stop them talking for long enough to avoid the risk of another row, long enough surely for the chemistry to kick in. 'Yes,' she said.

'You like the idea?'

Well, anything was worth a try, Suzi thought. 'It's brilliant. You're brilliant.' And as for Suzi, she might mess up big time in the men department, but she could still be a matchmaker made in heaven, she decided.

Estelle hadn't meant to go to the garret flat after work, but something Suzi had said, had made her think. *You should still talk to each other at least.* Suzi was right, of course. It was childish not to talk, not to let the man you had loved for so many years know what you were thinking, feeling.

She walked out of the shop, registered the presence of her Mini

Mayfair, did a double-take and then swore softly. The car had a flat, front nearside.

She hesitated, but there was nothing she could do about it now. She'd deal with it in the morning, maybe ask Liam if she could borrow the footpump to get enough air in it to make it round to the garage.

Liam . . . Could they talk?

Why not? Estelle made her way along West Street towards Pride Square, pulling her jacket closer around her. They were both adults – allegedly. And Liam, whatever else, was not telepathic. If he was as confused as Suzi seemed to think he was, if he was anywhere near as depressed as Suzi said he was, then he deserved some explanation.

Estelle felt a pang of . . . what? Love? Humanity? Friendship? Whatever, it was enough to make her stop at the off-licence to buy a bottle of wine. Liam was too disorganised to have any in the flat, and it would save them from going out somewhere too public for proper talking. The wine would be a peace offering, of sorts, she decided, and conversation was always easier after a glass or two.

She took her change and the brown and gold carrier bag and set off down North Street. Not that she had any intention of going back to him – she would make that clear from the outset. She would merely tell him – in a calm and reasonable way – that although she still cared for him, would always care for him, she was tired of being second best to whatever might momentarily catch hold of his passions, tired of waiting for Liam to give her some time, tired of being taken for granted, tired of running scared, half-waiting for him to leave.

It would help him, she decided, groaning as the first drops of rain fell on her head and stained her vivid pink sarong, in any future relationships with the opposite sex. When the time came, of course. She pushed this thought away, quickly, before it could spoil her mood, this strange sense of optimism.

But why not? Because she was getting there, wasn't she? She was managing on her own, creating a space to live in that was hers, thinking up new ideas that reinforced her independence as well as hopefully helping the future of Secrets In The Attic. And she was doing it without Liam. That was important. She'd never managed alone before.

She got to the big Victorian terrace, rang the doorbell and waited. No answer. 'Damn.' Estelle couldn't believe that after all this planning, he wasn't even here. And now it was bucketing down, and she hadn't brought her umbrella. She was bare-legged, wearing her roman sandals, the pink sarong, a T-shirt and a thin jacket. She must be mad – it was still only May and this was England, after all. She shivered as the wet carrier bag from the off-licence brushed insinuatingly across her bare flesh. 'Bugger it.'

She had a choice, she realised. She could go in, shelter from the rain, pour herself a glass of wine and wait for him. And why not? She had her key, a lot of her stuff was still in the flat, and she was pretty sure he wouldn't mind. Or she could give up, go back to her new flat above the shop, leave it till another night.

No contest. It wasn't in Estelle's nature to give up, so she delved in her multi-coloured rucksack for the key to the outside door, let herself in, and shook off the worst of the rain. If she went back to the flat above the shop she might never summon up the courage to come here again, and the chance would be wasted, the chance to put things right.

She would wait for him inside, she decided. She had the wine, didn't she? He would come home tired, cold and wet and she would surprise him. She smiled at the thought, curiously excited at the prospect of seeing him again – her love, her Liam, the only man she'd ever wanted. No, she wouldn't go back to him. Not yet anyway. But talking – they could still do that, couldn't they?

Chapter 11

The following day, Suzi noticed that Estelle was being very heavy-handed with some rather delicate china.

'Have you seen Liam?' she asked her, thinking of the Arts Centre tickets.

'You could say that,' Estelle replied.

'And did you talk?' Something, Suzi realised, was wrong here. She was no mathematician, but surely three and three didn't make four and a half?

'We did not.'

There was also a certain something in Estelle's expression that reminded Suzi that redheads had notorious tempers. As teenagers, Estelle and Liam had fought tooth and nail, but over the years, Estelle, at least, had calmed down. However, she didn't seem too calm right now. Suzi winced as another piece of china shuddered from its impact with the table top.

'Any particular reason why not?' Suzi asked, half-wishing she hadn't brought the subject up.

'Let's just say,' said Estelle, 'that the first part begins with an A and ends with an A and the second part is something I'd like to throw her into.'

Suzi frowned. She wasn't sure she was up to anagrams at this time in the morning.

Estelle muttered something as she went out the back.

'What was that?' Suzi asked, thinking she'd misheard.

'I said, he's a cheating bastard,' Estelle repeated. 'And you can tell him that from me.'

Hmmm. So far, Suzi reflected, the matchmaking didn't seem to be going too well.

Michael fed Samson, Delilah, Castor and Treacle, picked up the local paper from the doormat and sat down with a cup of strong coffee at Suzi's kitchen table to confront the situations vacant columns.

He realised, of course, that it had been naive of him to expect to live from the profits of gigs alone, when he had no established circuit, no record of performances, and when he was in competition with other artists who were tried, tested and came from Dorset. He realised too that he should have looked for a day job to tide him over, that he had no right to sponge off Suzi and that at this moment in time he felt like a spare fart.

But the fact was – despite what he'd told Suzi about applying for jobs – Michael didn't want one. This was an obvious disadvantage when it came to job-hunting. But he simply wasn't interested in a run of the mill job. He was fed up with being bossed by little men with big egos, to whom time-keeping was a religion – especially hard to take when he'd spent so long working for himself. And now? He didn't want his life to be like that, damn it. He wanted to sing, he wanted to be creative for a change, he wanted to be free. 'Really free, really free,' he mumbled, recalling some punk hit from the 70s.

Consequently, he half-heartedly ringed a couple of ads with red felt-tip – mainly for Suzi's benefit when she looked at the paper later – but when he picked up the phone, it was the number of The Hardy Arms in Dorchester that he punch-dialled. He'd left a tape there yesterday, the landlord had been friendly enough, and if he could tell Suzi he had some more work when she walked in through the door . . . well, surely that would ease the tension between them? And unfortunately he was not talking sexual tension here – resolved or otherwise. He was talking cut-the-atmosphere-with-a-bloodied-knife type tension.

But, no, the landlord told him, he hadn't had a chance to listen to it yet. *I'll call you . . .*

Michael was despondent when he put down the phone. Now, even if the landlord decided Michael had talent, he would also have him labelled as a needy man.

Samson came over and rested his jaw on Michael's knee in sympathy. Michael rubbed his ears and the dog slobbered gently over his jeans. Shit, another pair for the wash, thought Michael. He should do all that himself, but he hadn't got round to it yet, had no idea where Suzi kept such things as washing powder or ironing board. 'What d'you want, boy?' He looked into Samson's big brown eyes. 'A walk?'

Samson's tail shot into action. 'A walk it is then.' Better, at any rate, than staring into space. And a hell of a lot easier than walking a goat. Michael sighed as he got to his feet. He had expected to feel at home here, to fit effortlessly in with Suzi's routine, to be appreciated for what he brought to the household.

But, come to think of it, what did he bring to the household? Michael picked up his cup and washed it out in the sink. He had no money left to make much of a financial contribution, he seemed to have temporarily misplaced his sense of humour, he got pissed off whenever Liam came round – in fact, he felt like a bloody lodger. Worse than that, the whole balance of their relationship had changed. He felt Suzi was merely putting up with him, treating him as a duty not a pleasure, relegating him somehow to the role of another mouth to feed, another pet to look after. He was aware that he'd said he'd look for somewhere else – but surely Suzi hadn't really meant that? Surely she was happy to have him around? Otherwise, he thought, what was the bloody point?

Samson was getting excited, snuffling and letting out the odd gruff bark. Even Delilah had picked up on it. She was whimpering and had moved to the door, bright eyes expectant, tail a-wag. The least I can do, Michael thought, is walk the bloody dogs.

He reached up to pluck their leads from the hook on the wall, and as he did so, spied some orange tickets sticking provocatively out of an envelope, poked between a jar of cinnamon sticks and dried chilli on the top shelf of the open kitchen cupboard. He stared at the envelope for a moment. Clearly, it was Suzi's property, but she hadn't said anything about going to a play or a concert. Maybe she'd forgotten to mention it, he decided, shooting a surreptitious look at Castor, who was perching on the window-sill, apparently intent on cleaning her paws but also sending the occasional superior glance his way. And if Suzi had forgotten to mention it . . .

He dangled the leads in the air, thus provoking another yelp of frustration from Samson . . . then he should find out for himself what they were for. Check the dates and so on in case they missed whatever it was. Suzi was so scatty. He shouldn't let any tickets she'd bought go to waste.

No sooner had lengthy justification been arrived at, than Michael reached up in one swift movement, extracted the orange tickets from the white envelope and read the top one. IN CONCERT AT THE ARTS CENTRE, he read, THE BLUES SISTERS, followed by the date – and they hadn't missed it.

Bloody great! Michael flipped the tickets into the air. He loved the Blues Sisters, Suzi knew that . . . So obviously it was intended as a surprise . . . for his birthday maybe – a bit early, but that was hardly her fault, she wasn't responsible for the band's itinerary.

His spirits lifted as he opened the back door of the tiny cottage and whistled to the dogs, who bounded and sprang respectively over the step and into the back garden. Hester pulled at her rope (no way, José, thought Michael) the hens scattered with matronly clucks of disapproval and Michael set off at a fast pace for the riverbank, pouting his lips, doing his Marc Bolan impression and singing 'Hot love'.

Estelle wondered what on earth had possessed her to agree to this.

Erica Raddle had asked her and Liam months ago to 'help out' at the under-9s tennis tournament. These under-9s being the kind of under-9s (from good breeding stock, tennis-playing families) that Erica no doubt hoped would become (Chestnut) Grove Tennis Club's future. 'It means so much to them,' she'd said. 'They may be young, but they care desperately.'

In Estelle's opinion it was the parents who were the desperate ones, knowing perhaps that little Fenella or Nathan would very likely give up the sport when they reached their ninth birthday, in favour of discos, roller-blading or just hanging out. Knowing it might be their little darling's only claim to fame, their one-minute wonder, their opportunity for a picture in the local rag. So it was no surprise, Estelle supposed, glancing at the small figures dotted about on the green hard courts (no one trusted them on grass) that they took it seriously. This wasn't a game. This was war.

On court were Christabel Archer and Daisy-Jane Maddison. Both could serve over-arm, which was a plus. Both could hit the ball if it happened to come near them (which it usually did, since under-9s hadn't yet grasped the fact that the idea was to return the ball out of their opponent's reach) but neither was prepared to run.

This too was par for the course, Estelle thought, wincing as Daisy-Jane's female parent shrieked, 'Run, Daisy-Jane, run!' far too close for ear-comfort.

'Thirty all,' said Estelle, picking up an orange transition ball and throwing it to Christabel, since these young players also apparently believed that tennis stars in the making should not have to do such menial tasks for themselves.

'Thirty all?' she heard from behind her. 'Are you sure?'

Estelle spun round to glare briefly at Erica Raddle. She really wasn't in the mood for grandmotherly input. 'Yes,' she said, with more aggression than was perhaps strictly necessary. But who could blame her for being aggressive – after what she'd been through? First Liam and then her car.

She turned her attention back to the battleground. 'Ready, girls?' And fixed a smile of encouragement on to her face. Be encouraging at all times, they had been told. Positive reinforcement retains enthusiasm, develops self-esteem, sends out the right signals.

'Jolly good,' Estelle said vaguely to no one in particular. 'Off we go then.' She almost added a 'Tally-ho', but decided that this would be going too far.

Daisy-Jane was blowing her nose loudly as Christabel served into the body. She dodged at the last minute, the ball clipped her shoulder and her eyes filled with tears.

'Take two,' said Estelle briskly. She felt rather than heard Erica's snort of disgust from behind her. And she didn't care. She wasn't in the mood to care. All right, so it was a lovely day and the sun was shining (in her eyes); all right, so she was somewhere she loved to be. But even the charm of Chestnut Grove Tennis Club couldn't lift her mood today. This morning she had got her car to the local garage, only to be told by a cheerful mechanic that the puncture was in the wall of the tyre and she'd have to fork out for a new one.

He was very helpful, felt the need to explain everything in tedious detail and even showed her the air bubbles.

'How come?' Estelle had assumed she'd run over a piece of glass or a nail or something.

The friendly mechanic merely shrugged. 'Kids?' he speculated.

Kids . . . As Christabel served again, Estelle was distracted by the sight of Liam striding past, towards the neighbouring court, two little darlings in tow. He was wearing a pair of black 501s that were particularly close-fitting around the bum, and an open-necked shirt. He looked incredibly sexy.

'Hiyah!' He waved, grinned, thrust a hand through his untidy dark curls.

'Bastard,' she muttered.

Christabel, Daisy-Jane and all were looking at her expectantly.

'Forty thirty,' she said.

There were howls of anguish. 'Thirty forty,' she amended. 'Sorreee.' Last night she had waited for Liam for what had seemed like hours, drunk the entire bottle of wine, fallen asleep, and woken at midnight, alone, cold and rather drunk.

Christabel served into the net.

'Don't throw it all away, darling!' shouted Erica with some passion.

'Deuce,' Estelle declared as the second serve suffered the same fate.

'Heavens, Christabel! Honestly!' from the wings.

Followed by, 'You've got her now, Daisy-Jane. Go for it, babe!'

Were they fostering a sense of healthy competition in these youngsters, Estelle wondered, letting her gaze drift over to Chestnut Grove's honey and cream clubhouse and all the parents and children clustered on Erica's barbecue patio. Or just creating problems for adulthood – indigestion or heartburn perhaps? Irritable bowel syndrome? Suicide? 'Sudden death,' she said, following this line of thought and deciding that this was what she would like to give Liam. There were no advantages played in children's tennis.

Estelle re-crossed her legs and shielded her eyes from the sun. After all that wine, sun was not required as a feel-good factor. Why couldn't the day be more typical of English springtime – an uncompromising grey sky, perhaps, to reflect her mood?

She had washed her wine glass, got rid of the empty bottle and tried not to wonder where the hell he was (and with whom). She had adjusted her crumpled pink sarong, located the foot pump in the kitchen cupboard, staggered down the stairs, opened the front door to the Victorian terrace.

She had seen the rain, and . . .

Christabel's next serve was good, bouncing wide and out of Daisy-Jane's reach. 'Game,' said Estelle, relieved. 'And set. Jolly well done!' Hopefully that was sufficient encouragement.

She had seen Amanda Lake's red convertible, parked on the other side of the road, two heads close together in conversation, one dark, one blonde, illuminated by the light from the street lamp above.

They were obviously sharing an intimate moment and equally obviously about to go up to the flat. Estelle shuddered as she thought of her lucky escape. Liam certainly hadn't wasted any time in finding a replacement. Talk? She'd like to clock him one, the rotten bastard.

Suzi had popped out to the baker's for one of their yummy pizza slices, and was on her way back to the shop, when she got distracted by a sign outside The Bargain Basement. She groaned and took the biggest bite of pizza she could manage. THE BEST AND BRIGHTEST IN TOWN. FABULOUS PRICES . . . BECAUSE YOU'RE WORTH IT.

The door was closed, but she could see people milling around inside (people never milled around in Secrets In The Attic – there were never enough of them) and she could even hear some tacky background music that sounded suspiciously like Abba's 'Waterloo'.

'No class though,' growled a voice by her side.

Mouth full, Suzi spun around. No crumpled linen today – Josh Willis was wearing denim jeans and a battered leather flying jacket with fur collar. And his cat's grin.

'Hrmph.' Suzi stalked back towards her own shop, unable to say a word – partly because if she spoke she'd spit pizza at him, but also because she couldn't believe his nerve.

'You're in a different market place,' he continued, following her.

'Well, our market place is deserted,' she said at last, wiping her mouth with the paper napkin and opening the door of the shop. 'And what's the point of class if nobody wants it?'

'Fair point.' He sat down on the edge of the counter, long legs crossed at the ankle, hands thrust in the pockets of the flying jacket.

He seemed, thought Suzi, to take up an awful lot of space. And what was he doing here? She'd made it plain that she no longer wanted to do business with him, and he had made it equally plain that he wouldn't be visiting her again. It was for the best, she had told herself, trying not to think of his smile.

'I thought you were going to Germany,' she said now. That was where she had pictured him, driving his big white van, flogging furniture to tall, rigid men with blue eyes, blond moustaches and no sense of humour.

He shrugged. 'Not until the van's full up.' He eyed the writing desk in the corner and Suzi thought she could see the pound signs flashing in the pupils. Hah!

'I haven't changed my mind,' she said. She wanted him to go. And stay. His presence was unsettling; she felt drawn to him and didn't want to be. He was, she was sure, bad news. And if he was associated with Stan and Terry, it was probably bad news of the tabloid variety.

'Shame.' But he didn't seem to care much one way or the other. She supposed it was silly to imagine he was depending on their stock. After all, he'd never even come to them before; he must have a lot of other contacts who were more than willing to let him shift their furniture for them.

Like, 'Perhaps you should buy some bargains from the boys next door.' Suzi couldn't resist the jibe. She still felt a prize idiot for telling him so much. 'Best prices in town, you know.'

'I do.' He stared at her long and hard and she felt sure she was colouring up like a schoolgirl. 'Buy from them, I mean.'

'Oh.' She'd asked for that, she supposed. 'Tea?' she asked, to distract herself.

'Lovely.' He grinned.

Suzi was hoping for a few minutes' respite while she waited for the kettle to boil, but to her dismay, Josh Willis heaved himself off the counter and followed her into the tiny space that served as a kitchen and led out into a passage and the loo. And there wasn't enough room for him.

He leaned against the fridge door and she had to reach past him for the kettle and tea bags. Her head was level with his chest. The close proximity didn't seem to bother him but Suzi found she was getting short of breath and had developed a worrying case of the shakes in the leg department. She should, she decided, have had an earlier lunch.

'Do you know Stan and Terry well?' she asked, re-arranging mugs, plates and other paraphernalia in an effort to make the kitchenette look vaguely hygienic. At least, to his credit, he hadn't tried to hide the fact that they'd done business together.

'Well enough to know they're the lowest of the low,' he said cheerfully. 'Knocker boys. They specialise in chatting up old biddies who want nothing more than a cup of tea and a chat, and don't realise they're getting ripped off in the process.'

Suzi had thought as much. But, 'What does that make you then?' she challenged.

He laughed at her expression. 'Someone who's ready to take whatever business opportunity he's given. I only buy some of the stuff they have on offer. I don't know where it comes from.'

'Do you care?' she challenged. Because it was all very well to turn a blind eye — but what about integrity?

His eyes narrowed. 'I'm not the conscience of men like Stan and Terry. They do what they do. And —'

'You take advantage of it.' Suzi wasn't ready to let him get away with that one.

At last he nodded, as if conceding her point. 'Does that make me a bad person?' he growled, leaning down towards her.

Suzi looked into the grey-green eyes. He was laughing at her again. 'I don't know yet,' she said honestly. All she did know was that she'd never met a person like him.

He laughed again, took the cup of tea she offered him and strolled back out into the shop. 'Fancy coming to a car boot sale with me this afternoon?' he asked.

'I've got this place to run,' Suzi said quickly, clearing a space for her own tea and wishing a customer would come in. What did he want from her? Had she encouraged him? Did he want more than tea?

He gulped the hot liquid. 'What about your business partner?'

'Otherwise engaged.'

'No one else you could ask?'

Suzi looked around the sunflower-yellow interior of the shop and thought of Michael. He had nothing else to do – so far as she was aware. He really didn't seem to do anything much these days, apart from lounge around the cottage half-heartedly, looking through the situations vacant columns of the local paper and watching daytime TV.

It was getting to the point, she thought sadly, where she longed for him to be out when she got home, so that just for once she would have her cottage and her animals to herself. He was beginning to irritate her too – she'd snapped at him twice last night, and the hurt look in his eyes had stayed with her, so much so that later she'd held him close in bed, willing herself to feel something, anything other than sorrow. 'I'll try,' she told Josh.

She dialled the number of the cottage. Would he be there? Bound to be. But did she want him to meet Josh Willis? And was the boot fair a good idea? Was she mad to even consider it?

'You've got to get out and about a bit more,' Josh was saying. 'Find out what your average man in the street is wanting to buy, wanting to sell.' He picked up a delicate porcelain figurine and put it down again. Point made, Suzi thought. When they'd started, they'd bought almost anything – just to fill up the shop.

She replaced the receiver as it rang on. Reprieved . . . And, 'I thought you said this was a different market place,' she protested.

'So?' He grinned. 'Maybe you should find yourself a new one. Like one that appeals to more people.'

He had all the answers, didn't he? 'Anyway, I can't make it after all.' Fate, she thought. A let-off. 'Maybe another time,' she heard herself add. What? When would she learn to keep her mouth shut?

He finished his tea and plonked the cup down on the counter. 'Tomorrow morning?' he suggested.

'What?'

'Tomorrow morning. Early start. There's a good one on in Charmouth. I could meet you here at seven-thirty.' He flicked at the wind-chime by the door and it rang merrily.

'Seven-thirty?' she squawked. 'On a Sunday morning?' She wondered what Michael would say to that. Help.

He shrugged once more. 'I'll come by on the off-chance,' he said, as he left the shop. 'Think about it, Suzi.'

And she would, Suzi realised, watching him swing off down the street towards the car park. She would probably think of little else, damn it.

The time for the finals had eventually arrived, tea in the form of Earl Grey and home-made scones and coconut cake, courtesy of Deirdre Piston, had been served in the conservatory and on the patio, and Liam was looking for Estelle.

Eventually he found her, outside on the steps, gazing dreamily up at bloody Nick Rossi. He lingered for a moment, half-expecting her to make some excuse and come over, but instead, she flashed Nick an intimate smile and moved in closer. Then to Liam's horror, she reached into her rucksack, took out her diary and said something that sounded like, 'Friday evening, hmm, let me see . . .'

Jesus Christ! He stormed back into the clubhouse. She must be seeing him regularly. She certainly hadn't wasted any time. Or maybe . . . his stomach felt like a stone, he was surprised he could even walk . . . she had been seeing him before she left. Maybe . . . he shuddered . . . that was *why* she'd left.

Back in the clubhouse, Deirdre was busily collecting cups. Erica Raddle was at her side, and Liam was sure he heard the words, 'Purple and green acrylic,' as he strode past.

'Purple and green acrylic,' Deirdre echoed.

'Like Wimbledon.'

He turned around. 'What?'

Erica didn't bat an eyelid. She clapped her hands. 'Time for the grand finale,' she said. 'And may the best players win.' She flashed an encouraging, horsy smile towards Christabel Archer. 'Girls' final first then?' And bustled past Liam, who, along with the other umpires, had unfortunately promised to stay for the medal presentation.

Purple and green acrylic?

By the hard courts, chairs had been laid out earlier by Deirdre. Liam spotted Amanda, already seated, an empty chair beside her. He hesitated. He hadn't exactly been avoiding Amanda today, but neither had he sought her company. Their drink the other night had left him with a strange sensation somewhere around the groin area. A guy would have to be crazy not to have the hots for her, but it didn't feel right. He wasn't sure what she was up to; he only knew that the moment she'd driven away, she had disappeared just as clearly from his mind.

At the sight of Liam, she did her finger-waggle and indicated the empty chair. It would have been rude to ignore her, so Liam nodded, smiled and edged his way through, still looking out for Nick Rossi and Estelle. No bloody sign of them . . .

'Who's your money on, darling?' asked Amanda as he sat down.

She was lovely, she was being friendly and Liam tried to get into the mood. 'The one that sounds like something out of a herb garden,' he muttered, glancing across at the green hard court, at the two little girls posing for parents' cameras as they received their last-minute instructions, at the view beyond of Pridehaven and lots of blue, blue sky and sea.

'Lavender?' Amanda giggled. 'I agree. That would put Erica's nose out of joint.' She put a hand on his arm and he looked down at her perfectly French manicured fingernails.

Any man, he thought, would be flattered to have this sort of attention from a girl like Amanda. Any man would be excited by the touch of her hand, by that smile clearly intended for him alone.

So why the hell did he keep looking at her and wishing she were someone else – someone with a vivid cloud of dark-red hair, velvet brown eyes and a lop-sided smile? Why did he so much want her to be Estelle?

Chapter 12

Suzi switched off the alarm before it had the chance to wake Michael. He was sleeping on his side, facing her, snoring very softly, his wispy fair hair not quite covering the bald patch on the centre of his scalp.

Despite her throbbing head, Suzi smiled. It was a fact that irritated Michael beyond belief; no point telling him that baldness could signify virility. Michael and every other man she knew would laugh in her face.

She crept out of bed, pulled on the blue fleecy robe that was a little worse for wear and showed how much she liked snuggling up to the dogs and cats first thing, and went into the bathroom. It was a shivery sort of morning – well, it would be at six-thirty, she reminded herself, putting tentative fingertips to the spot just above her left eyebrow where her hangover seemed to be centred.

Six-thirty . . . What a horrible thought. She had an hour before she was due to meet Josh Willis, which in itself was ridiculous since Suzi never needed an hour to get ready for anything. And besides, she hadn't definitely decided she would even go, had she? She could be getting up for a glass of water, she could have set the alarm for any number of reasons. Yes, well . . .

She pulled the robe in closer. How frustrating it was, she thought, not to have the option of saying to oneself, I'll have to go – I said I would. Because she hadn't. He had given her a clear choice; she could change her mind (if she'd made it up in the first place) even now, with no questions asked. But this degree of self-analysis so early in the morning was doing nothing for her hangover.

Suzi peered cautiously into the mirror above the wash-basin. Everything looked more or less intact. If it's raining, she told herself, I won't go. I'll creep back into bed next to the man who is supposed to be my lover, hold him close and forget car boot sales and Little John lookalikes. But if it was sunny . . .

She approached the blind with some trepidation. It was navy-blue and facing west, so you couldn't tell . . .

She yanked it up and blinked. The pain in her temple increased. But there was definite sunlight on the other side of the frosted glass and not a raindrop in sight. So she'd go.

She pulled open the shower curtain, narrowly missing the bottom shark blissfully swimming round in circles at the base of the mobile that hung, along with sea-horses and a copper unicorn, from the ceiling. What about Michael? She felt the familiar guilt. Was she off her head? And talking of heads, did she have time to wash her hair?

If Samson doesn't leap up when I come down the stairs, she thought, as she climbed gingerly into the shower – it was very early, so he was bound to still be asleep – she'd give it a miss.

She lathered her hair with shampoo almost without thinking, felt the hot pressured water rain on to her neck and shoulders. Lovely. Already feeling better, she reached for the conditioner. And if Michael woke up before she left – he was a heavy sleeper but she could switch the hairdryer on and that would increase the odds – then she wouldn't go.

Fairly virtuous . . . Suzi rinsed off the conditioner, feeling it, silky smooth as it floated from her scalp and slid down her back. Where was she going with all this? And why was she getting herself so worked up? It was nothing. Michael didn't seem to mind her going to a car boot sale on a Sunday – why should he? she reminded herself crossly – neither had he minded Liam turning up unannounced last night. Not that Liam ever did any announcing, she thought wryly, he didn't believe in giving her the option of saying no. And after they'd eaten, Michael had even washed up the supper things, so that she and Liam could have a heart to heart. Yes, Suzi thought, Michael's mood had definitely improved. That was good, wasn't it? Only . . . Why?

She tipped back her head, closed her eyes and felt her hangover drifting away from her. He'd sat there last night on her old sofa looking for all the world as if he was hugging some special secret close inside – instead of merely stroking the cat. But still, later, they hadn't made love. Oh, what should she do about Michael?

Squeezing her favourite shower gel (olive and elderflower) on to a natural sponge, Suzi soaped herself generously. Last night had been – almost – like past times. They'd all had a bit too much to drink, Michael had got out his guitar and they'd sung a few of the old songs – Liam and Suzi joining in lustily, if not tunefully. They'd gone on until they ran out of lyrics, until Samson, Delilah and the two cats had all left the room in protest, until Liam had cried a couple of maudlin tears for an absent Estelle and until Suzi had remembered that maybe she *might* be getting up at six-thirty the next morning.

Liam was still sleeping it off downstairs and Suzi had managed just over four hours. She must, she thought now, want to go to this car boot sale pretty badly.

Ten minutes later, hairdryer in hand (it was selfish, she decided, to wake Michael purely on a whim) Suzi went downstairs to be greeted by a joyful Samson who clearly thought his luck had changed.

'Sorry,' Suzi told him. 'I'll feed you, but a walk's not on offer.'

As a precaution, she glanced back up the narrow stairs behind her and then back to Samson. 'I've got a tall, red-headed stranger to meet,' she confided, kissing his neck. So that was it then, her options had decreased to one — she must be going to the boot sale after all. And why the heck was she still feeling bad about it?

Suzi glanced at her watch as she rounded the corner at Pride Square. The Square was deserted and even the swish-slap of her trainers on the pavement seemed to echo in the silence. But then, it would be silent at seven-thirty on a Sunday morning, she reminded herself. Most people had the sense to stay in bed.

After all that rushing around (what on earth had possessed her to wash her hair?) she'd still be five minutes late, she realised. She might even have missed him.

At this thought her step quickened and she consciously slowed again. She would not look as if she were hurrying, she would not look as if she were worried, she would look as if she were simply out for an early morning stroll, damn it. Besides, she could see now that he wasn't waiting outside.

As she got to the shop, she rubbed her cold hands together and wished she'd worn a warmer coat. Her denim jacket had seemed the right kind of casual note to play, but . . . she shivered, it was feeling pretty flimsy right now.

To pass the time, she walked a bit further along the pavement, glanced in at the window of The Bargain Basement, saw their garish BECAUSE YOU'RE WORTH IT sign, and looked quickly away again. Bargains or not, she'd like to bet Stan and Terry wouldn't be up at this unearthly hour on a Sunday morning.

She glanced up at the window of the flat above Secrets In The Attic. Would Estelle be up and about? Probably not, and her curtains were still drawn, but Suzi dodged into The Bargain Basement's doorway just in case. If Estelle were to see her, there would be far too much explaining to do.

Explaining that was beginning to seem rather pointless, since Josh still hadn't arrived. Suzi was just thinking that she might as well go back to the cottage, collect the dogs and have a proper morning walk along the river down to the harbour, when a battered white van rolled up beside her, the window was wound down in the old-fashioned way and a red head appeared at the driver's window.

'I wouldn't stand there if I were you,' growled a familiar voice. 'Stan might think you're planning to nick his stock. Or his brilliant line in marketing.' He laughed. 'You might even get a bucket of water thrown over your head in the name of healthy competition.'

'Sssh.' Glancing furtively up towards Estelle's window, Suzi came out of cover and ran round to the passenger side via the rear of the van. It was freckled with rust, splattered with dirt and someone had thrown a slice of cucumber that had stuck to the back window and was now decomposing nicely.

She climbed in and flashed him a quick smile, but to her irritation he didn't immediately drive away. 'Why sssh?' he mocked. 'Who lives up there? You and your husband?'

'I'm not married.' Suzi fastened her seat belt to hide her embarrassment. 'And my business partner lives up there if you must know.'

He raised his eyebrows into a question. He was wearing the flying jacket again today, and a pair of faded denim jeans.

'Estelle Howard. We're joint owners,' she explained.

'Ah.' He glanced in the rear view mirror, revved the engine but still didn't move off. 'Now it all becomes clear. The same partner who doesn't want to sell the stock?'

Suzi nodded, wishing he'd just get on with it.

'So don't tell me . . .' He grinned the cat's grin. 'She doesn't want you to go to a car boot sale today, because she doesn't want you to buy any either?'

'No, of course not. I mean, she does. We're always looking to buy new stock. It's just that . . .' Why did he have to make things sound so complicated? And why weren't they moving? 'Shall we go?' She flicked him a challenging look. 'Or were you planning to stay here all day?'

Estelle was flitting around Secrets In The Attic moving furniture, creating space for her jewellery display. She'd placed an ad in the local paper, DON'T LEAVE IT TUCKED AWAY IN A DRAWER, and had organised some cheap leaflets on the same theme to shove in letter-boxes. With some difficulty she eased the grandfather clock further into the corner until the pendulum gonged in protest. Sure, the ad had meant taking a leaf from Stan and Terry's advertising campaign, she knew that. It was their style, but clearly their style worked, so what the hell.

She brushed the dust from her hands on to her parrot-green and yellow baggies and folded her arms as she surveyed the shop floor. She'd already bought some of the jewellery outright. Other pieces — because, as Suzi kept reminding her, funds were low — she'd taken on a sale or return commission basis.

Moving over to the safe, she pressed the combination and pulled out the box of jewellery. Not a bad stash so far. She sifted through it. She'd avoided obviously antique-y items like pocket watches that might have value but little use in today's market. Instead, she'd concentrated on wearability.

She picked up a clasp and admired the smoothness of the pale ivory. Because this jewellery was to be worn. She held the clasp up to the collar of the old silk shirt she was wearing over a green vest top. Nice.

She would display it, Estelle decided, on black velveteen. And maybe include a children's section – little girls loved long beads that swished and rattled as they walked, and it would give them something to look at and try on while their mothers concentrated on what *they* wanted for a change. She had a feeling that this could turn things around for Secrets. And let's face it, it had to.

The phone rang and she answered it. 'Car?' She frowned. 'My car isn't for sale.' Weird. That was the third call today. What was going on? Why would anyone imagine her darling Mini Mayfair was for sale?

Lurking at the bottom of the box, she found a couple of jewelled hatpins. Victorian probably, she thought, examining one of them under her microscope. More women were wearing hats these days and antique hatpins would be a popular accessory, she was sure.

She began checking pins and clasps, sorting out those pieces that needed work other than cleaning and polishing. She had a clear vision of a shop that specialised in beautiful jewellery – old and new. Estelle smiled slowly. With a section for each decade perhaps, right up to the present day.

Drawing out a narrow box, she opened it carefully. Inside were Shelagh Rossi's pearls, creamy and perfect, cool to the touch, tiny at both ends, building gradually to one gorgeous globe in the centre. And there was more to come . . .

Estelle felt a little guilty at being the recipient of Shelagh's jewellery, especially since Nick had told her about the money problems his mother was experiencing, and her utter refusal to consider selling or even opening up the house on the hill to the public, as he'd suggested. Nick, it seemed, was ploughing the majority of the money he earned as a business consultant into the place. 'But I often wonder,' he had told her, 'if it's even worth saving.'

What *was* worth saving? Estelle looked around the shop. This place was for starters. And it wasn't too late. It meant so much – her chance to achieve something on her own, her bid for independence, her bolt-hole – for that was what it had become. And she'd do her damnedest to save it.

But Liam . . . well, their relationship was now clearly beyond saving. The fact that he'd been sitting with Amanda at the end of the under-9s tournament, her hand on his arm – Amanda's little gesture of possession – had told Estelle everything that she needed to know. Everything in fact that she'd known already, she reminded herself, since she'd seen them together outside his place. Liam and Amanda Lake were now a couple. So much then, for his high and mighty principles. He was seeing someone who had never had to work for a thing in her entire life.

Estelle picked up the ring she'd bought last week from a little old lady whose eyes had filled with tears as she'd handed it over.

'Are you sure you want to let it go?' Estelle had asked her, for this was the part of her job that she hated. As with Shelagh Rossi, too often the reason that people sold their jewellery was because they needed to. They needed the money for more basic necessities – heating, food, shelter. Memories had to go . . .

Sure enough, 'I have to be practical,' the woman had told her. 'But it's hard, my dear.'

'Was it yours?' Estelle had probed gently. The tiny band of diamonds looked like an engagement ring, and was probably about sixty years old, so the period would fit.

She nodded. 'From my Harry,' she said. 'He died twenty years ago, but he's still with me.' Firmly, she pushed the ring towards Estelle. 'I don't need this to remember.'

He's still with me . . . Estelle twisted the ring around, so that the diamonds caught the light. Would everything always remind her of Liam? Abruptly, she got to her feet. One thing was for sure. She wouldn't be going to the garret flat unannounced again, to talk — or for any other reason. Estelle was not into humiliation, and the less she saw of Liam and Amanda, the better. It was over.

As she bent to move a porcelain chamber pot in closer to the grandfather clock, Estelle yelped and froze. A large house spider that had obviously been nestling under the shelter of the rim, remained equally frozen for a few moments, before scuttling towards the far wall.

Estelle took a few paces back, yelped again (this time silently) and cracked her shin on the Edwardian rocking chair. 'Damn,' she said.

The spider stopped dead. Was it wondering where to take cover? Estelle stared at it, and the spider stared back. They stayed like that for several minutes. Both of them were scared, Estelle told herself. She was scared because she had a phobia. And the spider? Well, the spider was scared for more obvious reasons.

Rather than stay like this for the rest of the day (for how could she move out of sight, leaving it free to scuttle off to who knew where?) Estelle reviewed her options. A few steps back would enable her to reach the phone whilst retaining a half view of four legs. Such a movement might spur him or her into action (she sensed it was a him, but couldn't be sure) but at least she'd be able to phone a friend.

'All right?' Terry — who was certainly *not* a friend — was standing in the doorway.

Typical, Estelle thought. He wasn't exactly a knight in shining armour. In fact he was wearing a suit that was too tight for him, and the man had a stomach on him that was impossible to hide.

No, I'm huddling by the counter in a state of panic and fear because a little brown insect might attack me. 'Fine.' Estelle smiled brightly. 'You?'

'Pukka,' Terry said.

What-a? 'Jolly good.' Estelle changed position and tried to avoid the temptation of checking on the spider. She could, of course, ask Terry to get rid of it for her. But that would hardly be a step forward for female independence, now would it?

'We was wondering if you'd had second thoughts?' He looked her up and down in *that way*.

Estelle returned the compliment, scanning the purple-patterned tie, allowing her eyes to linger on the fat belly with an expression that was – she hoped – even stronger than distaste. 'About what?'

'Your lease.' He exhaled loudly. 'We can't help noticing you don't exactly get 'em flocking in, and we need the extra space, see?'

Bloody cheek. For a moment, Estelle almost forgot the spider. 'We deal in quality,' she said, her voice dangerously low. 'We don't need to have people *flocking in*.'

'So you don't have a money problem in the world, then?' he sneered. 'You always pay your bills on time, you're not even in arrears with the rent?'

Estelle stared at him. What did he know? And more to the point, how did he know?

'Hypothetically speaking, of course.' Terry's pale eyes widened into innocence and he spread his arms wide.

Enough. Estelle had had more than enough. 'I prefer plain speaking to hypotheticals,' she said. 'And I don't like whatever little game you're playing. If you think you can come here –'

'Now, now.' Terry held up a fat, warning finger. 'Don't jump to conclusions, young lady. That could be dangerous for all concerned.'

Bloody dangerous, Estelle thought. For you. She might not be able to cope with a spider, but there was no way on earth this man and his obnoxious partner would get the better of her and Suzi.

'And by the way . . .'

'Yes?'

'Would you take an offer on the car?'

'Car?' She followed his gaze – to the windscreen of her Mini Mayfair parked outside. 'What the hell . . . ?'

'Things must be bad.' Terry, damn him, was grinning all over his pouchy face. 'If you even have to sell your transport, love.'

'I have no intention of selling my transport.' And she most certainly was not his love. With that, Estelle stalked out to the car, ripped off the 'For Sale' notice from the windscreen. £500 she read. A BARGAIN. Hah bloody hah. It didn't want to come loose. She tore at it. Some bastard had stuck it on.

'Surgical spirit,' Terry said helpfully, as he passed her. 'That'll shift anything.'

She ignored him.

'Kids, probably,' he added.

Estelle thought of the flat tyre. Kids? She went back inside the shop. The spider was still there. Independence be damned. Who could she phone for insect rescue? And more to the point, what the hell was she going to do about Stan and Terry, and how were she and Suzi supposed to pay this month's rent?

Chapter 13

Suzi was conscious of a wave of sadness as Josh parked the battered white van outside Secrets In The Attic.

The morning had begun with him giving her lessons on how to approach the car booters. God, she'd thought, he made them sound like a breed apart. She'd learned how not to alienate or crowd them, but to pinpoint bargains as they were unloading, and snap them up before anyone else had a chance to do so. According to Josh Willis, it was an art. It sounded like manipulation to Suzi, at the very least.

'They're a load of vultures,' she said, hanging back as the dealers flocked *en masse* to the contents of a promising-looking blue transit.

She watched as Josh eased his way through, chatting laconically, hands thrust casually in the pockets of his jeans as if buying stock were the last thing on his mind. And she smiled as he emerged with an old Brownie camera.

'Collector's item,' he said. 'The guy just wanted to talk photography for a moment or two.'

'And you were happy to oblige.' Suzi took it from him and examined it with interest. 'Being the opportunist that you are.'

He grinned and took her arm, leading her towards the next car-load, already parking up. 'At least I'll go home with something to show,' he said. 'Unlike you.'

Suzi shrugged. To be honest, she wasn't bothered if she went home with nothing. If Estelle had her way, they would soon be running a jewellery store, and decent jewellery was scarce in car boots.

'You're not pushy enough to be an antique dealer,' he teased.

'Good.' Suzi was conscious of his firm grip on her arm. She looked down at his hand, seeing again the fine sandy hairs, observing the shape of his fingers, the square cut of his nails.

But despite herself, Suzi had been unable to resist – getting into the swing of things, joining in the chit-chat, pulling out her purse. And by the time Josh took her off at midday for a big breakfast at a local café on Charmouth beach, she'd acquired a few small bits of 40s and 50s bric-à-brac, and several pieces of jewellery that were not made of plastic or glass and that could, Josh assured her, be easily sold on for a profit. It had not been a wasted morning. In fact, she'd had a great time.

When they got back to the van, parked up the hill, Josh had pointed along the granite cliff pathway. 'Fancy a stroll?' He had taken off his flying jacket and slung it over one shoulder.

Suzi knew she should be getting back, she knew there was no reason in the world why she should linger on the cliff, the beach or anywhere else with this man, and she didn't see the logic in walking up a steep hill and getting tired and out of breath, when you just had to come back down again. A stroll indeed . . .

And yet she found herself wanting to prolong the day. Over breakfast they had discussed antiques, the countryside and ways of keeping fit. (Suzi's take on that one was that she knew she must exercise, and she did exercise – playing tennis and swimming in the sea being her two virtues in that department – but she had to spend a long time psyching herself up for any of it. Far easier, she'd always thought, to curl up with a good novel, far too tempting to just potter in the garden instead.)

She now knew that Josh liked animals, organic vegetables and travelling. But Suzi was curious. She wanted to know more about what really made Josh Willis tick. The personal stuff like – did he have a significant other? How many significant others had he had in the past? And family background – brothers, sisters, children . . . ? If she stuck around, there was more chance of finding out, she decided. And besides, the best thing to do after a fry-up, was walk it off. So, 'Why not?' she said, and they'd set off for the path that led towards Lyme.

As they trudged uphill, Suzi broke the silence. 'Tell me about yourself.' The direct approach seemed to work best with this man, and you couldn't get much more direct than that.

He didn't respond with the predictable, *what d'you want to know*, but instead gave her a rundown. 'Brought up in Hammersmith, parents working class, one older brother. Hated school, left when I was fifteen, travelled round Europe.' He spoke in staccato phrases, and she could tell that his breathing – like hers – was becoming more shallow with the effort of the climb. She hoped her legs would hold out.

'Why did you hate school?' she asked him.

'Because school was a big London comprehensive,' he said. 'Where the priority's staying alive.'

Enough said. Suzi surveyed the bulk of him as he negotiated the cliff path beside her. He was surprisingly light on his feet for such a big man. She remembered the moment of close proximity in Secrets In The Attic's tiny kitchen and shivered. 'Don't tell me you were bullied. I wouldn't have thought you'd have problems in that direction.'

He grinned. 'I was a late developer. And shy.'

'Shy?' She laughed out loud. Red hair did not go with shy. And she didn't think she'd ever met anyone with such an air of confidence.

'Believe me, I was.'

Suzi stumbled on the rocky path and with a complete lack of self-consciousness, he stopped and tucked her arm through his. She hesitated for a moment, but he obviously meant nothing by it, so she relaxed into his rhythm and they continued in step, breath coming even harder now. Suzi felt her calf muscles waking up, as they stretched to adjust. She could smell the leather of his jacket, mixing with the scents of the gorse, the sharp salty tang of the sea below and the damp earth on the path underfoot.

'So after you travelled around Europe, you became an antique dealer?' she asked as they paused at a gap in the hedgerow to survey the view below.

He let go of her arm and she moved a short pace away. Charmouth beach stretched out behind them, a strip of sand and fine shingle, a few pin-men walking over the bridge that crossed the river Char, the car park almost a quarter full with day trippers, Suzi supposed, a lot of them probably hopeful fossil-hunters. The sky was clear and despite the wind, it was warm. Suzi lifted her face to the sun. It had turned into another glorious spring afternoon.

'Nope.' He moved closer to the edge, looking down at the almost vertical drop, until she wanted to grab him and yank him back to safety. 'I came to antiques pretty late in life. It's the open spaces that have always appealed to me.'

How old was he, Suzi wondered. Late forties? About ten years older than she? 'Me too,' she said dreamily. 'Open air and freedom. Wide spaces. Landscape.'

He stared at her. 'You feel like that too?'

She nodded. Though she'd never really thought about it that way before.

'So what did you do before that?' she asked him, pretty astounded at her own boldness.

But he didn't seem to mind all the questions. He thought for a moment, still looking down, as if for inspiration. 'Barman, builder, landscape gardener. Anything that came along.'

He moved back towards the path and Suzi followed. As she'd thought, an opportunist.

'Anything that didn't tie you down?' she guessed. She had half-expected him to take her arm again, but he showed no inclination to do so. And why should he? She was capable of negotiating the path for herself, they were no longer climbing in any case, since the path had levelled out (thank goodness) and of course they hardly knew one another. She also sensed that he enjoyed walking alone. His stride was long, the stride of a loner, and something in the grey-green eyes as they flickered to take in the occasional snatches of seascape below, told her that he would be wary of anything – or anyone – that might restrict his freedom.

'If you like.' He wasn't giving much away. 'I'm not married if that's what you're asking. No live-in lover, though I've had my share in the past. No children.' He turned to look at her. 'You?'

Suzi hesitated. Thought of Michael as she'd thought of Michael several times during the day. She had told Josh she wasn't married. But, 'There is someone,' she said.

Josh Willis only grinned his cat's grin. 'There's always someone.'

Now, Suzi was sorry that the day was over, that any moment Josh Willis would be driving off in his van bound for home – wherever that was, and then for Germany. Would she ever see him again? She didn't like the thought that she might not, felt certain that she should have said something, anything, to forge some link of friendship between them. She liked the man. She appreciated his confident, laid-back, see-what-tomorrow-brings attitude to life. And that was all, she told herself firmly, that it was.

Next door, Stan was pasting up GRAND SALE notices. 'Good grief,' Suzi said. 'Now they're even cutting the price of the bargains.'

'A stunt.' Josh dismissed this with a wave of one hand. 'Maybe you should pull a stunt of your own.'

'Like what?' Suzi felt more gloomy then ever. She wasn't sure she was up to stunts. Stunts sounded far too exhausting.

Josh seemed thoughtful. He pulled at the short beard, peppered with strands of gold, copper and white. 'How about doing an antiques roadshow?' he said, holding her bag so she could open the shop door. 'That would bring the punters in.'

'Antiques roadshow? Like on TV?' Immediately, Suzi could picture it. People from Pridehaven and beyond queuing up to have their attic secrets held, examined, valued by the experts. Queuing? Who was she kidding?

'Yeah. Why not?'

Well, there was an obvious problem. 'We don't have a resident expert,' she pointed out, turning the key in the lock. Estelle had learned a lot in the short time they'd been running the business – but hardly enough to be an authority.

'Don't look at me.' He followed her inside, having to duck to avoid the dream-catcher whose feathers brushed at the top of his head. 'I'm self-taught by a combination of Miller's Guide and the dealers on the circuit.'

Suzi didn't believe this for a minute. 'I bet you could do it,' she said. 'Especially if you had me and Estelle backing you up. Making tea, disappearing to look things up for you, that sort of thing.' And Estelle could surely do the jewellery and smaller pieces.

He still looked doubtful, but Suzi was fired up with the idea by now. 'You could waffle, at least.'

His eyes widened in mock horror. 'I thought honesty was your policy in this place.'

'Waffle is what happens when honesty goes off at a tangent.'

They both laughed. 'We'll have to talk about it,' he compromised, handing back her bag.

That was enough for Suzi. 'Now, over a cup of tea?' Perhaps it was crazy, but she didn't want to see that white van driving away – not yet at least. And if a stunt like that would help save the shop, then it was her duty to get it organised pronto.

'I've just made a pot if you're interested.' From the back of the shop, Estelle's dark red head peered around the doorway. She eyed Josh with undisguised curiosity. 'And I hope you haven't bought any more furniture, Suzi, because we've got too much in this place already.' She sighed. 'If only we could get rid of some of it.'

Suzi ignored Josh's raised eyebrows. So, she had lied. She'd had her reasons, but she could hardly backtrack now and say that yes, they'd love him to buy some of their stock, and that she'd only changed her mind before because she'd thought he was working with Stan and Terry, aiding and abetting them in some dastardly plan to ruin Secrets In The Attic. Never mind the cheap melodrama. He'd think she was off her trolley.

'So this is the partner who doesn't want to sell the stock?' Josh enquired. 'Aren't you going to introduce me?'

'Yes, of course.' Wondering quite how she was going to wriggle out of this one, Suzi mumbled, 'Josh Willis, Estelle Howard.' Maybe he was Estelle's type. They were both redheads, which gave them something in common, though Josh was more wild ginger mixed with crazy carrot and Estelle smooth auburn-mahogany.

Maybe if Josh had been walking on a cliff top with Estelle, he would have pulled her close to him, run his fingers through her mass of gorgeous mahogany-red hair and kissed her hungrily on the – . Goodness. Suzi stopped her imaginary scenario right there. What was she thinking of?

She gave herself a mental shake just as another figure emerged from behind Estelle. He'd obviously been up in the flat and had come to see where Estelle had got to. Oh, dear. 'And this is Michael,' Suzi said.

Chapter 14

The silence, as they walked down West Street towards Pride Square, could be cut, Suzi thought, with the proverbial. And it was nothing like the relaxed silence she'd experienced this morning – with another man, she thought guiltily. Other men and women carried on adulterous affairs for years without being found out. She wasn't even married, only living with a man who'd invited himself into her life and yet she was found out at the very first boot sale. Typical. Though there was nothing, she reminded herself, to find out. But where, she wondered, had the day swept off to? And what had happened to her in the process?

She was aware of Michael's angular, loping movements – beside her and yet miles from her – and it made a strange contrast to the easy rhythm of the man she'd been walking with on the cliff earlier this afternoon. It depended, she supposed, on whom you were in step with. And right now, she was not in step with Michael.

'Michael?' She glanced across at him. The wind had brushed the fine strands of fair hair away from the bony planes of his face. His mouth was set into a tight line of suppressed anger and his brow was fixed in a frown. He was not, she realised, a happy man. Her fault.

'So who's that guy?' he said, as they rounded the square, past the kids lounging on benches by the water fountain, smoking, drinking coke, chewing gum, talking in loud teenage vernacular on their mobiles. Sunday afternoon in Pridehaven, Suzi thought.

'His name's Josh Willis.'

Michael glared at her. 'I don't mean what's his name. I know his bloody name, you introduced us. I mean, who is he?' His stride lengthened and Suzi ran a few steps to keep pace. They passed the library, the town hall, the hippy and gift shops, all closed.

Who was he? Suzi sighed. 'He might be taking some of Secrets' furniture over to Germany for us.' OK, so she wasn't telling it how it was. But how was it, exactly? It was still a business relationship. Josh Willis had not given her any sign that they could ever be anything more than friends. Why should he? And why should she even be thinking about it?

'But who is he?' Michael swung down the path by the church that led through the graveyard and down to the riverbank. 'How did you meet him for a start?'

Suzi followed. The flint walls of St Catherine's were in shadow, the stained glass of the window dull and lifeless. Soon, she thought, after its parishioners had consumed their tea and toast, scones and crumpets, they would venture out once more. The evening service would begin and the church would light up again – with voices, brightness and a little hope.

'He came into the shop.' Suzi remembered her first sight of him, the business card placed on the counter, pushed towards her, the grey-green eyes, wild hair and short copper-red beard. The suggestion – heaven help her – of mutual benefit. 'He's an antique dealer. He had a business proposition to put to us, that's all.' It sounded, even to Suzi's ears, extremely unlikely.

Sure enough . . . 'A business proposition?' Michael sneered. His arm swung out at the brambles at the side of the path. A thorn snagged on the sleeve of his jacket and he pulled it roughly away, careless of any damage.

Suzi felt herself losing patience. 'Yes – a business proposition,' she said. 'Buying some of our furniture and selling it in Germany. Like I said.'

Michael didn't reply.

Suzi forgot about the guilt cocktail she'd been swallowing lately and felt only self-righteous anger. 'What's the big deal?' She stopped walking, looked into his tight, angry face. What right did Michael have to suggest whatever he was suggesting, to cross-question her like this about what was *her* business – hers and Estelle's. And *her* life. She had never asked him, she reasoned, to take such a part in it.

'He's the big deal,' Michael snapped back.

Suzi flicked open the latch of the gate and strode down the path towards the bridge. 'So now I can't talk to anyone of the opposite sex, is that it?' she shouted back at him, the wind lifting her words, seeming to give them a hysterical edge that she had not intended. Above her the gulls swooped and soared, screaming at them, laughing like batty old women. The path was overgrown – the long grass whipped at the legs of her jeans, her feet in their trainers trampled buttercups, thrift, thistles, regardless. 'I can't do business with men?' She laughed. 'Hey – that's a bit restricting, you know, it cuts out fifty per cent of the population. I could be done for sexual discrimination. And all because my boyfriend's jealous to the point of paranoia.'

Michael caught up with her in an instant. He put his hand on her shoulder, and she slowed as she felt the pressure through her denim jacket. 'What do you expect, Suzi?' he said, twisting her round to face him. 'Some guy turns up in your shop. You don't know him from Adam. He could be . . . I don't know, some maniac, a stalker or something.'

Suzi hadn't thought of it like that. She realised that when she'd gone to lunch with Josh, she had not been in the least afraid, only curious. Curious and compelled – but she couldn't tell Michael that. She moved away, glancing sideways at him, resisting that pressure. 'I knew he was OK,' she said shortly.

He dropped his hand. 'How? ESP?'

'I just knew.' And whatever was happening here, she would not allow Michael to question her judgement like this, to take over, as he seemed bent on doing. To dictate to her. It wasn't fair. It wasn't anything she'd ever wanted.

Suzi walked on. She could smell the dampness of the river now, feel the moisture in the earth beneath her feet, giving more easily under the weight of her body. Trusting Josh Willis was her decision – and her problem if she turned out to be mistaken, of course.

Michael's voice softened. He seemed to be pleading with her, though she didn't know for what. 'Even if you were right,' he said, as they reached the blue bridge. 'Even if the guy is OK, it's a bit much, Suzi.'

'What's a bit much?' She negotiated the wooden planking, leaned over the parapet of the bridge. The river was high today, the swollen water moving fast, the long hair-line sweep of the reeds bent into worship by the force of the wind, and no ducks to be seen. Perhaps she was being unreasonable, Suzi thought. Michael was probably right. It *was* a bit much.

'Going off with him, God knows where.' His voice had hardened again, and Suzi heard herself responding in kind.

'We went to a car boot sale, for heaven's sake,' she muttered. 'It was work.' And afterwards, she thought? That walk along the cliff. Was that work?

'For the whole day?'

'We were –'

'Yes?'

Suzi walked on, wanting now to be at home, in the cottage, out of the firing line, she supposed. 'I don't know . . . talking.'

Michael scuffed at a stone on the path with the toe of his desert boot. 'Oh, right, talking. Yeah . . .' His head was down now. He looked, Suzi thought, like an overgrown child, kicking out at something he didn't understand, had no control over.

'Michael —'

He swung round at her. 'But you didn't tell me about him, did you — that's a bit odd, wouldn't you say? And you didn't tell me you were going to the car boot sale with him either. Never mentioned his name in fact. Come to think of it, you never leave at that time of morning to go to a bloody car boot sale. And —'

'I didn't think it was important.' But of course it was.

They reached the gate that led to the back garden of the cottage, and Suzi opened it, relief swamping over her at the familiarity of it all, her herb kitchen garden, Hester straining at her rope, the hens restless and scrabbling for food. The sun was going down and everyone would want feeding — which would be a distraction at least, she thought.

'Not important? Like I said, Suzi . . .' Michael took a deep breath, shutting the gate after him. 'What's going on?'

Later, after the animals had been fed, after Suzi had spent an hour in the bath trying to soak it all away, after they'd opened a bottle of wine and she'd started preparing an omelette, she tried to tell Michael how she felt.

'I never asked you to move in,' she said. Perhaps not the best way to start, but she had to try and be honest, she owed him that much. 'I did say that it was only for a while.'

Michael got two plates out of the cupboard. 'I see. So that's how it is.'

'No . . .' Lightly, she touched his arm. 'You don't see – yet. But I'm trying to explain.'

'You want me to move out?' He looked so helpless standing there, holding two yellow plates, one in each hand, like some sort of sacrificial offering, that Suzi felt overwhelmed by tenderness.

'No.' She'd spoken too quickly. She took the plates from him, placed them on the table, grasped his hands. They were cool to the touch, and her mind spun back to that afternoon, to the warmth that had rushed through her as Josh Willis had linked his arm into hers. Stop it. She had to stop it. The idea was ridiculous. There *was* no idea . . . She was just lonely and confused, wondering what had happened to herself and Michael. OK, it had never been exactly a rock-of-Gibraltar-like security, but she'd enjoyed him, he'd enjoyed her, they'd had a laugh and she'd never looked at another man. Until now, that is.

'I'm not saying that,' she went on. 'I'm saying that I didn't ask you to move in. We barely discussed it, you just assumed and I tried to let you know that it wasn't permanent.'

He looked confused now. 'But I thought you wanted us to be together as much as I did.'

Oh no, Michael, she thought. I never wanted us to be together as much as you did. That much, at least, she knew. And she was sorry – but she couldn't help her own feelings. 'I was happy with things as they were,' she told him. She was moving their hands in the rhythm of her words, as though this could emphasise their meaning, make things clear for Michael, who didn't seem to understand. 'I like my freedom, I suppose. I wanted to see you, I liked our times together.' She took a breath. 'But I was never looking for commitment.'

Michael just stared at her. 'What are you saying?' he asked at last, his voice bleak.

Suzi let go of his hands and got the eggs from the side. Freshly laid, one of the many benefits of keeping hens in your back garden.

She broke them and whisked, gently. What was she saying? 'That I don't want to be tied down,' she told him. 'That I'm not sure things have been going too well since you've moved in here. That it's all too much too soon.' She added the herbs – sprigs of thyme and rosemary from the kitchen garden. 'I'm saying that I want to live my own life.'

'Without me?' Michael looked desolate.

'Not necessarily.' Though she couldn't help wondering. It rather depended on how – or why – they had stopped being lovers. And how – or why – they'd become some parody of an old, established – sexless for God's sake – couple. And that wasn't all. She steadied her breathing.

'I don't want twenty questions, jealousy, all that sort of stuff.' She looked him full in the face. 'I want my independence.' Perhaps it was some failing in her, that she couldn't live with a man, couldn't allow a man to take over any part of her life. That she fought back when she felt dictated to, that she felt easier and most at peace when she was alone in her cottage with her dogs and her cats. But whatever it was, Suzi reflected, it was better that Michael knew now rather than later.

Michael though, was still focused on the events of the day as he saw them. 'Just tell me there's nothing going on with that guy.' He drained his wine glass.

Was that all he cared about, Suzi wondered. Was it OK for their relationship to have no prospects – just so long as she hadn't humiliated him by seeing someone else? She poured oil into the pan. 'There's nothing going on.'

'And in the future?'

'Michael, stop it!' She felt trapped. Didn't he realise? Perhaps she was being unfair to him. But he was pushing and push-ing and she couldn't stand it any longer. Shaking, she poured the egg mix into the sizzling pan. The aroma of heating eggs, thyme and rosemary drifted up from the hob, almost making her giddy.

Michael was hunched at the kitchen table now, chin resting on folded arms, eyes accusing. 'I'm surprised you bothered with those bloody concert tickets,' he said.

'What concert tickets?' She followed his gaze to the envelope on the shelf above the worktop. The orange tickets were just discernible, peeping out of the top. Anger at the fact that Michael had obviously been rooting around among her things, fought briefly with guilt. He thought the tickets were for him and Suzi, that much was clear. Well, he shouldn't have looked at them in the first place.

'Those are for Liam and Estelle,' she told him starkly. Perhaps she was wasting her time and money, but it was *her* time and money and why shouldn't she do something for her own brother and closest friend? 'I was hoping to get the two of them together again. I thought, you know . . .' She caught a glimpse of his crestfallen features as she scooped the edge of the omelette up with her spatula and allowed more egg to run through underneath, oh hell, '. . . if music be the food of love and all that.' They belonged together, didn't he see?

Michael had stood up and was standing beside her at the hob. 'You don't love me, do you, Suzi?' he asked.

Suzi studied the pale blue eyes. Even now, she couldn't say the words, couldn't hurt him. 'What's love got to do with it?' she floundered.

'Everything.' He took the spatula away from her.

Suzi buried her face into his chest. She could feel the bones of his sternum through the denim shirt he was wearing, sensed his hesitation as to whether or not he should hold her.

'You're trying so bloody hard to get your brother back with Estelle . . .' At last she felt his hand, stroking her hair, smoothing

159

away the rough edges of her day, trying to make it better '. . . and in the meantime . . .'

'Yes?' She looked up at him, the tears not far away.

'You and I are falling apart,' he said.

Chapter 15

It had been a long and trying day, and Liam was attempting to wind up the rehearsal. He hadn't got round to doing his laundry, so no clean shirt this morning, and running out of fresh coffee hadn't improved his mood – the piss-poor instant available in the staff room was not something with which any poor sod should start the day. The kids had played him up during the mandatory RE, the head had bollocked him about the literacy testing results, and now Bradley Jacobs and Marcus Weatherby were taking advantage of the long-time war between the Capulets and Montagues by creating a pretty convincing war of their own.

'Ouch! Jesus!' Marcus had let loose a punch in the direction of Bradley's ribcage.

'Hey, Marcus. I thought I said no contact.' Liam jumped on to the stage and stepped between them.

'He bloody elbowed me in the face,' complained Marcus. 'Sir.'

'Don't swear,' Liam snapped.

'You said get in there and look like you want to kill him, Sir.' Bradley performed his customary flick back of the hair. 'I was only acting.'

Titters from the wings and the flash of a mini skirt and long, bare legs, announced the side-line presence of Jade Johnson.

'Jade,' Liam yelled. 'They're fighting because of you. You're supposed to be looking shocked and scared. You're Juliet, remember.'

Juliet smiled at Marcus (who was not her Romeo) in a manner that could only be called provocative, and stuck out one hip. Liam was aware of the buzz of teenage sub-text. Someone's mobile went off.

'I thought I said switch off all the bloody mobiles,' yelled Liam, leaping down from the stage again.

'Oooh, does that include mine?'

Liam swung round to face Lorraine Johnson, who was sporting a batwing leather jacket teamed with what looked like black PVC trousers and high-heeled gold sandals. Ye Gods. 'No.' He smiled briefly.

'Ready, babes?' she called.

No, she bloody well wasn't. And if she must pick her daughter up after rehearsals, why the hell couldn't she wait outside in her car like all the other parents, Liam wondered. 'Can you give us a minute?' he said.

She consulted her brassy gold watch. 'Sure. No probs.'

Liam turned his attention back to the fight scene. It was supposed to evolve from a dance – with Juliet spun from one to the other of them, her smile for Romeo the spark that created the action. 'From the top.' He looked around. 'Jade!'

Jade, who seemed to be involved in some sort of complex semaphore communication with someone on the other side of the stage, stopped abruptly and tottered in on her platforms.

Liam shook his head in despair. 'You can't dance in those,' he told her. 'You'll twist an ankle.'

'He's right, babes,' put in Lorraine Johnson. 'Wear your Le Roc shoes.'

Jade scowled at her parent. 'I didn't bring them.'

'Barefoot then,' Liam suggested, losing patience. 'Music, Crystal?'

Crystal pressed the play button, the song began, Jade pulled off her platforms, and was duly twirled by first Marcus, then Bradley, then back to Marcus again. At this point she put out just the tip of her tongue and ran it over her lips. In what was probably schoolboy instinct, Marcus grabbed her bottom, Jade giggled and thrust out her breasts, and Liam threw his hands in the air.

'Hold it, hold it!'

'He bloody well was,' muttered Bradley.

'Marcus is supposed to be your cousin,' Liam reminded Jade. 'That . . .' He pointed at Bradley, 'is Romeo. He's the one you're in love with, in case you've forgotten the story-line.'

'I'm not sure about this Juliet stuff, babes.' Lorraine Johnson flapped the arms of the batwing coat so violently that Liam half-expected her to take off. 'I thought this Shakespeare was a highbrow sort of a bloke.'

Before Crystal Woods could leap into the breach with her once-weekly request to take over the part of Juliet, Liam took charge. 'On to the fight scene,' he said. 'Hold his lapels, so . . .' He jumped back on to the stage and demonstrated. 'Move with your fist, like so. Bradley, you move back. Push his shoulder, like this, then back. No contact, remember. But it's got to look convincing.'

The two boys glowered at one another.

'Good,' Liam said dubiously.

Ten minutes later he was as satisfied as he would ever be. 'That'll do.' He pushed his hair back from his face and wondered if they would ever get the play finished in time. What with this and his training programme for CG's, it was no wonder he couldn't find time to do the bloody laundry.

He started to clear up, moving chairs, getting the stage ready for tomorrow's morning assembly, as his cast began to drift away. The caretaker had complained that clearing up after drama was not in his contract, and Liam knew that any power struggle between caretaker and headmaster could only have one outcome. Sure enough, the head had spoken to Liam – and now Liam did the clearing up himself.

'But *everyone's* going,' He heard Jade move into wingeing mode. 'I *can't* be the only one not allowed. It's not *fair*.' Life isn't fair, Liam thought.

Behind her a group that included Marcus, Bradley and Crystal, were hovering, awaiting the parental decision. The hostility between the two boys appeared to have temporarily abated – for which Liam was grateful, he didn't want the production to turn into a blood-bath – but, being experienced in the handling of young teenagers, he couldn't help but be suspicious of Jade's role in all this.

He was dimly aware of Jade's mother's capitulation, Jade's assurance to her parent of lifelong love, and then the fact that . . . hell, he was now alone in the school hall with Lorraine Johnson. He thought of what Amanda had said about recognising her as a man-hunter and tried not to panic. To avoid looking at Lorraine, he looked at the still lifes of various pieces of fruit that the year 6s had been drawing yesterday and which were now proudly displayed next to the shortlisted designs of the sports day programme. He felt a bit like a lemon himself. He was a grown man, for heaven's sake. How could he be frightened of a parent?

She lit a cigarette from a flashy gold lighter. Liam considered pointing out to her that it was not appropriate for a school hall to smell like an ashtray in morning assembly, but he daren't risk saying anything that might delay her departure.

He was just about finished moving chairs and had looked at as much fruit as he could take, when she made her move. 'I wondered if we might have a little talk,' she said, taking a few steps closer.

Liam eyed the gold sandals. 'A talk?' Since when had his voice risen by an octave?

She nodded, blew out smoke through red lips. 'Man to woman, woman to man.'

'Sure.' Liam grabbed a chair and placed it between them. Ridiculous, perhaps, but better to play safe since gender had been mentioned.

She smiled. 'Not here, silly. In the pub. I'll even buy you a beer.'

Liam couldn't think how to say no. He tried, 'I really don't think –' but got no further.

'Please,' she said. And it wasn't a question. She waited for him by the swing door, a certain look in her eye.

'Just a quick one then,' he said. After all, she was clearly an important influence in Jade's life. And at all costs, as Amanda had said, the show must go on.

Estelle yawned loudly and put the reference book about antique jewellery that she'd been reading, down on the table by the worn red couch. A feeling of restlessness was ticking away at her. It was only six o'clock. She could eat her chicken-with-basil-and-sundried-tomatoes-for-one, and drink some of the Italian white chilling in the fridge, but it seemed too early to settle into another evening staying in alone.

Another day in the shop, another evening in the flat above . . . Estelle frowned as she stared at the blue carpet. That was worn too, frayed round the edges. She mustn't let it become a routine, she decided, she must get out and do something, make some sort of contact with the outside world.

She could, she supposed, go down to her local. But the Bear

and Bottle was an old-fashioned pub and therefore not terribly single-woman-friendly. And the alternative just along the road, The Seagull, would be crammed full with a younger generation she knew she wasn't part of any longer. Good grief, that was a depressing thought. When exactly had she switched generations – and how come she'd never noticed?

A walk, she decided, getting to her feet, trying to remember where she'd put her suede ankle boots. Not practical perhaps, but she loved them and wearing them always gave her a boost. A walk would provide the fresh air and exercise she probably needed, give her an appetite, maybe even the confidence to nip into the pub. She pulled on her jacket. She would walk down to the harbour, watch the boats for a while, and try not to think about Liam.

Liam was looking round the pub, feigning an interest in the dried flowers hanging from the oak beams, searching for an out-clause, increasingly desperate now. He had so much to do, for God's sake – a pile of English exercises to be marked by tomorrow, a lesson plan for science to be sorted. He had to eat, he had to find a clean shirt for tomorrow, and the flat was a mess. At this rate, he'd be up all night.

They'd sorted out Jade and Romeo and Juliet – this had involved him assuring Lorraine Johnson that there would be no 'funny business' going on, that he would look out for Jade's interests and ensure that her reputation and everything else remained intact.

It had also – unfortunately – entailed Lorraine placing a bony hand on his knee as they sat up at the bar and was now threatening to lead to the telling of her life story.

'I must be off,' Liam said firmly, trying to get up.

'Don't leave me . . .' Her lipstick was smudged and her mascara had run. She ordered another drink and Liam realised belatedly that she must have had a few before she came to the rehearsal.

'Not for me,' Liam said firmly.

But she ordered it anyway, with a, 'jus' five minutes, go on, y'can spare five minutes . . . Pleash?'

Liam sighed. 'Just five minutes,' he agreed.

Lorraine spent the five minutes telling him that her husband worked all the hours God sent, that she suspected his work to be more vital to his existence than she was, that when he wasn't working he liked to go down the pub with his mates, and that he couldn't perform in bed like he used to.

'Well, never mind,' Liam said, rather ineffectually. 'Things can only get better.' He couldn't help feeling sorry for her. But it wasn't his problem.

'You know what I mean,' Lorraine began.

'Do I?'

'When I say that a woman like me has needs.'

Liam began to panic again. 'Yes, I mean, no. I mean –' What did he mean? What did *she* mean?

'You see, the thing is . . .' Lorraine said, still slurring.

'Yes?' Alarm bells began to ring.

She leaned closer. 'My husband just doesn't understand me.'

Estelle walked out of Secrets In The Attic, automatically checking her green Mini Mayfair as she did so. Since the incident of the 'For Sale' sign, since the flat tyre, OK, if she were honest, since that last little chat with Terry, she'd been wondering. Was it all coincidence? She didn't think so somehow.

She was just approaching Pride Square and the Bear and Bottle, when Liam came hurtling out as if he were on fire. He was dressed in teaching gear – dark blazer, charcoal trousers, cream shirt and grey tie, though the shirt was unbuttoned at the neck and the tie was loosened and set at a rakish angle. There was no one else in sight, and yet Liam looked hunted. And desperate.

He glanced wildly from left to right, seeing her almost immediately. 'Estelle!' To her surprise he rushed across the road. 'Thank God!'

'What is it?' Her first sensation was one of pleasure – that he should be so obviously glad to see her. And then she remembered Amanda.

'Nothing, nothing . . .' He glanced behind him, grabbed hold of her arm.

Estelle flinched. Nothing? She had often imagined them getting together to talk, but never quite like this. He was very close. Too close – she could hear the shallowness of his breathing, smell the Liam-scent that held the faint shimmer of sweat from the energies of Liam's day.

'Where are you going?' He began moving, very quickly, propelling her at the same time, down South Street.

'For a walk.'

'Mind if I tag along?'

'Do I have any choice?' But Estelle disentangled herself all the same. She was being used – that much was clear. And yet she'd wanted to see him, hadn't she, wanted to have the chance to talk things through? To her intense irritation, just being with him felt good.

Liam shot her a look of such tenderness that Estelle almost stopped walking. He had always been able to make her dysfunctional with just a glance, just a word. A load of old flannel, she supposed it was – though she had never thought that then. It had always seemed so special – the way he spoke to her, the way he was with her. She sighed. But when you realised how many other people were susceptible to his charm, the glow kind of faded. It was very different being one of many.

'How are you?' he asked, as if he really cared.

'Fine,' she said automatically. She wouldn't give him the satisfaction of knowing about her restlessness, her nights in alone, the sense of isolation she sometimes felt when she awoke in the mornings at 4 am – always half-looking for him as if he were in her very blood. 'You?'

He looked a little awkward, and she instinctively glanced over her shoulder, back towards the pub, just as Lorraine Johnson walked out. She looked strange and disorientated, her hair askew, her step unsure. Drunk? Estelle walked more quickly, matching Liam's stride, hoping the woman wouldn't call out or follow them. It seemed to her that Stan and Terry, Lorraine and Rita were haunting her, always there, always looking at her with knowing eyes, all seemingly waiting for her to make some stupid mistake, for the business to fold, so they could come in and take over.

'I'm OK,' Liam was saying, as they turned by the church. 'Busy, you know.'

Estelle knew. Liam would never change. He would always be busy, always cram too many things into his life, so that nothing got the time or attention it might deserve. That, she reminded herself, was half the problem.

As they walked on, Liam seemed to relax – at least, she thought, as far as Liam ever relaxed. But every couple of minutes he would tear his fingers through his dark curls, Liam's gesture of confusion, or nervousness, frustration or anger. Something, she knew, was bothering him. But he wasn't going to tell her, was he? She was no longer his confidante, the one he turned to. Instead, there was such an awkwardness between them now – even in the very space between their physical bodies that seemed to grow more distant as they walked on down the path. The silence between them was creating a pain in her chest. It was awful. They seemed to have nothing to say to one another.

And he had made no effort to see her since she'd left, Estelle reminded herself. For Liam, it was certainly over.

'Sorry I didn't get to talk to you at the tournament,' Liam said at last, as they ploughed their way though the undergrowth to the riverside path. They had not crossed the blue bridge and so were walking on the other side of the river to Suzi's cottage. It was a mild evening and every so often a cloud of tiny gnats appeared to murmur in front of their faces. Estelle cleared them with an impatient wave of the hand.

Was that an intentional reference to Amanda? Was he gloating, wanting to remind her that he no longer had any need of her company? He could certainly have walked away from Amanda any time he liked, if he had indeed wanted to talk. 'No problem,' she said brightly. 'I was busy anyway.'

'Oh yeah – you were, weren't you?' He shot a sidelong look in her direction and Estelle knew he was thinking of Nick Rossi. And why not? He had Amanda. Why not let him think that she and Nick were an item, that someone – and someone pretty hunky at that – wanted to be with her.

As they approached the harbour, the path grew less wooded and the earth more soggy as the river widened into two large tributaries leading down towards the sea. Liam helped her over the soggiest bits and the final stile; they crossed the harbour road, and made their way down, over the massive pile of rocks. Above them the seagulls were soaring. Graceful creatures in flight, Estelle thought, watching them. But so darned noisy, especially in this, their nesting season. On the various roofs of harbour buildings, the young gulls could be seen – grey, fluffy and oddly almost the size of adult birds already.

'These boots . . .' Liam said, looking down at her feet, 'weren't your most practical decision.' And every so often he reached out a hand to help her jump, to make sure her footing was secure, his eyes intent as he gazed at her, making her shiver to his touch.

She could see the pulse in his throat throbbing, and she wanted to kiss it, wanted to run her fingers through his mass of dark curls the way he kept doing. She looked away.

'Sometimes I think I'd love to leave this place,' he said, as they came to a standstill, to the northeast of the harbour.

Oh yeah, Estelle thought, watching the boats. Some were on their last legs, unpainted, rusty with disuse, others were new and bright, resonant of sailing clubs, gin and tonics, regattas. Nearer to them, on the beach, were the fishing boats, drawn up on to the shingle by metal winches, crammed with nets and lobster pots, tarpaulins, oilskins, knives. The smell of the sea was ripe here, with leftover fish – not left for long by the gulls – with the faint oily sweetness of tar contrasting with the salt crusted on pebbles and shells and the grainy acidity of the damp sand. And beyond the fishing boats, the coastline wound its way, sandstone to the east, grey granite to the west, the fringe of Golden Cap clearly visible in the distance, the shore line of Chesil beach reaching out its long, long arms.

'But you never will,' Estelle said softly. Liam was a part of Pridehaven and only he had made it so. She could see the love in his eyes, even now, as he spoke of leaving and yet looked out to his sea, thick and blue-green tonight, tipped with highlighted spume, to the sun that was slowly setting on the horizon.

He turned towards her and for a moment she imagined he was about to take her in his arms. The rush of the tide seemed to move in rhythm with his words. 'Would it have made a difference?' he said. 'To us?'

'Perhaps.' There would have been fewer things to compete with, Estelle supposed. No Pridehaven, no landscape of memories, no

Suzi to take up his time and emotions. But there would have been other things.

She moved away, not wanting to be too close. She couldn't think about being in his arms, when those arms had been holding another. Estelle's kind of love was total – that had always been the trouble. She loved him with a force that was all-consuming. She would have given him anything, everything . . . But she also wanted to be loved like that in return. It seemed to be the only possible way.

Liam picked up a pebble and chucked it towards the sea with some force. 'I never thought this would happen to us.' He sounded angry. He tore his hand through his hair, glared at her as though it were her fault.

'Neither did I,' she heard herself saying.

'I thought we were safe.'

'Nothing's safe.' She'd always known that. How could you put your love and trust in a person while that person had legs with which to walk away? She'd learned that from an early age, hadn't she, that night on the blue bridge? Was it any wonder she'd resisted marriage, children, making herself more vulnerable? It was true – nothing was safe.

And in her heart she reminded herself of how quickly he had found a replacement. Of the blonde and dark heads in Amanda's car the night she'd gone to the garret flat. You and me, she wanted to say to him. What's happened to you and me?

'I loved you,' Liam told her.

Estelle noted the tense. 'That's all in the past,' she confirmed. Though she wanted, suddenly to cry.

'Is it?' But Liam looked distracted, as though he were thinking about the school play, tomorrow's classes, or even maybe of Amanda, Estelle thought.

She took her courage in both hands. Now or never – and

she couldn't quite get her head round the never. 'Maybe, some time,' she said cautiously, '. . . we could get together to talk things through.' She heard the cry of a baby gull wanting food. 'Maybe that might help,' she added. For she sensed that he was troubled – if not as troubled as she.

'If that's what you want.' He smiled then, a special smile that took her back in time to their first months together.

Unable to resist, she smiled back at him and in that moment she knew there was something they still shared, would always share. The bond had not been broken. She heard the lash and lap of the waves on the rocks. It was almost as if the last weeks hadn't happened at all.

'Tonight?' she suggested. 'We could go for a beer.' Or back to her flat, share the meal for one and the Italian white. She could picture him there, sitting on the worn red couch, see them – heaven help her – making love. Oh, God. See them as they used to be.

He hesitated, chucked another pebble towards the sea. 'I can't tonight, Estelle,' he said, speaking in a rush. The wind took his words and bounced them mockingly around the harbour, for all to hear. 'I've got these lesson plans and –'

'It doesn't matter.' She moved away once more. Damn it. Why had she allowed him to get to her again? Done the giving again and had it slammed back in her face.

'Another time?' he was saying. 'Can we do it another time? Please?'

'Maybe.' But she wasn't sure they ever would.

Liam moved closer, put an arm around her and pulled her to him.

Estelle resisted. He smelled of the sea, or maybe it was that the sea was here, all around them, and they had absorbed its fresh, salty perfume.

'I miss you,' he said.

Estelle's body froze into one huge knot of tension and desire. Would he kiss her? They were close enough. If she turned, just slightly . . . Would he ask her to come back to him? She waited. His eyes glazed as he looked at her, it seemed to Estelle that he knew her so much better than she could ever know herself. She waited.

Nothing. Even the gulls seemed to have stopped screaming. And after a moment, in a gesture of pure self-preservation she pulled away once more. It was all very well to say she was managing – but it was clear that something had gone from her life. She was busily pretending to herself and everyone else that it wasn't an important something.

But the trouble was, without Liam and his love, she felt so alone.

Chapter 16

Bradley Jacobs had unexpectedly informed Liam at the last rehearsal of *Romeo and Juliet* that he was *pretty ace at tennis, Sir*.

Liam didn't believe him, but on the other hand thought, nothing ventured nothing gained, and so invited him along to the next coaching session at CG's.

Liam had not, however, expected him to have Jade Johnson in tow. He was in jeans, she was wearing an Adidas T-shirt and unzipped fleece, an extremely short white tennis skirt and trainers with laces tucked into the sides. Her blonde hair was pulled away from her face into a plait, and her smoothly foundationed teenage face wore a coy expression. Bradley just looked smug.

Liam was not glad to see her. He might need more tennis players to help save CG's and bring it into a Socialist new millennium, but not at the price of that mother of hers. Disruption was Lorraine's middle name, and OK, he was terrified of her too. He could see her now, flapping around the courts in her batwing leather coat, screeching that this tennis lark was a bit dodgy, *babes*, and when would Jade be ready to go home? Not to mention, Liam thought darkly, the fact that her husband didn't understand her.

It had been cowardly of him he knew, to wait until Lorraine

Johnson had gone to the ladies, before asking the landlord of the Bear and Bottle to give her a message saying he'd been urgently called away. But the woman was a piranha. She wanted to swallow him whole.

Ah well. Deciding to make the best of it and relieved at least, to see a glimmer of sunshine breaking through the high clouds, Liam began collecting up the balls, ready for the next exercise. He was unwilling to think of what had happened that night, of leaving Estelle, of returning to the garret flat alone to stare and stare at that lesson plan. Four hours' sleep he'd had, and with all this going on, it wasn't enough. He had suitcases under his eyes, still no clean laundry and a brain that was becoming more dysfunctional by the second.

Estelle . . . She obviously thought it was over between them. She'd said so in words of one syllable. And she'd pulled away from him when he'd tried to hold her. Shit . . . But how could he not want to hold her, Liam reasoned. When she was so close, when he knew that by reaching out a hand he could touch the cloudy wildness of her dark red hair, when he could almost taste the musk of the scent she wore? But she'd pulled away, damn it.

And if he'd thought it would make any difference, despite the workload that was waiting for him that night, then he would have stayed with her – of course he would, he was aching to. But what would it have achieved? She was the one who had left. If she wanted to come back, if she even thought there was a chance . . . she'd have let him know somehow.

'All right?' Jade passed him a ball to put in the ball cage.

Hardly, Liam thought.

'Mum said I should show willing.' She glanced over at the others – Gazza, Stunt and Tiger as if assessing their eligibility, and briefly at Diane Parker and her friends Julie and Helen. From a more competitive angle, Liam guessed.

He sighed. This, he did not need. 'Have you ever held a racket before, Jade?'

'Oh, yes, Sir.' She batted mascara-ed eyelashes at him and twirled the racket she was holding as if she were making a fashion statement. An expensive racket, that had, no doubt, been especially purchased by her awful mother for the occasion, Liam thought.

'Hmm.' He decided to leave it. If she was too terrible and couldn't even hit the ball, he'd have a quiet word later and persuade her to be a cheerleader instead.

'Up the other end then,' he said, waving them to the far side of the green hard court. He still hadn't tried them on grass and that was a no go area today as it had been raining and the grass would cut up and be treacherous. 'We're going to practise chip and charge.'

'Is that what they do at Uncle Sam's?' joked Bradley, earning a giggle from Jade. If that was his best attempt at humour, Liam thought to himself, then he could forget it. This was serious business.

For the next few minutes, he got Tiger to serve, while he demonstrated the technique. 'Chip and charge is particularly useful on the second serve,' he said, running on the spot, trying to keep alert, knowing he'd lost their attention already. Jade was standing very close – too close – to Bradley Jacobs; Diane, Julie and Helen were inspecting their nails, fiddling with their ear-studs and picking their teeth respectively, and the rest of the boys were staring at Jade as she now stripped off the fleece and tossed it towards the wire netting that bordered the courts.

On second thoughts, Liam reflected, perhaps a cheerleader like Jade was not a great idea. She was too much of a distraction.

'Start running in a little way as he serves ...' He had to concentrate here because over the past few weeks, Tiger's serve had become a bit of a rocket – if an erratic one. 'Chip and charge up to the net!' Slightly out of breath, he returned to the service line.

Diane, Julie and Helen began to clap. 'I'll never be able to do it, Sir, will you, Hels?' said Julie.

'Just have a go,' Liam urged. In his experience, the main benefit of any coaching session was the practice involved. He didn't seriously expect them to make use of the technique in a game.

This time, Liam served, watching in despair as one by one they totally messed it up. They either charged too quickly, meaning they were at the net before the serve came over and therefore in an impossible position to make any kind of return, or they forgot to charge at all.

Last to come up was Jade and Liam tossed her a serve of such powder puff velocity that it barely made it over the net. Jade however, got on to her toes, chipped and charged, ready for the volley.

Liam was so surprised that he didn't manage to get it back to her at all. There was another bout of clapping – this time mainly from the male players.

'You've played before,' Liam gasped. That would teach him to make assumptions.

'Well, I blatantly wouldn't have come along otherwise, would I, Sir?' Jade asked reasonably, running her fingers suggestively along the net tape.

'Try it again.' It could have been a fluke.

Liam served – not so softly this time – and held his breath.

Once more, Jade chipped and charged.

Liam returned the ball, hard and fast to her backhand, knowing she wouldn't have a chance, but if he were honest, trying to retrieve a small piece of his coaching ego.

Jade volleyed it with a punch of triumph, completely out of his reach. More cheers.

'How *much* have you played before?' After the initial ego-bruise had faded, Liam felt a wave of euphoria. Jade could be his joker in the pack.

'Mum started me with this coach bloke when I was three,' Jade said, twirling the racket with aplomb. 'Short tennis with a soft ball. No thanks to that.'

'You played when you was three?' Gazza was eyeing her through his thick black-framed glasses with obvious admiration. He pulled up his sleeves and adjusted the belt of his jeans. Liam suppressed a smile.

'I didn't get on to a full-sized court till I was almost eight,' Jade confirmed, clearly enjoying the increase in attention. A true perfomer? Liam wondered, as she straightened her shoulders and stuck out her chest. The Adidas T-shirt heaved.

'Only eight?' he murmured.

'I was always big for my age,' Jade informed him. 'My coach thought I could handle it.'

Liam too had no doubts on that score. But the question was – could anyone handle Jade Johnson? 'Do you still have coaching?' he asked.

'Yeah.' She nodded towards the clubhouse. 'I don't come here, though. Mum says it's too tacky.' She smiled at Bradley with obvious affection.

'Tacky?' Liam murmured. Her *mother* said it was too tacky? He felt a rush of defensive pride. Chestnut Grove might need an injection of cash. It might not boast the best coaches or the smartest surroundings. The showers weren't renowned for their power, the furnishings had seen better days and the hard courts needed re-surfacing. But despite all that . . . He looked down the hill to Pridehaven and the horizon beyond. Despite all that, it was his favourite place to be.

And how come, he wondered, that Bradley Jacobs had come

into favour? Did this augur well for *Romeo and Juliet*, or could it be a disaster? Just how friendly should Romeo and Juliet be?

'Dad says I should give it up,' Jade went on. 'He says Mum's always trying to pretend we're something that we're not.' Another racket twirl. 'If you get what I mean.'

Liam nodded. He got exactly what she meant. And it was precisely that kind of snobbish attitude towards the game of tennis that he wanted to eradicate. He collected up a couple of balls and chucked them into the ball cage beyond the base line. Tennis should be played by anyone – money and social status notwithstanding. That was the ethos he'd like to see more firmly in place at CG's. Liam glanced across at the honey-bricked clubhouse and glass conservatory. Tacky, eh?

Jade was still talking. 'He says that netball was blatantly good enough for his sisters and it should be good enough for me,' she said. She scuffed the soles of her trainers on the green hard court and did a half-twist. 'As if . . . But Mum wins all the rows.' She winked at Liam. 'She always gets her own way, Sir.'

What did she mean? Liam hoped it had nothing to do with him. However, this was the longest speech he'd ever heard Jade make, and he was beginning to think that despite everything, maybe she'd be a half-decent contemporary and upfront Juliet after all. She was a natural – a drama queen in the making.

Michael tucked the postcard between the coffee jug and the tin of ginger biscuits on the wooden surface of the garden table. But, *Out of sight* . . . and so on was too much to hope for. And he needed it here in close proximity, to remind him.

He picked up his guitar and strummed a melancholy minor chord, then another. Castor the cat, sunning herself by the greenhouse, yawned, stretched and went back to sleep; the hens fluttered a little, and Hester carried on chewing grass as though nothing had happened. That just about summed it up, Michael thought.

The postcard had been sent to the shop. That might indicate subterfuge ... Michael strummed more violently, or it might, and hopefully did, mean that *he* – the big guy with attitude – didn't know where Suzi lived. That was something. And did he know, Michael wondered, about himself, Michael? Was it – as she said – a business relationship, or was it an affair? Almost as bad, was it something in between, still exciting, still unknown, with everything to come?

He could just see the card's blue background poking out from behind the coffee jug. Not of a German sky, but a Far Side cartoon – the kind you could get anywhere in any language probably, of a gleeful dog trying to persuade a gullible cat to enter a tumble drier marked CAT FUD.

Hardly original, Michael thought, watching Castor and thinking how unlikely it was that either Samson or Delilah would have the brain power to lure *her* to such a fate. Cats, after all, were far superior in intellect, more spiritual too than their doggy counterparts who would be anybody's best friend for a chocolate bonio.

Michael hit B flat. He had found the postcard in her underwear drawer. How significant was that, he wondered. She could have put it there with the idea that if she stuck it on the fridge with the others, Michael would flip (he had, after all, teetered over the edge of controlled jealousy after the boot sale episode.) Or she could have put it there because this Josh Willis was a secret. Because she cared. Or because ... she wanted him close to her underwear?

Michael flinched as he played an off note. No. She had said there was nothing going on, and it must be true. Suzi wasn't the type. There wasn't an ounce of deceit in her body. *So why hadn't she just thrown the postcard away?*

Michael heard the faint voices that signified walkers heading along the riverbank path. Mainly, it was just people from Pridehaven who used it to cut through from the town to the harbour, but he supposed it would be holidaymakers soon. Suzi had told him that the worst thing about living in Pridehaven was the summer rush. The town might not be pretty enough to be a tourist attraction in its own right, but caravan sites, hotels and guest houses drew them into Dorset, and cafés kept them on the streets with their cream teas, apple cake and fudge.

He sighed, pulling the postcard out of its semi-camouflage. The text was dreary rather than personal, the writing big and loopy. There was an anecdote about travelling over the border in his van and being stopped at customs — hardly stand-up material, Michael reflected; the information that a gate-leg table had sold for more than 'we' expected. Michael frowned. And a reference to the 'open spaces' that give a 'little bit of freedom' to the traveller. God knows what that was all about.

Bloody hippies, Michael thought crossly. They never grew up, always thought the world owed them a spliff and a good time.

How could he get her back? Michael played another chord, decided it sounded quite good, and made a mental note. If he'd lost her, that was. 'Want you back for good,' he murmured. Oh, Jesus, no, that was Take That, he'd have to find something more original.

A butterfly landed on the glass of the greenhouse, shimmering there for a moment in the sunlight. A Red Admiral, he thought it was, the kind of butterfly you no longer saw in town gardens, if you saw any at all.

Michael struggled with the melody. She couldn't say he wasn't trying to build up a new career. He had four pubs booked now — regular dates of once a month, one in Pridehaven, one in Burton Bradstock, one in Seaton and one in Dorchester.

And who knew who might be at any of those gigs? There were so many people in the music business – not just talent scouts, they were a bit of a myth – but guys on the record-ing side and other musicians after a new band member. People who knew other people. Contacts. It was probably just a matter of waiting for his lucky break. He was only forty. It wasn't too late.

Michael put his head to one side and listened. Whoever it was had walked on. The garden was quiet again, the faint rustle of the reeds and sluice of fast flowing water the only sounds to be heard above the occasional scrabble or clucking of the hens, the stringy creak of Hester pulling on her rope.

In a minute, he'd put the postcard back in the drawer, he decided, just in case Suzi turned up unexpectedly. He wouldn't want her to think he'd been looking through her things – especially after what had happened with those concert tickets.

And he wouldn't normally root through her underwear drawer, he told himself. He wouldn't root through anyone's underwear drawer, and unfortunately Suzi wasn't the type for silk and stock-ings, frills and thrills in that department. She was no nonsense; black cotton thongs were about as sexy as she got. No, he'd been looking there, because he was scared, and Suzi would never understand that. Never understand his fear that one day it would be all he'd have left of her, her things and a morning alone in her cottage, knowing he had to leave.

Ouch. Another wrong note. Michael was going for loneliness and the music was telling him pain . . .

And besides, he'd really messed up with the concert tickets, because why should she have bought them for him and her? Why should he expect any such thing? He should be doing that kind of stuff, instead of depending on her for food and shelter, instead of acting like a parasite, buying the occasional take-away and imagining that balanced the books. She had never told him she wanted to share her worldly goods with him – like she said, he'd assumed, and he'd assumed wrong. He hadn't listened either. He'd been a bloody fool, in fact.

Suddenly the tune came together in his head, and Michael played it a couple of times, changing a chord here, altering the rhythm there, intent on the song and almost unaware of the dark clouds gathering force in the sky above him, though at one point he put down his guitar to pull on an old blue sweatshirt draped on the back of his chair.

Castor woke again, got to her feet and stalked gracefully into the cottage to find the warmest corner. But Michael worked on. He had already woven a couple of his own songs into the act – the funny thing was that he'd never gone in for songwriting much before, but this was a creative place.

He let his gaze wander past Hester to the river beyond. He loved taking the dogs down the riverbank path to the sea, walking with them right over the cliff to Burton Hive. He was becoming an outdoor person, Suzi's sort of person, while Suzi was spending her days festering away in an antique shop. Odd, but it had never seemed quite Suzi somehow.

'Someone else not you'. The song title came to him. Because that was what Suzi seemed to have become.

At last Michael put down his guitar, just as the first few drops of rain fell. He loved the taste of the salt air on his tongue, the sound of the waves creeping across the shingle. He felt at home here. He shivered. He didn't want to leave.

He knew he should get himself and the guitar back inside the cottage – the wind had picked up and there was clearly a downpour on its way. Even the hens were all inside the hen-house now, and Hester had that resigned look in her pale eyes that usually forecast bad weather. But he lingered, relishing the freshness in the air, using the moment to wonder about his future, his future with Suzi. If he had one . . .

She had said she wanted more independence, she had said she wasn't sure she wanted him living full-time at the cottage – that it was early days for their relationship, too soon to make any commitment. Michael leaned forwards, his elbows on his knees. He'd messed up. So, OK, he'd look for his own place – though it wouldn't be easy without a day job, without money in his pocket. Suzi knew that. Suzi understood that much at least.

He watched a thin-legged spider weave its fragile way through the long blades of grass. A harvester. The garden was a wild, cottage garden, crammed with herbs, meadow flowers, and plants that had sprung up from seeds blown from the riverbank – poppies, thrift and buttercups. In the far corner, Hester held sway over the small patch of lawn, to one side the greenhouse sheltered Suzi's strawberries, aubergines, peppers and tomatoes, to the other side were the hens and the cockerel in their narrow, dusty run.

. Michael got to his feet. It was the planning that had gone wrong, he decided. He should have got things organised here before he upped and left Fareham. But it wasn't too late to make things right. When he had more money from performing, there wouldn't be a problem. He and Suzi would survive this – they had to.

He watched the dark clouds dispassionately as they thickened, seeming to drop lower, closer towards him. It wasn't over. That night, after she'd gone with Willis to that bloody car boot sale, Suzi had folded against him, Michael, and said she needed . . . Needed what? Needed him? Michael hoped so.

He'd held her that night and felt the rush, had tried, while trying not to try, because that was the trick. They had made it, made love, and he was glad. But somehow . . .

He picked up the postcard, which was wet, the ink beginning

to run, as the rain splattered on to the table, on to his chair, his guitar, his hair.

Why hadn't she thrown it away? Somehow, he had still felt like second best.

Liam scowled as he spotted the tall, tightly packed figure of Nick Rossi strolling out of the clubhouse accompanied by four lads. They were all members of the tennis club, of course, had probably all been playing since childhood. And they all had aquiline profiles, thin lips, insipid eyes – the easy, blond, confident good looks that Liam always associated with family money that had never had to be worked for. The opposition. He addressed Rossi. 'Need some practice, do they – your lot?'

'Hardly.' Nick shrugged as he glanced towards the next court. 'Girls too?' he enquired.

'Yeah, well, I assumed CG's could vaguely be called politically correct,' Liam said, though it was undeniably true that Erica Raddle and Deirdre Piston were doing everything they could to nullify this image. He could see them now, inside the conservatory, sitting at one of the tables that looked out to the tennis courts, Erica probably mouthing away as usual while Deirdre took notes of her pearls of wisdom.

'No problem for us,' Nick said, still watching Jade.

'She's only twelve years old,' Liam snapped. And as he spoke, the thought of this creep with his Estelle hit him so hard that he gripped his racket until his knuckles went white. He had to, otherwise he'd floor the smug bastard.

Rossi shrugged again. Liam would love to rip that shrug from those broad shoulders, love to make him care.

'When do you think you'll be ready for the tournament?' Rossi pulled out a black leather Filofax from the zipped pocket of his sports bag and regarded Liam cooly. The implication was clear.

'Anytime you are.' Liam groped in his tatty black briefcase on the ground at his feet for his own battered red diary.

As they fixed a provisional date for mid-season, Liam looked up to see Tiger hit an easy volley into the net. He winced, but knew Rossi had seen it too.

Sure enough, he raised his eyebrows. 'Looks like you've got a long way to go,' he remarked.

'Maybe we'll surprise you.' How could she tolerate him? The guy was so bloody obvious. Liam realised he was grinding his teeth again. He took a deep breath, looked towards Gazza who was . . . 'Put that bloody fag out!' he yelled.

Nick laughed. 'Let's wait and see. C'mon boys . . .'

Boys? More like androids, Liam thought, with their identical white joggers and cream, zipped fleeces.

'Hugh and Barnaby up the other end. James and Oliver, this end. May as well warm up a bit . . .' Nick pulled off his sweatshirt, slung it casually over one shoulder and smoothed his layered blond hair back into place.

Hugh and Barnaby? Liam smirked, tried not to watch them, but did anyway, his glance drifting over to the far court and then pulling back again, his ear attuned to their banter. They were showing off for his group's benefit, he could see that much, playing long sweeping ground strokes, smashing serves into court, going for shots that were on their way out anyway, not playing the percentages and not giving a stuff. They didn't have to, thought Liam. They were a different class. In more ways than one.

'We need to practise some volleying,' Liam told his lot, thinking of Tiger's gaffe. He demonstrated the grip as Deirdre scuttled out of the conservatory brandishing a tape measure in one hand and a clipboard in the other. 'C'mon, Jade – let's show them.' He tossed a couple of balls to her, which she volleyed, crisply and neatly with the precise punching action required.

'Hammer grip,' she told Bradley fondly as he tried to follow suit and missed the ball completely. 'I'll show you.' She took hold of his hand.

'You can show me too, if you like,' came the call from one of the lads on the far court. Hugh, Barnaby, whoever, they all looked the same to Liam.

'Gosh, and me!'

'Bugger off,' said Jade.

Deirdre dropped her clipboard.

'That one looks a little low ...' Erica was standing in the doorway of the conservatory, issuing instructions. 'Check it, will you, dear?'

Deirdre and her tape approached the net in question.

Erica was droning on. 'Once the re-surfacing on the top courts is done ...' she was saying.

Liam did a double-take. Had he heard right? 'Re-surfacing?' he yelled back at Erica. 'What re-surfacing?' He strode towards the conservatory.

Erica bared her teeth. 'On the top courts,' she said, arms akimbo, polyester blouse crackling.

It took Liam a moment to absorb her meaning. 'The courts used exclusively by the tennis club?' He was at the door now, close enough to count the red veins on Erica's horsy face.

'Precisely. Green and purple as per Wimbledon seems to be the consensus.' She went to shut the door, but Liam got there first.

'What about the courts used by the youth club?' he demanded, his voice dangerously low. She had gone too far this time. Who the hell did she think she was? 'And whose consensus is green and purple?'

Erica sighed one of her gusty sighs. 'We've taken advice, Liam,' she said. 'It's that or blue, because of visibility, you know. And we can't be blue.'

'Why the hell not?' Blue sounded just fine to Liam. The kids would like blue, for a start. It would be different, something un-fusty, bright and that bit Continental, to attract them on to the courts.

'Chestnut Grove has always been green.' Erica was looking dangerously close to explosion point.

'So?'

'And although we have some private sponsorship, there's not enough, I fear, to re-surface *all* the courts.'

'Private sponsorship? Where the fuck did that come from?' Liam too was wound up now, good and proper.

Erica winced. 'An anonymous sponsor has decided to remain so for a reason. I can't say more at present.' She tapped her nose.

Liam leaned closer. 'And what I'd like to say – just in case you've forgotten – is that all decisions are supposed to be made at Committee.'

'Naturally.' Erica folded her arms. 'And in the meantime, Simon is continuing his research into the green and purple issue.'

'And when,' growled Liam, 'is the next meeting?' He'd give her green and purple issue.

Deirdre – who had completed her net-checking and was now standing a safe distance from Liam, ready to leap to Erica's defence if necessary – consulted her clipboard. 'The 2nd of next month,' she announced.

That date rang a bell and it only took Liam a moment to remember why. 'I've got a parents' evening,' he said, slapping his forehead with the ball of his hand. 'Can't you re-schedule?' But he knew even as he said this, that Erica would be thrilled he couldn't make it. Why should she change the date when her main objector wouldn't be there to stop her getting her own way?

'I'm afraid I can't set a precedent,' Erica confirmed, baring her teeth once again, turning away from him and taking a step inside.

'A precedent,' Deirdre confirmed.

Damn and double damn. Liam glared at Deirdre, knowing that this was unfair, that mousy Deirdre had no voice in the matter and probably no opinions either. If Erica told her to lie down and wave her legs in the air, she'd probably bark with delight and bake a batch of fruit scones while she was doing it.

He returned to the court, unsurprised that his lot had all stopped playing, and were now standing around smoking, chewing gum and drinking coke. On the night of the parents' evening he'd have to get Suzi down here to find out what was going on. Or God knows what they'd decide in his absence. Green and purple?

'Let's wind it up then,' he said, since they'd clearly decided to do just that and anyway there was a huge dark cloud squatting threateningly above them. On the far court, Rossi's lot had warmed up and were now playing a game of doubles. As he watched, a near-perfect serve was somehow returned, but too high and punished by a smash worthy of Tim Henman.

Liam groaned. Nick Rossi and Erica Raddle – the enemy. They held all the cards and weren't even playing by the rules.

Was he fighting a losing battle? For the first time Liam allowed himself to consider this possibility. He ground his teeth once more. Well, if he was, he was bloody determined to give it all he had. No one would be able to say he hadn't gone down fighting.

Chapter 17

'I thought that diamond choker was special.' Nick Rossi was glowering at his mother.

Estelle shifted awkwardly on Shelagh Rossi's flowery chintz sofa. She was trying to stay focused, but undeniably, she'd had a shock. The note was folded, tucked into the zipped compartment of her multi-coloured rucksack. She could read it at any time. But not yet, not now.

Shelagh had invited her here to provide a valuation for some more jewellery and a couple of pieces of furniture. But Nick, clearly, wasn't happy.

'All my jewellery is special.' Shelagh eyed her son calmly. 'But one has to prioritise.'

'Prioritise?' Nick folded both arms and face as he turned away to stare out of the elegant French windows. It was a view that deserved a little more appreciation, Estelle couldn't help thinking. A stretch of parkland beyond the patio with its statues of two regal lions. A path that led down the green slope to some stone steps and an ornamental pond with fountain, full, she knew, of slim, swift, iridescent carp, weaving their way through the lily pads. She knew this, because Shelagh had shown Estelle round her precious garden on Estelle's last visit to the gothic house on the hill, her pride evident at every step, every border, every plant.

'What happens?' Nick went on, 'when we get down to the clothes on our backs? What's your priority then, Mother?'

'Silly . . .' Shelagh poured tea into the dainty cups on the table beside her, but Estelle couldn't help noticing that her hand was trembling slightly. 'We have so many things we don't really need.'

Nick took the few strides necessary across the thick white pile of the carpet, to reach his mother's wing-back chair. 'You may not *need* your diamond choker, Mother,' he said, standing in front of her, demanding her attention. 'But you've always enjoyed wearing it, getting it out of your jewellery box, touching it, admiring it, hmmm?'

He was confronting his mother, yes, but Estelle noted the gentleness in his voice as he spoke, the affection evident in his eyes as he looked at her. But Shelagh, Estelle observed, would not look back at him.

'True,' she conceded at last. 'But a diamond choker around a scraggy old neck isn't quite the thing.' She smiled at Estelle. 'Wouldn't you say so, my dear?'

Estelle wasn't sure she wanted to get involved in this moment of discord. She could advise on value, but hardly whether or not it was beneficial to sell the family treasures. And as for scraggy, though Shelagh was in her late sixties, she remained an elegant woman. She was slim and held herself upright, her hair was white but still luxuriant and cut in a flattering, modern style, and her eyes were almost as blue as her son's.

'It is beautiful,' Estelle said, turning the choker to catch the light. 'And I can see Nick's point. If you're fond of the piece, it does seem a shame to sell it.'

Shelagh shot her a sharp glance. 'Are you saying you don't wish to dispose of it for me, my dear? Because I could always –'

'Of course I'm not.' She shouldn't let her emotions interfere with the professional requirements of the job, Estelle reminded herself. She could earn a hefty commission from this sale, and the reasons behind the selling should not be her concern. 'I'm more than happy to help,' she said. 'If you're sure.'

Nick took a step towards her and rested a hand briefly on her shoulder. 'Rather you than anyone else,' he said. 'But it's the white elephant we should be selling.'

Ignoring him, Shelagh added milk from a tiny jug and passed Estelle her tea.

Estelle took it. 'White elephant?'

'He means the house.'

Of course, Nick had already told her that the house was eating up all the money his father had left them, most of what Nick earned and now apparently, the proceeds of the sale of his mother's jewellery too. But ... Estelle's gaze drifted up to the ornate, corniced ceiling. The creamy plasterwork was chipped, but the ceiling, adorned with cherubs, trumpets and bunches of grapes, was still impressive in its grandeur. Yes, she could see why Shelagh didn't want to sell up. It was quite something.

'He should have more respect for his father's memory,' Shelagh went on conversationally. 'This place is all we have left of him, you know.'

'I do have respect.' The dainty cup looked ridiculous in Nick's large brown hand. He could crush it so easily, Estelle thought. And come to that, he could force his mother to sell up if he wanted to. Without his help, surely she would never be able to stay here. The guy had loyalty then, too. He must have, to stand by and watch his earnings being swallowed up by something he didn't even want.

Estelle had to admit that since meeting his mother, her opinion of Nick Rossi had changed. He wasn't just your typical arrogant, athletic, tennis club hunk. Far from it. He was a caring and generous man. As well as being drop dead gorgeous, of course.

'And I shall stay put for as long as I'm able,' Shelagh said.

Subject closed. Estelle wondered how many times in the past they'd had the same discussion. Each time, Shelagh would probably dig her heels in deeper and each time, Nick would become more frustrated. And how long would it be before she gave in? When the last piece of jewellery had been sold to provide an amp or two more of electricity to seep its heat through draughty windows and doors, another gardener to keep borders weeded, hedges clipped, trees pruned? Estelle felt sorry for them both. But Shelagh Rossi, she knew, would have to give in eventually.

GIVE IN TO THE INEVITABLE — that's what the note had said. Estelle could still picture the words, had to stop herself from pulling the note from her rucksack. Black capitals scrawled on a sheet of pink notepaper. Pink, for heaven's sake . . . LEAVE BEFORE YOU HAVE TO.

Estelle had stared at the words for some moments before taking in their meaning. At first she'd thought it was some bizarre flyer – addressed to *The Occupier*, from an estate agent or sales team, perhaps. *Give in to the inevitable – buy a MUST HAVE 100% secure burglar alarm for your shop.*

But it wasn't that, of course, because it was handwritten not typed and though the envelope was blank, Estelle knew it was intended for Secrets In The Attic, for her. And it was a threat. Another threat? The anger had surged through her. LEAVE BEFORE YOU HAVE TO. And it surged through her now, just thinking about it.

She hadn't told Suzi yet. She hadn't even told her about the puncture, or the 'For Sale' notice on her car – just a prank perhaps, kids having a laugh. She was still telling herself that, not thinking of Stan and Terry and their not-so-veiled threats. The phone number of the shop was easy enough to find and her phone in the flat merely an extension.

But now she'd been sent this note, she would tell her everything, Estelle decided, placing her empty cup on the table in front of her and smiling at Shelagh Rossi. She must complete her business here and then go back to the shop. Yes, she would tell Suzi, because not only was Estelle angry, now, she was also beginning to get scared.

Suzi was walking along the riverbank path, wrapped in a big blue beach towel, on her way back to the cottage, when she saw Estelle coming towards her. She noted her friend's expression of relief when she spotted her and waved, though not without a twinge of anxiety. They saw one another every day – so why had Estelle come visiting?

'I thought you were out,' Estelle said.

'I was.' The sea had been cold but bracing. Lately, Suzi had been using it as a stress reliever after work – the chill of the waves helped her forget that since coming back from Germany, Josh Willis had barely bothered to get in touch. Suzi shivered.

The fact that he'd sent her a postcard had appeared significant at first. Though now when she looked at that card, it seemed both brief and impersonal. Apart that is, from the mention of open spaces and freedom, something they'd spoken of that day on Charmouth cliff, something that had seemed to mean a lot to him. But who could tell?

Still, the physical exertion of swimming against the tide made her too tired to worry – about herself and Michael, about the shop, about Liam and Estelle. And about whatever Josh had or hadn't done, damn it.

'Can we talk?' Estelle seemed even more restless than usual.

Suzi frowned. As she'd suspected – more problems. She held

the gate open for her friend 'You can shout at me while I take a shower,' she told her. 'And open a bottle of wine. Now tell me what's up.'

By the time Estelle had explained about the puncture, the 'For Sale' sign, the little chats with Stan and Terry, and Suzi had seen the note Estelle carried in her rucksack – and made it wet, incidentally – they'd almost finished the bottle.

'I suppose that kind of thing happens to cars when they're parked on the main road,' Suzi said doubtfully.

'What, in Pridehaven?'

'Well, why not?' Why not, because it was a sleepy seaside town more like a village where people were friendly and didn't vandalise one another's cars, that's why not. 'We're very close to The Seagull,' Suzi added, trying to reassure her. The pub next door to The Bargain Basement was always full of kids who didn't look old enough to be there, while the sound of rap and hip hop thumped rather than drifted their way from six until late every night. The pub, Suzi reflected, thinking of her noisy flying neighbours, was aptly named.

'They're not shifting us, whoever they are,' Estelle said, squaring her shoulders and glaring at Suzi as though she were responsible. 'Are they, Suze?'

And Suzi, though she wasn't sure that she shared Estelle's dedication to antiques, agreed with her. 'So what should we do?'

She towelled her hair with more aggression than was strictly necessary. It wasn't easy, was it, to cope? To run a business and make a living, not to mention handle all this kind of stuff. 'Go to the police?' She almost suggested they ask Liam's advice but one look at Estelle's face persuaded her that this was a bad idea. Perhaps the concert at the Arts Centre might rectify that particular situation. At any rate, she thought, it was worth a try.

'We can't prove anything,' Estelle reminded her. She looked thoughtful. 'But the thing that bothers me the most . . .'

'Yes?'

'Is how on earth did Terry know what a financial mess we were in?'

He wouldn't have, would he? The more Suzi thought about it after Estelle had gone, the more she couldn't say for sure. Who else was a common denominator? Who else knew their problems and knew Stan and Terry?

She thought of the one brief telephone conversation they'd had since his return. His, *Hi. How's tricks?* had been perfectly light and casual, as if Suzi were merely some vague acquaintance, which of course, she reminded herself, was exactly what she was.

'I'm fine,' she'd told him. Though she didn't feel it. She felt helpless and strangely at odds with herself these days, as though she were a spectator of her own life.

'And how's business?' he had asked her.

'That's fine too,' she had replied, maintaining the light tone that she hoped matched his. Only, why had he wanted to know?

They had finalised the details for the roadshow. And that was that.

Would he have told Terry how badly they were doing? She had no idea. One lunch, one breakfast, one walk, one car boot sale, didn't add up to much. Oh, yes, and one postcard. The truth was – if Suzi were honest with herself – she hardly knew the man.

Chapter 18

'They don't show you this sort of stuff on the TV,' Estelle muttered to Suzi. 'The antiques roadshow lot have valuable attics.'

The three of them were in Secrets seated behind two trestle tables, facing the open door of the shop. During the afternoon various people had wandered in, listened to Josh and Estelle's advice and wandered out again. Though what all this was doing for the business, Suzi wasn't quite sure.

'Yeah. This is more car boot sale than valuable attic.' Suzi watched Josh break the news to the owner of yet another chipped 70s dinner service that they were not holding the find of the century in their hands and that actually, the floral plates and bowls, pretty though they were, were worthless. As was most of the other stuff that had passed through their doors – ply coffee tables, cracked glass vases, old photographs, broken toys, tacky jewellery . . . you name it, they'd seen it today. And no, she didn't want to dwell on the thought of car boot sales.

'Go on then,' the owner of the dinner service challenged Josh, polishing one of the plates with the sleeve of his threadbare jumper. 'How much would you give me for 'em – tell me straight.'

'I'm sorry.' And he did look sorry, Suzi noted, wondering

about Josh's acting abilities. 'Dinner services like this one are not a particular interest of ours.' He pulled up the sleeves of his crumpled linen jacket and leaned forwards, his elbows on the table.

Suzi noted the 'ours'. Josh Willis appeared to have become a partner. She pushed this thought from her mind the second it crept there.

'You could try next door,' put in Estelle, earning a quick flash of the cat's grin from Josh. 'They'll buy anything.'

The dinner service man looked across at her sharply, but Estelle's expression was as innocent as Josh's, and the man merely gathered up his treasures and left the shop. The song of the wind-chimes seemed to follow him out of the doorway.

'Coffee?' suggested Suzi, feeling redundant. Out of the three of them, there was no doubt who was the least knowledgeable about antiques. And it wasn't just that. All morning she'd been torn between wanting to talk to Josh and wanting to keep out of his way. And she hadn't managed either. She had merely hovered, while he sat there larger than life. Larger.

'Could murder a cup,' he told her cheerfully.

'Me too,' echoed Estelle, leaning closer to him to point out something in the *Miller's Guide*.

Fine. Whatever. Suzi hurried away to the tiny kitchenette. She'd made up her mind to be cool, so it was all to the better if Estelle and Josh were hitting it off. Apart from what Josh had or hadn't done . . . It was madness. She, Suzi, was living with another man and she was far too sane to be carried into the realms of fantasy by some Little John lookalike in a crumpled linen suit, who had happened to take her to a car boot sale . . . She filled the kettle. And to lunch . . . Spooned instant coffee into two mugs, dropped a green tea bag into another. And for a walk on the hills . . . Damn it.

She waited for the kettle to boil, cut herself off from the banter going down in the shop. It was ridiculous to imagine that she'd missed him.

Suzi took the drinks back in, recognising the tight grey perm of Mrs Barnaby, who wore a facial expression to match.

'My nephew, Nigel,' she was saying in introduction to Estelle, who had, Suzi knew, seen a fair bit of her until Stan and Terry had come along and bought all the pieces Estelle had made offers for. Mrs B. had been conspicuously absent from Secrets In The Attic ever since.

'I couldn't resist bringing this in,' she said, as Nigel put the table he was carrying down in front of them. 'Hoped you'd let bygones be bygones, dear. My selling to them next door, I mean.'

Estelle shrugged. 'No hard feelings on my part, Mrs Barnaby. That's business. You're entitled to sell to whoever you like.' She moved closer to the table and stroked the grain of it with a fingertip. 'Ebony?' she asked Josh.

He did the same and frowned. 'Ebonised to simulate ebony, I'd say.'

'I thought they'd be fair,' Mrs Barnaby continued, as though the history of the table was nothing to her.

'And they weren't?' Suzi tried to sound off-hand. Surely it had to be Stan and Terry trying to get them out of Secrets? Who else could it be?

'It was the furniture,' Mrs Barnaby was explaining, as Josh got up, to prowl around the table in his biscuit-coloured suit, one moment muttering to Estelle or to himself, the next moment pulling at his short red beard or leaning over the table to leaf through the pages of one of his reference books.

'She was done,' said Nigel. 'I told her that chest was worth two hundred of anyone's money. Beautiful piece of walnut that were. Dealers like that lot next door should be –'

'Too late now, dear.' His aunt took his arm.

But Nigel was stubborn, Suzi would say that for him. He stuck out his chest and pulled in his stomach. 'It's never too late to give someone a piece of your mind,' he told her. 'There's such a thing as trading standards. Mebbe even the police.' Estelle and Suzi exchanged a glance and Josh looked up.

'Preying on vulnerable members of our community.' By now, Nigel was well into his stride. 'Elderly folk who don't know no better.'

Mrs Barnaby blanched at this.

Suzi wondered if Mrs Barnaby's furniture had ended up in Germany and if so, how much Josh himself had paid for it. She shot him a meaningful look but he ignored her and returned his attention to the two-tiered table.

'Simple, classical design,' he said.

'How much is it worth?' Suzi asked. It was about time he was put on the spot.

'Maybe about £500 in auction,' he said, without looking up.

Mrs Barnaby merely shook her head and glanced ruefully towards The Bargain Basement. 'He seemed like such a nice man,' she said. 'Three sugars in his tea. I teased him.'

'Would you be interested?' Nigel asked Estelle. 'In the table, I mean.'

'Not for more than £300,' she said.

Suzi registered the flicker of approval in Josh's grey-green eyes.

'I'd have to advise auction if you wanted a chance of getting its true worth,' she went on.

Mrs Barnaby sighed. 'Though he wasn't pleasant about you, my dears,' she said.

'Oh?' Suzi and Estelle exchanged another glance.

'Inflated prices were mentioned.' Mrs Barnaby looked around

the shop as if searching for evidence. 'And I'm sure he said you wouldn't be in business for very long neither.'

'He's got a bloody nerve.' Estelle's fists clenched.

Suzi cast her a warning glance and shoved one of their Sotheby's leaflets (for credibility, Josh had said) towards aunt and nephew. 'We plan to be around for a while yet,' she said sweetly.

Suzi had already started packing up when an elderly gentleman with a stick tip-tapped his way into the shop. 'You are still doing the roadshow?' he enquired as he got to the counter. What hair he had left was grey and slicked back from a wide forehead.

'We certainly are.'

The man reached into his pocket. 'My late wife's,' he said simply, as he placed a lapel clip carefully on the counter.

After a few moments, Suzi realised that both Estelle and Josh had gone very quiet. Estelle's colour was high as she examined the piece of jewellery under her microscope, Josh was frowning and flicking through yet another reference book. Suzi raised her eyebrows. Clearly not tat then, that was something.

'Rock crystal,' Estelle said, after an eternity.

That didn't sound too great to Suzi. She got on with what she was doing.

'And in the centre . . .' Josh's voice was low, 'unless I'm mistaken, a line of rubies.'

'Burmese rubies.' Estelle laughed – slightly hysterically, Suzi thought. 'Precious stones in a natural setting.'

'It's signed,' the old man said.

'I know.' Estelle's voice was hushed now too, almost reverential. 'And made in France. See the control mark.'

By now Suzi twigged that both Josh and Estelle were looking at her expectantly. 'What?' She came closer. 'Is it worth much?'

Josh and Estelle exchanged a glance that was close, Suzi thought, to being conspiratorial. She tried to suppress the ridiculous stab of jealousy. As if Josh Willis had anything to do with her, as if she'd discovered him, as if he meant something . . .

'It's a platinum clip,' Josh said, speaking as if to a child.

So?

'And these,' Estelle pointed, 'are diamonds.'

Now Suzi was beginning to get the point. Clearly this was a coup of some sort, a kind of grande finale for their afternoon roadshow. 'That's good then, yeah?' She looked from one to the other of them.

'It could be worth up to two grand at auction,' Josh told the old man.

Suzi blinked.

'I couldn't sell it, though, lad,' the old man said. 'I wanted to show it to you, and it's nice to know. But it's too special, y'see.'

Too special. Suzi watched his eyes mist with tears, listened as Josh told him about insurance, urged him to take care on his way home. What was it like, she wondered, to have a someone who was as special as that? Would she ever know?

Suzi remained subdued as they packed up, barely listening to the conversation being tossed around between Josh and Estelle. She heard Estelle try and offer him some money in payment for his services, registered that he'd refused on the grounds that they couldn't afford it and anyway he'd had a bloody good time.

'Call it a favour,' he said.

Ah, but what would he want in return? Suzi wondered. She was beginning to see ulterior motives everywhere, but at least it might stop her from being so flipping gullible.

It was after six when everything was sorted, the tables put away and the shop looked vaguely like an antique shop again. Well, like a shop anyway, Suzi decided.

Josh turned to her. 'Fancy a drink – to celebrate?' he asked.

'Not really.' She half-regretted the words as soon as they were out of her mouth, observed his look of mild surprise, the slight narrowing of the grey-green eyes. She was supposed to be seeing Michael play – but it wouldn't have been hard to find an excuse; she'd been doing it often enough lately. Yes, and feeling guilty too. How did you tell someone to go? Someone who hadn't done anything wrong, someone who cared for you? Why couldn't life and love and that kind of stuff be more organised and logical? It wasn't exactly fair. And she knew that she wasn't being fair either.

He hesitated. 'Estelle? How about you?'

She seemed to be considering the invitation. She looked at Suzi, who shrugged to indicate that it was all the same to her. Fat chance. She was heaving with jealousy and Estelle should be able to see that. She was supposed to be her best friend, wasn't she? But she couldn't stop her. There was no way she could tell Estelle that Josh might be the missing link between their financial problems and The Bargain Basement. How could she? It wouldn't do much for her credibility as a responsible business partner.

Anyway, Estelle was already putting on her jacket. 'Beats going up to an empty flat,' she said. 'Bear and Bottle suit you?'

Josh didn't even look at Suzi as they walked out of the door. 'The Bear and Bottle suits me just fine,' he said.

Chapter 19

Michael knew that it was a mistake to play to an individual. The audience was the thing, and Michael's act depended on building a rapport. But it was hard, he found, as he played his favourite Bob Seger number, to stop looking at Suzi, who was seated at a small circular table over in the far corner of the pub.

She had arrived back at the cottage late this afternoon after her roadshow thing, in a very strange mood. Agreed to come tonight to his gig at The Brunswick in Seaton, with an, 'of course I'm coming', and a deep frown. As if, he thought, she didn't usually find some excuse or other to back out of it. And in a way, he couldn't blame her.

She had changed into some black jeans and a clean top, waved some mascara in the general direction of her lashes, run her fingers through her spiky dark hair and announced herself ready.

Yes, she was here, but . . . Michael launched into the chorus of 'Still The Same', she was preoccupied, only half-watching, occasionally taking a sip of her beer, even more occasionally glancing his way with a vague half-smile that could have been meant for anyone. Not really here at all.

Was it anything to do with this bloody antique dealer guy,

Michael wondered, almost forgetting the first line of the next verse. She'd been jumpy and so hyped up before this roadshow of theirs you'd think it was going on the telly, not just some half-baked scheme to draw customers into the shop. He had a sudden thought – one he didn't like much. Maybe *he*'d been there – this Willis character.

But then . . . Michael finished the song and accepted the applause from the small crowd – gathered at the bar and seated at the dozen or so tables scattered in front of him, with a small bow. She had been preoccupied for a while now. When pressed, she insisted it was just the shop, but other than that she wouldn't discuss it.

Wouldn't discuss very much at all, he thought. She'd changed, or they'd changed. 'Someone else not you' . . . He began to play the song he'd composed sitting in the garden of Suzi's riverbank cottage. The words were even more resonant now than they had been then, the song had become integral to his act.

As he played, he watched her, tried to spot a flicker of recognition. But there was nothing. Christ, Suzi hadn't even twigged he'd written the song for her. Were things that bad between them?

As the last notes died away, the applause was enthusiastic. Nice that, Michael thought, for one of your own songs. He grinned as he scanned the faces. Gave a guy a real buzz.

He launched into a Chris Rea number, 'Fool if you think it's over', to finish the first part of his set. He usually enjoyed this one but tonight it only made him feel depressed. He hadn't played it lately, though he couldn't for the moment remember why.

Things with Suzi weren't too hot, he had to admit. On the surface they behaved like a couple living together. How did a couple living together behave? Michael frowned as he thought of Estelle and Liam – passionate whether they were kissing or fighting, and now seemingly split for good. Though that wasn't

Suzi's style, he knew. She was kind. She avoided confrontation. She hated hurting anything – or anyone.

But all the deep-down stuff seemed to have fallen apart. Like the talking – the talking had changed from telling one another about their week away, taking apart the world around them to . . . Jesus, what to have for dinner? And as for the loving . . .

As he played, Michael noticed the side door of the pub open to admit the blonde. She paused mid-entrance, and he took his attention away from Suzi long enough to register that she was wearing black knee-high boots and a tight lycra-style mini dress. Sexy, he couldn't help thinking. Her make-up was faintly gothic – dark eyeliner, touches of violet around the lids. She always had this independent look about her – she never seemed bothered about being alone.

She glanced round, caught him looking, waved and smiled.

Michael decided to ignore her. This was only Seaton, but he was beginning to feel that she was following him round the country.

As he moved smoothly into the chorus, his voice caught and he remembered why he hadn't played the song for ages – he couldn't always get to that note, unless . . . Christ, he was in the wrong bloody key.

He could see, as he tried to extricate himself from the situation with an unscheduled musical break, that both the blonde and Suzi had noticed his gaffe. Suzi was looking concerned, but the blonde was smiling broadly with those dark painted lips of hers, mouthing something he couldn't quite make out. Ah well, in for a penny.

'Wrong bloody key,' Michael announced, getting a laugh and a round of applause as he did a quick hop backwards, changed key and continued.

Encouraged, he performed a Catherine wheel-like movement with his right arm, strumming the guitar every time his splayed fingers passed it. It was something that he often did when he was mucking about – but hell, this audience were laughing. They liked it. 'Hey . . .'

He took a step further on the rickety stage he wasn't used to, inadvertently hit one of the prongs of the microphone stand with the toe of a desert boot, saw, as if in slow motion, the microphone spring back, felt it deliver him a sharp blow to the chin.

'Ouch! Bloody hell!' At first he wanted the ground to open up for him. Then he registered the continuing laughter, the smiles, knew in a second that they were on his side. And milked it. Boy, did he milk it. He staggered slightly, sank to his knees, continued playing. It worked. They loved it.

'Clever stuff.' The blonde was on to him before he'd even slipped the guitar strap from his shoulder.

'How d'you mean?' Michael had one eye on the blonde, one on Suzi, who had gone to the bar to get them both a drink.

'That part of your act – the larking around.' She eyed him suggestively over the rim of her wine glass. 'I like it.'

'You do?' Despite himself, Michael was pleased.

'Uh huh.' She half-turned around. 'I see your girlfriend's here tonight. Serious with you two, is it?'

Michael wasn't sure of the answer to that one. 'We live together,' he said, realising too late how ridiculously pompous that sounded.

But the blonde only smiled, the tip of a pink tongue appearing as she bit at her lower lip. 'Have you played it yet?' she asked.

'It?' Not 'Lay Lady Lay', he hoped.

'That song you wrote, "Someone Else Not You", have I missed it?'

'Yes.'

'It's good.' She sounded sad. 'I like the lyrics.' And she moved off without another word.

Michael had a feeling that she understood. And he was thought-ful as he made his way through the archway towards the bar and Suzi.

'What happened?' Suzi handed him his pint. 'I thought you'd lost it back there.'

'I was thinking of incorporating it into the act.' Michael took a large gulp of Best. The more he thought about it, the more it made sense. 'Lee Evans type of humour, you know. Slapstick music.'

Suzi seemed doubtful. 'It makes you look –'

'Stupid?'

'Unprofessional.' Suzi swung her bag on to her shoulder and led the way back to the small circular table in the corner. There was an orange wall light burning just above her and it lent her skin a kind of fiery glow. She sat down on the seat cushion of the bench. 'But it's up to you,' she said. 'It's your life.'

Michael felt as if the table was a million miles in diameter. How had they travelled so far apart? And what the bloody hell did she mean by that remark?

The night before the dress rehearsal of *Romeo and Juliet*, Liam was at home in his garret flat when he received a phone call from Amanda Lake. He had, he realised, very mixed feelings about her. When he was with Amanda, he always felt something was expected of him – that he should be more confident, more worldly wise, richer or better looking. That he should, perhaps, take her in his arms and make passionate love to her.

One of the reasons that he hadn't done this was the mixed signals he was getting. He looked at the tuna tagliatelle for one that he was about to shove in the microwave. It contained fresh basil and parmesan apparently, but did not fill him with desire.

At times, Amanda almost threw herself at him, showering him with compliments, every word an innuendo, every look a flirtatious one. But at other times she was an indifferent ice maiden. And another reason, the bigger reason he knew, was Estelle.

He looked gloomily around the narrow galley kitchen. Estelle who had made every meal time an occasion – even a take-away from the chippie down the road had been loaded with salt, vinegar and fun, with Estelle. Estelle, who had kept the flat clean(ish) and tidy(ish) and been there for him every night to smooth out the wrinkles of his day. God, how he missed the woman.

With some difficulty, he dragged himself back to the conversation with Amanda. What was it with her? She hadn't exactly been making a nuisance of herself. But she kept appearing – driving past the school gates in her red convertible just as he was leaving, sounding the horn, calling, 'Darling, how are you? Call me!' Before tearing off again. It wasn't doing a lot for his street cred with the kids.

He had phoned her a couple of times – more through guilt than a desire to see her, and listened to her ansafone before hanging up. But he was always slightly relieved that she wasn't there. Perhaps, he decided, it was simply that he knew he wasn't in her league – and nor did he want to be. She did, after all, compromise his Socialist principles.

'Darling,' she purred over the telephone line. 'I haven't seen you for yonks.'

Liam winced. Grabbing a fork, he stabbed the polythene cover of the tuna tagliatelle. A cream and orange mushy mountain – piled on one side of the tray only – stared back at him. Liam almost chucked it straight in the bin. 'I've been busy,' he said, 'You know, the play and everything.'

'The play!' Amanda made it sound like arts production of the year. 'Heavens! I'd almost forgotten.'

Liam wished he could forget. He also wished he hadn't just reminded Amanda. He put his gourmet meal in the microwave and pressed the right buttons.

Sure enough, 'You will get me tickets? Two tickets?'

'Well . . .'

'Please? You did promise me, darling!'

Liam wasn't sure that he had, but he also couldn't see how to get out of it. 'It'll bore you to death,' he said. 'I'm sure you've got lots more interesting things to do.' Like cocktails with Fenella whatshername or something? He watched the thing that was gradually resembling tuna and custard rotating in the machine, more unappetising with every spin.

'Nonsense.' Amanda became brisk. 'And you can give me the tickets the day after tomorrow.'

'The day after tomorrow?' What now? Had he forgotten something that he shouldn't have? Was his life slipping out of his control? Had it in fact ever been in his control in the first place?

'We're going to have dinner together,' Amanda told him in a voice that would accept no argument. 'I'll pick you up at eight.'

Liam knew he was being weak and pathetic, but he couldn't think of an excuse, let alone how he was going to pay for the sort of swanky place she'd want to go to. She probably had no idea of a teacher's salary. The microwave let out a smug *pinggg*.

'Good,' Amanda said. 'And I'm so looking forward to the play on Saturday. In fact, I can't wait.'

Liam could, though. He opened the microwave door and surveyed this evening's gastronomical delight. He could wait for ever if necessary.

Chapter 20

Estelle wasn't sure how Suzi had got her here in the foyer of the Arts Centre. But here she was, clutching a concert programme, her bag and the ticket Suzi had given her. She wasn't even that much of a fan of the Blues Sisters. But when she'd tried to get out of it, Suzi had become quite narky.

'It's the least you can do, Estelle.' She had stood, legs planted slightly apart, her small frame upright (and uptight, Estelle thought) hands on hips, fierce eyes blazing.

Estelle knew perfectly well what had rattled *her* cage. 'He asked you first,' she pointed out. 'And you said, no.' What had got into Suzi? If she fancied Josh Willis, why didn't she just go for it? Obviously it wasn't that easy, and she'd have some sorting out to do, but if she didn't think she had any future with Michael, then why the heck had she let him move in? Estelle was fond of the guy, but he and Suzi were hardly a match made in heaven.

And if – and it seemed a big if right now – Suzi *didn't* fancy Josh Willis . . . Estelle adjusted the shoulder strap of the long indigo dress she was wearing with soft leather sandals and a blue and white wrap-over coat. If she didn't fancy him, then why had she minded Estelle accepting his invitation? It was only to celebrate the roadshow day after all. He wasn't exactly Estelle's type. But then again, who was, apart from Liam? And she thought Suzi was confused?

'I'm not interested,' Suzi had snapped.

'Even if I told you he talked about you all evening?'

'Even if he did a handstand on the table.' But Suzi's expression softened. 'So what did he have to say?'

That she was impossible and infuriating and a hopeless business woman. That he had no idea what she wanted and suspected that she had no idea either. What he hadn't said and what was obvious, was that he fancied her like crazy. 'I thought you weren't interested,' Estelle had teased.

At that point, Suzi thrust the orange concert ticket towards her. 'I bought this weeks ago,' she said. 'Just go – will you?'

Now, Estelle showed her ticket to the usher and followed him to Row C. She located her seat and noted that the place next to it was empty. She supposed it would be occupied by Michael, which was OK, though Estelle didn't know why Suzi had to be so secretive about it – unless she was seeing Josh Willis on the sly and wanted to keep Michael preoccupied elsewhere. That didn't sound like Suzi, though – she was not the conniving type.

When the lights went down and the band came on stage, there was still no sign of him. Estelle sighed. What had she let herself in for? Was she so desperate to get out of the flat?

Then various occupants of the row began rustling sweet packets and moving coats, getting to their feet to allow a latecomer to make his way through.

'Sorry, sorry,' he muttered as he eased past. Until, 'Bloody hell. What are you doing here?'

Estelle cursed Suzi. She should have known. Maybe Suzi was the conniving type after all. 'The same, I would imagine,' she said tersely to Liam as people around them started ssh–ing and sighing, 'as you.'

★   ★   ★

All through the set, Liam was conscious of Estelle's body next to him, in a way he was sure he'd never been conscious of it when they were together. She was wearing one of his favourite dresses, her auburn hair a thick loose mist around her shoulders and she smelt faintly of musk. Just enough, Liam thought. Just enough.

Her bare arm lay flat on the arm-rest between them, the palm slightly raised, as if threatening a clenched fist in the future. He smiled. Estelle's armour. The trouble was, she had so much of it, he didn't know where the accessible bits began. Her arm could be accessible, he wasn't sure. He burned to touch it, hardly heard the music from the band on stage, focused as he was on the warmth that seemed to radiate from her. Estelle . . .

At the interval, the house lights went up and Liam continued to stare, hypnotised, at the fine golden haze of hair on those pale arms, as she clapped her palms together. He felt like he was falling in love with her all over again.

She turned towards him, frowning at his scrutiny. 'What's Suzi playing at? And why are you staring at me like that?'

'Sorry.' He didn't want her to think he'd lost it completely. But by now, Liam, who had called Suzi every unflattering name he could think of in the past hour, as he rushed from the dress rehearsal of *Romeo and Juliet* – where everything that could go wrong, had – was feeling more cheerful. It did him good, he realised, just to be near this woman. Whyever had he let her go?

And it was a relief to be away from *Romeo and Juliet*. It had been a nightmare. Bradley and Jade, who had been getting on so well, had had an almighty slanging match just before the death scene, whereupon the sleeping Juliet told her Romeo (who was just about to kill himself for the love of her) to, 'fuck off, why don't you, dick-brain?' albeit under her breath. A phrase that Liam couldn't help suspecting had originated from her maternal parent. Romeo proceeded to drink the poison, sinking to his knees with the words, 'I always knew you was a slag.' At this, Jade rose prematurely, but instead of stabbing herself to death with a dagger, stepped over her Romeo (treading on his wrist, in the process) and stormed off the stage in a huff. Romeo then indulged in a few unconvincing death throes, the words, 'blatantly a well-rotten bitch,' hot on his lips.

Not quite, reflected Liam, the effect he'd been looking for. Something seemed to happen to year 7s when it came to the summer term, but metamorphosis was far too pleasant a concept. Almost overnight, they looked like teenagers, talked like teenagers, behaved like teenagers, as if the most important thing in their young lives was to leave childhood way behind them.

Sad really, Liam thought. Though he knew they were just kids underneath it all. Just kids pulling on some armour like most adults did every day of their lives. Armour . . .

He forced his gaze away from Estelle and back to the stage of the Arts Centre. Meanwhile, Crystal had lost the music tapes twice – though Liam suspected this to be her revenge for not being picked to play Juliet – Marcus forgot almost all of his lines, and during the final dance sequence, Jade fell off the stage. Her 'who the fuck did that?' was almost drowned by the strains of 'what now, my love?'. But not quite.

As the applause for the Blues Sisters' first set died down, Liam tried to remember if a) he'd brought his wallet with him and b) if it contained any money.

'It'll be all right on the night.' Suzi had witnessed the last half-hour of the dress rehearsal, but seemed to be a lot less sympathetic to her brother's problems than usual. 'Now for God's sake hurry up or you'll be late,' she added.

All very well for her, Liam had thought, as he threw on a clean, un-ironed shirt and headed for the Arts Centre. She didn't have Tony Andrews breathing down her neck. Not to mention, of course, the high embarrassment factor of Amanda's promised presence at the performance proper. Liam had shuddered, groped in his pocket for Suzi's ticket – still there – thought with trepidation of this dinner with Amanda tomorrow night. Could he cry off? Think of a believable excuse, like he was dying or something?

The wallet was in his back pocket and Liam was pretty sure it contained a tenner.

'Let's get a drink.' He grabbed Estelle's arm and propelled her along the row. 'We can talk to each other at least.'

'I don't know what's got into Suzi,' Estelle continued to complain, pausing to apologise to a woman in a scarlet jacket and the bald-headed guy beside her. 'Why does she have to interfere?' She went with Liam, but pulled her arm away as she did so.

'Because she loves us?' Liam suggested. Estelle was narky all right. She did not want to be here and she did not want to be with him. But what could he do about it?

They walked through the open glass-panelled door and into the bar. 'White wine?' he asked.

She nodded, gazed into his face for a moment, seemed about to say something, and then looked down at her feet. 'People should be left to sort out their lives for themselves,' she said at last.

'If they can.' Liam turned around to order the drinks. There were about thirty people waiting and only two white-shirted barmen doing the honours. He sighed. The question was – could he and Estelle?

Back home in bed, Michael tried to make love to her as Suzi had known he would. It was, she realised, watching the shadow of the candlestick on her dressing-table thrown into relief by the bedside lamp, something to do with the performance. With Michael's performance at the pub tonight, something to do with the high it gave him, the sensation of power. Perhaps, she thought, it gave him the courage he required.

Did it need courage? Suzi felt Michael's hands, gentle on her back. The two of them were naked, lying like spoons in the double bed, Suzi facing away from him, towards the window, as she usually did. What, she wondered, would Freud have made of that?

Michael began with a sweep of his fingers over her shoulders, thumbs soft in the crevice beneath her shoulder blades, and moved down to her waist, his hands a little too unsure, the pressure too light on her skin. Suzi closed her eyes. How she longed for a firm caress. Though maybe – who knew? – a firm caress could become a dangerous one; one that you couldn't ignore.

His hand reached for her breast. Suzi tried to relax into him, to go with the moment. This attempt at togetherness had become a rarity; each night he left her alone with her thoughts had become a relief. Not, she reflected, how it was meant to be.

And yet . . . His fingers were on her nipples now, stroking, urging her into compliance, into desire. Something stirred within her. Suzi sighed and reached a hand back towards his thigh. A signal. Please, she thought. Please let it work out between them, let her and Michael be content with whatever they had. She didn't want danger, didn't want it as part of her life. She was scared.

She had never, after all, allowed a man so far into her world, into her home, the way she had allowed Michael. Though as a matter of fact – her fingers caressed the length of his thigh, aware of the roughness of the male skin, the coarseness of the hair – it had been Michael who had made it happen, Michael who had given in his notice, arrived on the doorstep of the cottage, needy, like one of the animals she had rescued. Michael, then, who had forced the relationship to change. But Michael would not, she reminded herself, have reckoned on it changing into this.

Suzi nestled her body closer into his, her buttocks cupped deep into his groin. Her hand rested on the sharpness of his hip. Michael would never have reckoned on Suzi's reluctance, her resistance, she was sure. She might welcome the needy into the riverbank cottage, but she could no more admit her own need, than fly.

Michael kissed her shoulder, his lips moving in a predictable pathway down her spine. Suzi groaned. This was enough. Forget Josh Willis – how could she ever be sure of a man like him? She was not, she decided, cut out for love – not at any rate the kind of love that made sane men and women give up everything up to and including their independence, not the Romeo and Juliet kind of love that she had seen in Liam and Estelle. After all, once you'd had it – look at how hard it obviously was to manage without it.

No, she didn't think she was capable of that sort of love, and she certainly didn't want it. And she wasn't in love with Josh Willis – like she kept telling herself, she hardly knew the man.

So Suzi turned to Michael and looked into his eyes. 'Now,' she said.

The river was dark beneath them, a fat snake weaving and rippling through the reeds and under the bridge.

'Do you still think about it?' asked Liam.

Such was their understanding – *had* been their understanding – Estelle corrected herself, that she didn't need to ask him what he meant.

'I still think about her,' she said.

'And?'

Estelle sighed, leaned more heavily on the blue bridge that was evening-damp under her palms. 'I still think about the way she did it,' she admitted. 'The moment she did it.' Because Liam was Liam and knew it all – everything, at least, there was to know about Estelle. And because she imagined if she said it starkly and

out loud, here, where it had happened, then it might – one day –
have the grace to go away.

'And still blaming yourself?' he persevered, his body dark and
stranger-like in the night-time.

What was it to him, Estelle wondered. He had said and done
everything he could over the years, to rationalise why a five-year-
old girl could not be held responsible for the death of her own
mother. Especially when that mother was a drinker – OK, a lush,
Estelle corrected herself again, for what was the point of pretending? Whatever demons had haunted her mother, made her what
she was, made her so unhappy that a bottle was the only escape, she,
Estelle, would never know about them now. She had not been old
enough to offer any comfort, let alone be confided in.

Until one evening when that mother had leaned too far over
the bridge. Or launched herself into the water, Estelle wasn't even
sure. But she did know that even at five years old, she had felt the
misgivings of a certain understanding.

And Liam was right, what could she have done? Too late to
pull her back. Her mother's skull smashed on impact on the rocks
that lay just below the surface of the fast moving river, rocks that
were just visible when the water was low – smooth and slimy
with lichen.

'There's always something that could have been different,'
Estelle told him, as she had told herself many times. She tried
to look into the depths of the river that had taken her mother's
blood, but the water remained untouched and innocent – dark
and chocolate-smooth.

'Like *what if*?' he almost jeered.

Estelle turned. She could just make out the twist of his mouth
in the darkness.

He went on. 'What if you'd said you wanted to go home five
minutes earlier, what if you'd insisted on holding her hand?'

'Yes.' Estelle moved a step away. Why should he understand? He had not had that close contact with death, had no idea of how it felt to watch your own mother die, how it was to stand there, helpless, screaming, how you could torment yourself in the years that followed.

Liam grabbed her by the shoulders, twisted her round to face him. Taken aback, Estelle stared into the shadows of his face, but it was too dark to make out the expression in his eyes. 'What if I'd been the one with her?' he demanded.

'Huh?' Had Liam finally lost his sanity, she wondered.

'What if I had gone out with your mother for a walk. What if I was five years old and I'd been with her and the same thing had happened?'

Estelle tried to pull away. 'Don't be stupid. You didn't even know her.'

But he held fast. 'It's not me that's stupid, it's your bloody what if game that's stupid. So come on, what if I'd been the one?'

Estelle gave up, slumped against him. It was simpler not to fight him, too easy to rest against the warm body that still, damn it, felt like home. 'You'd have done the same as me,' she muttered into his jacket.

'Yeah.' He forced her away from him again, denying her need. 'Because there was no other choice for a five-year-old. Got it?'

'Maybe.' She didn't want him to make her face it, even think about it. She didn't want to be here. She wanted to lay her head on his shoulder and pretend nothing had changed.

'And what would you think of me?' he persevered. 'If I'd been the one? If I'd been with her when she died?'

Why wouldn't he be quiet, just be quiet and let her rest? It had been such a strange evening, seeing him there at the Arts Centre, realising that this was a ploy of Suzi's. Why? To get them together? Estelle had always imagined Suzi half-jealous of what they had. Herself she had seen as an interloper, pushed out of a brother and sister bond that had often seemed too close to admit another. She had even imagined Suzi to be one of the problems that held herself and Liam apart. If only Suzi could have found a special someone . . . she had often thought.

And yet now it appeared that Suzi wanted them to be back together, Suzi had gone to great lengths to try and sort it, Suzi – as Liam had said earlier – simply loved them both and wanted them to be happy.

And now this. Enough surely to cope with the close proximity of Liam, without Liam suggesting a late-night stroll after the concert, without Liam bringing her to the blue bridge, laying all the mother guilt trip on her again. She rubbed her eyes. Damn Liam for bringing it all back.

'Estelle?' He spoke quietly, his voice soft and low in the night air. Around them were the usual night-time noises, the occasional hoot of an owl, the ripple of some life form in the river below, the rush and drag of the tide, just audible in the distance. Noises that Suzi, in her riverbank cottage just down the tow path, would be all too familiar with.

'I wouldn't think anything bad of you,' Estelle admitted.

'You wouldn't think it was my fault?'

'No.'

'That I should have stopped your mother from falling?'

'No.'

'You wouldn't think that I could have pulled her back at the last moment?'

'No.'

'Shoved myself in her way as she fell?'

'No.'

'Thrown myself into the water so that I got there before her?'

'No.' This was getting silly now. How on earth could anyone possibly have –

'Somehow got my body between her and the rocks?'

'No!'

'Stopped her from killing herself?'

'No!'

She began to shake then, not a trembling but a jerking movement that racked her whole body. And she cried. Huge tears that seemed unlike any she had shed for her mother before. And Liam held her. Not like he had held her in the past, but as if he were holding her very soul, every part of her touching him, every inch of him moulded to her, to her needs, to the fear that had never been expressed before. The tears seemed to rip their way out of her, clung to her cheeks, finally were absorbed by him in some sort of absolution.

'Let it go, love,' Liam said. 'Let it go.'

It was half an hour later before they made their way back down the pathway, through the gate and past the church, the graves pale and eerie in the moonlight. Half an hour, in which time Estelle knew she had moved on. Just a step, but an important one. She'd still grieve for her mother, grieve for what might have been; she'd still hold her memories, for they were hers alone. But the guilt had been somehow swept away in the current that led down to the sea. The guilt had gone – perhaps for good.

'Are you going to invite me up to see your new flat?' Liam teased, as they approached Secrets In The Attic.

'Maybe.' There was a kind of shyness between them now, as if they'd reached a point of no return. Estelle knew they'd have to sit and thrash it all out – why they had split up, what it would take for them to get back together. But she also knew it would be done, that she and Liam would not – not yet at least – be prised apart.

They got to the shop and at last, at last, he pulled her towards him into a kiss. She tasted the warmth of his lips, the sweetness of his tongue, began to close her eyes. And snapped them open again.

'Christ Almighty!' She pulled away.

'What?' He half-turned to follow her gaze.

There was broken glass on the pavement. The shop window had been smashed – a half-brick sat amongst the debris of Clarice Cliff and Estelle's semi-precious jewellery. It didn't look as if anything had been taken. But nevertheless, it was destruction. Destruction, vandalism, invasion of the worst kind.

'Kids,' Liam said, guiding her towards the door. 'We'll phone the police.'

'Not kids,' Estelle shouted. Suddenly it was all too much. Tonight, the tears, the purging, and now this. She felt stripped naked. She no longer had a sense of direction, a way to go.

She took a deep, shuddering breath. And then she screamed.

Chapter 21

'Where is he?' Liam growled, pulling the heavy brocade curtain aside and scanning the rows of wooden chairs that had been laid out on the dark wooden flooring of the hall. People were already arriving for the performance, being handed day-glo yellow programmes from selected prefects in school uniform, who had been practising saying, 'Good evening, Sir, Good evening, Madam,' all week.

And Marcus was nowhere to be seen. Liam tore a hand through his hair, paced up and down the small area of stage unoccupied by either kids or props. Tybalt was the most important player next to Romeo and Juliet. What would they do without Tybalt? Who would fight Romeo? (Though Liam wouldn't mind, after what Bradley had put him through at that dress rehearsal the other night, having a go himself.)

He frowned as he caught sight of his two star performers on the other side of the stage. What were Jade and Bradley doing whispering in the wings? Thankfully they no longer seemed to be at loggerheads with one another. But shouldn't they be in make-up? And there was such a thing as being too friendly. 'Psst!' He made angry gestures towards them, mouthed, 'Make-up.'

'Marcus and Bradley had a fight last night.' This was from Crystal, who had materialised beside him. She was wearing black leggings and a baggy grey T-shirt that did her matchstick figure no favours whatever and her hair was tied up in a pony tail that jumped to attention when she moved. She smirked. 'About Jade.'

Liam groaned. Just what he needed. 'Was he all right? Did he say anything?' Was he still on for tonight, he meant.

Crystal shrugged. 'Only that he wouldn't be seen dead in the play.'

'Oh, great.' For a moment Liam forgot his role of nurturer of young minds. 'Bloody great.'

'But he probably didn't mean it, Sir.' Crystal skipped off happily.

When did little girls stop being little girls and become so bitchy, Liam found himself wondering for the millionth time since he'd begun teaching. What happened to them between the ages of eleven and fourteen that made the most innocent, the most manipulative and the sweetest, the most spiteful?

But more important at this moment, who the hell could he get to play the part of Tybalt – and at such short notice? Liam realised dismally that there was no one. The only person who might know the lines was Crystal since as prompter she probably knew everyone's lines by now, but that would be stretching it. Still, what choice did he have? Girls played principal boys in pantomime, men had played women back in Shakespeare's day.

'Crystal!' He strode past the dinner table and chairs already positioned on stage, towards Bradley and Jade. Now, where did she go?

Bradley took a step backwards and put a hand defensively up to his face, as if he thought Liam was about to clock him one. And was he tempted . . .

'So you and Marcus have buggered things up for everyone, is that it?' Liam demanded.

'Sorry, Sir.' To give him his due, Bradley did look more than a bit ashamed of himself, unable to look Liam in the eye. He scuffed his dirty trainers across the floor of the platform, building up an impressive pile of dust.

'What are we going to do?' Jade's voice was high and shrill. Liam glanced at her. She was wearing the silver-grey evening dress earmarked for her first scene and she looked terrified.

'Get along to make-up, Jade,' he told her, recognising the signs of stage fright. 'Everything'll be fine.'

'I don't think I can.'

'Of course you can.' Liam didn't mean to snap, but he really didn't need this.

'I'm scared.'

Bradley put a comforting arm around his Juliet and looked up for the first time.

Her hero, eh, Liam found himself thinking, as he registered Bradley's face, and more particularly the picturesque black eye he was sporting. 'Jesus!' he said. Not so much ashamed – scared of being seen, more like. He looked like a street-fighter. He looked terrible.

'I'll just wear extra make-up, Sir.' Bradley executed his hair-flick, but the element of cool was totally destroyed by the plum-coloured bruise. 'No one'll notice.'

'I can't go on,' Jade wailed.

Liam lost it. 'It's only a fucking school production.' At the expression on both their faces, he forced himself to breathe slowly and deeply. He was an adult. He was in charge here. He was a sane and rational man. What did it matter if Tybalt hadn't turned up, Romeo had a black eye even before the fight scene and Juliet had completely lost her bottle? He'd faced worse problems in school productions – though he couldn't recall any right now.

'Make-up,' he said to Bradley. 'Jade – tell Crystal she can play your part, God knows she's asked me to let her have a go often enough.' And then he remembered he'd been about to ask Crystal to play Tybalt . . . He scanned the stage desperately, as if a stray Tybalt might emerge from the wings and save the day.

Jade hesitated. He could see her struggling. Not only would Crystal be wearing her costume and saying her lines, but as Juliet, she would also – for an hour and a half – have possession of Jade's Romeo.

'You've got three minutes in which to decide,' he informed her, crossing his fingers behind his back. 'I don't have the time to sort out weeping and wailing prima donnas.' And if she felt hard done by, tough luck, Liam decided. He was damned if he was going to let her wallow in her own self-pity and he'd had enough of women's tears and histrionics over the past few days to last him a lifetime. They might be from Venus and cook and iron like angels, but by God, where the heck did all these emotions come from?

He peered out into the hall again – the rows were filling up. He could already see Suzi, Michael and . . . Estelle. He held on more tightly to the tatty red curtain, tried to reach her by will power alone, but she was not looking his way, her head was turned towards Suzi, she was listening to whatever Suzi was saying. 'Shut up, Suzi,' Liam whispered.

At last he retreated with a muffled sneeze from the stuffiness of the curtain, forced himself to check the set, the music, the tiny cubby-holes being used as make-up areas by the two student teachers who had volunteered their services. They were lucky, of course, to have so much space, to have a platform that made such an excellent stage, to be in a school where drama was not allowed to be pushed off the curriculum by literacy and numeracy gone mad.

But no Crystal. Liam went to the back of the stage to look for her.

But despite the occasion, despite his mood, the thought of Estelle would not go away. It had seemed important, he reflected, to get through to Estelle, after the Blues Sisters concert. Suzi had given him the opportunity, and he was determined not to waste it, not to allow Estelle to drift back into his past, which was where she seemed to want to be.

At the end of the concert, he'd been looking for an excuse not to go home, a chance to spend more time with her, to talk, to walk. Then they'd got to the blue bridge and her mood had changed. Liam sighed. He had always felt that he'd failed her in some way – at least as far as her mother's death was concerned. And so he'd thought, *this time* . . . I want to make her see.

Liam eventually found Crystal back on stage practising high kicks that were threatening to send the dinner service crashing to the floor, and mouthing Juliet's lines to the back of the closed curtain, instead of organising the prompt chair and music tape. 'Crystal . . .' He frowned. 'I might need you to perform.'

'As Juliet?' Her eyes grew wide.

'Or Tybalt.'

And before she could make a run for it, he placed one hand firmly on her bony shoulder. 'Come with me,' he said.

But in the first make-up cubby-hole, Jade was sitting calmly on a wooden chair, a towel around her shoulders protecting the silver-grey dress. Julie Nelson, the student teacher, was applying scarlet lip-liner. Jade looked at least sixteen.

'Through there.' Liam ushered Crystal out of earshot. 'Well?' he asked Jade.

'I've taken one of Mum's pills,' she said, holding up her chin in defiance. 'Wasn't going to let that little muppet get her paws on Brad.'

'I'm relieved to hear it.' For a moment Liam pondered on the possible nature of the pills in question, but Lorraine Johnson wouldn't have let her daughter have them if they were dangerous, surely?

He hurried off. In the other cubby-hole, Bradley was beginning to look almost dashing, and there was no sign of his bruise.

'Concealer,' said the other student teacher, Carrie Jones. 'It's green and flesh. Evens out the imperfections.'

'Excellent.' Liam rubbed his hands together, although Crystal, standing behind Bradley, was looking somewhat subdued. Tybalt clearly didn't have quite the pull of Juliet.

'Sorry I'm late, Sir.' With admirable timing, an out of breath Marcus appeared, looking slightly flushed. 'We had to take the cat to the vet.'

Better and better. 'No problem.' By now Liam was feeling positively expansive. 'Get changed, get made up, quick as you can. Back to your music and prompt chair, Crystal. Do your best, everybody.' At last, everything seemed to be falling into place.

He strode back to the wings. Mind, he had thought everything was falling into place with Estelle that night by the blue bridge. Marvellously well. And it was, surely it was, until they'd got back to Secrets In The Attic, and she'd seen the smashed window of the shop.

From his position, Liam could see that Crystal was now sitting demurely in her chair, open copy of the adapted play on her lap, tape recorder beside her. He could hear the audience quite clearly now, the rustle of programmes and coats being removed, the scraping of chairs on the parquet floor, whispered conversations about whose son was what and whose daughter was doing the other.

Liam tried to relax. Estelle had seemed to go to pieces – he'd never seen her so upset, almost as if she'd gone into shock. He had taken her inside, a helpful neighbour opposite had provided brandy, he had phoned the police, contacted her twenty-four-hour insurance company, and in between he'd held her, looked after her, been there for her. What more could he have done? What more could anyone have done? Liam looked down. His knuckles were white and clenched, but whether this was pre-performance nerves or the memory he was re-enacting, he had no idea. Both, maybe.

It was the early hours before Estelle had at last fallen into an exhausted, white-faced sleep. And in the morning . . . he didn't want to think about what had happened the following morning. All that mattered was that Estelle had told him to go.

'Thank you,' she had said, as if he were some stranger. 'But I can manage now. I can manage perfectly well on my own.' God, she might as well have cut him up and had him lightly poached for breakfast.

It was enough to drive a man to drink, Liam thought, wishing he had a hip flask concealed about his person. Who could blame a man for choosing celibacy as a simpler way of life?

With a sigh, he went to check the progress of Marcus and his make-up, began to usher his actors on to the stage. 'Remember,' he said to Bradley and Jade, 'that you're in love.'

'No probs, Sir,' Bradley whispered back, squeezing Jade's bum.

'But not at first,' Liam reminded him.

He got them into position.

And at last they were ready to begin. Liam glanced at his watch – only seven minutes late – whispered, 'Go for it,' the curtain was pulled aside in a cloud of dust that glimmered in the glare of the lights, and the feast scene (now a dinner party with a murder mystery theme) began.

Liam realised he'd been holding his breath and exhaled loudly. Though he could no longer see them, they were all there in the blackness of the audience – Amanda and whoever she'd brought with her, Estelle, Suzi, Michael, not to mention all the parents, staff and even a representative from the local rag. At the end of the evening, Liam thought, he might just sneak quietly away.

But he didn't get the chance, because he was pulled on stage by Jade and Bradley during the final curtain call, given a round of applause and a vote of thanks by Tony Andrews, who smarmed and smirked his way through enough publicity material to keep the journalist happy, whilst managing to give the impression that he himself as headteacher had held the production together, just as he held the entire school together.

Afterwards, Estelle, Suzi and Michael gathered backstage to congratulate Liam and help clear up. Carrie Jones and Julie Nelson had provided a bottle of champagne and someone had rustled up some glasses.

'Well done! What a performance!' Suzi was all smiles. She accepted a glass. 'After that dreadful dress rehearsal, I couldn't believe it went like clockwork.'

Liam laughed. Suzi had not described it as dreadful at the time – but he had to admit that it had been bad, even by dress rehearsal standards. 'Apart from Juliet missing her entrance to the final dance scene,' he said.

'Asleep, was she?' Michael enquired.

'No, that was later when she dropped off on the couch during her fake death scene.'

'Too many late nights?' Michael downed his wine in one.

'She'd taken one of her mother's tranquillisers.' Liam had begun to wonder if they would manage to wake her sufficiently for her to kill herself properly in the final scene, or if they would have to rapidly re-structure the entire ending of the play. But fortunately, Jade had come to in time to plunge the dagger realistically into her heart. 'No, she missed her cue because she was snogging with Bradley in the wings.'

Suzi giggled. 'So that's why her make-up was smudged.'

Liam nodded. 'The wonder of teenagers. They either want to murder each other or they're madly in love.' Despite himself, he turned to Estelle. She had waved away the offer of champagne. Her face was even paler than usual and there were huge bags under her eyes. But she still looked beautiful to him.

Her smile seemed forced. 'It went well. You must be thrilled,' she said.

'And how are you?' Liam touched her arm.

'Yes, Estelle, that's exactly what I wanted to ask you.' Amanda and her father appeared from the other side of the curtain so abruptly, that Liam found himself wondering if they'd been eavesdropping, waiting for the ideal moment to enter. And it was quite an entrance. Henry Lake was dressed in a black dinner jacket and bow tie, whilst Amanda was looking stunning in a high-necked long, crimson dress more suited to the West End than Pridehaven Middle School. Her blonde hair was swept to one side, fastened by a silver comb and hanging in a cascade of gold over one bare brown shoulder.

'Liam told me all about it at dinner last night,' she went on, her baby-blue eyes perfectly innocent and unaware, her mouth a pink crescent of sympathy. 'A brick flung through your window? It must have been an awful shock.'

And judging by the expression on Estelle's face, Amanda had just delivered another one, Liam realised. Jesus . . . Had she said that on purpose? Did she have some ulterior motive that she certainly hadn't revealed at dinner last night? He shifted position awkwardly.

He'd almost cancelled that dinner date, but in the event it had been OK, just friendly, a pretty ordinary Italian restaurant, no strings and Amanda had paid her share, so he needn't have worried. The funny thing was that he'd found himself talking about Estelle. Because, yes, Amanda had this way of inviting confidences and afterwards you wondered how the hell she'd got so much out of you. But Liam had never dreamed she'd bring it up now. And to Estelle.

'It was,' Estelle said shortly.

'How are you feeling?' Amanda persisted.

'Fine.'

Dear God. Liam would remember the look Estelle shot him, and the way it made him feel, probably for the rest of his days.

In the pub afterwards, Suzi turned on him. 'What on earth was Amanda Lake doing at the performance?'

Liam shrugged. 'She pestered me for a ticket.' He tore his hand through dark curls that were looking even more crazy than usual, Suzi observed. In fact he looked like a mad professor in his corduroy jacket with the patched sleeves and the Rupert Bear scarf tied loosely around his neck. She softened. Liam had obviously been through the mangle the last few days. However . . .

'And what was that about dinner?'

He shrugged. 'It was only dinner, Suze.'

Suzi sighed. 'You realise you've probably blown it with Estelle,' she told him. And after all her hard work.

'There was nothing to blow.'

'Explain.' She knew she was cornering him, but she was concerned. Both Liam and Estelle looked wrecked. And Suzi couldn't accept that it wasn't true – that what they both needed was not simply one another.

'Suzi, I know you were only trying to help . . .'

'The concert?' And she'd had such high hopes.

Liam nodded. 'But I did everything I could that night – and more. She freaked, Suze, when she saw that window smashed. I don't know what else I could have done.' Hand through hair once more.

Suzi frowned, looked round the Bear and Bottle, which was quiet tonight. Perhaps she should have confided in Liam before. 'It's not the first thing that's happened . . .' And as Michael returned with the drinks, she proceeded to tell them both the whole story – about the puncture, the 'For Sale' sign on Estelle's car, the visits from Stan and Terry, and finally the hate mail.

'Bloody hell,' said Michael. His long legs were stretched out in front of him, as though – now that he played here – this had become his territory. Suzi hoped that this was the case. She wanted Michael to feel good about something.

Liam rose to his feet. He looked furious. 'Why didn't you call the police?'

'And say what? We don't have a shred of evidence that all this is anything to do with The Bargain Basement. It could be just kids mucking around, a bit of vandalism, nothing to worry about. That's what everyone thinks.'

'Until you piece it all together.' Michael said what they were probably all thinking.

'So if you can't prove anything –' Liam began.

'And if you don't want to go to the police . . .' Michael added.

Suzi saw the look that passed between the two men. 'We should give up Secrets?' she demanded. 'Let them win without even putting up a fight?' She might have expected such an attitude from Michael, who was so laid back she sometimes wondered if he'd have the energy to save his own soul from the devil. But not from Liam – Liam who would fight for any cause he believed in.

'I'm thinking of your safety,' Liam urged, as if reading her mind. 'Yours and Estelle's.'

'Try telling Estelle that.' Suzi glared at him – her brother, champion of the underdog. Where was that hero when you needed him?

Liam sighed. 'I don't think I'll be telling Estelle anything in the near future.'

'So you're just going to give up on her?' Suzi persisted. God, she was sick of self-pity, fed up with trying to make the two of them see sense. They'd just seen *Romeo and Juliet* for heaven's sake, and Suzi had seen the expression on Estelle's face when she looked at Liam. Nothing had changed. Nothing should have changed. What was wrong with the two of them? What did she have to do?

'You'll be seeing her at the American tournament,' Michael said into his beer, 'And at the dance.'

The other two glanced at him.

'Bloody hell,' said Liam, probably thinking of Estelle and Amanda. 'But before that, I've got the under-15s tournament and Nick bloody Rossi to contend with.'

'Rather you than me,' said Suzi. 'And now, if you'll excuse me, I need the ladies room.'

Suzi walked into the public bar, and was already half-way through the door of the ladies, when she heard a familiar laugh. More of a growl really. No. She jumped, let go of the door handle, took a step back, peered round the pillar and spotted Josh's big figure. Unmistakable. He was sitting at a table with two men. There was a basket of dried flowers on the window-ledge above. All three had pints of beer on the table in front of them.

'Josh,' she whispered, feeling herself almost pulled towards him, wanting to go over, to say hi, to apologise maybe for being such a moron after the roadshow. He might, after all, merely have mentioned their problems to Terry in passing. He would have no idea, she was sure, of what was going on. And she could hardly blame him for not phoning her when she had been such a miserable cow.

Excuses, excuses. She never stopped making excuses for the guy. Suzi sighed. What was the matter with her? Why did she want to talk to him, even be near him so much? How had she got so pathetic, without her even noticing?

She wavered, frowned at the two men sitting with their backs to her, one fair, one dark. Retreated quick as a ferret when she recognised who they were.

Josh Willis drinking in the pub with the enemy, with Stan and Terry, friendly as you like. She let this sink in. How much evidence did she need? Josh Willis who had seemed to be on their side. Josh Willis who she had hoped might become . . . what? A friend? More than a friend? No way.

She should, she realised, as she slipped into the loo, have trusted her first instincts about the man. And her second ones. And now? She would, for sure, have nothing more to do with him. She wouldn't give him a sandwich if he were starving. And she sure as hell wouldn't be giving him her last Rolo.

Josh Willis was involved in the plan to get them out of Secrets In The Attic. He had to be.

And what had she done?

Yep. She had helped him every step of the way . . .

Chapter 22

Estelle was aware that something was going down in the shop next door. She wasn't sure – yet – what it was, but Stan and Terry were very much in evidence – tight-lipped, closet-faced, striding outside, marching back in again. She could hear the drag of heavy furniture being moved around the floor, the occasional curse, and the slam of the shop door.

When she went outside to her car, she was confronted by both of them. Stan shot her a look of such weaselly venom that she recoiled, shocked, and hurried back inside. Terry didn't even look at her – which was unusual in itself.

Pretending she was unperturbed and deciding to ignore the early morning July shower, Estelle flung open the door of Secrets In The Attic so that the wind-chimes sang and the dream-catchers quivered. She felt compelled to make a statement. Bugger them all. COME IN AND LOOK AROUND OUR ATTIC, the sign on the door read.

Come on then, she thought, let's be having you. Perhaps if Stan and Terry witnessed a flow of customers to the shop, they might give up their little campaign.

She decided to re-arrange the jewellery while she was waiting.

If she had her way, she would get rid of all the furniture (and not replace it) and fill the shop with jewellery instead – antique, modern, from local designers, silversmiths and craftspeople. There was so much talent in the area. Besides, she was fed up with dusty old furniture.

She glared at an old wash-stand that had not made it to Germany and was equally unwanted here in Pridehaven. When, she wondered, would Josh Willis be heading off again? Perhaps he'd take a job lot – including the wash-stand? – if she could get Suzi to agree. Only, Suzi tended to have a collapse of reason when that man was around.

When Lorraine Johnson appeared on the street outside and began flapping around on the pavement, screeching and casting killer looks towards Secrets In The Attic, Estelle moved away from the window and tried to fight the rising panic. Her throat was dry and her hands were shaking. 'Up the workers,' she told herself unconvincingly, realising she sounded like Liam on a bad day. 'Don't let the bastards grind you down.'

She brought her fist down on the counter a little harder than she'd intended. She would not give in. No customers as yet but that was perfectly normal. Stan and Terry and their blousy wives couldn't hurt her – not in broad daylight anyway. And she wouldn't phone Suzi or Liam – especially not Liam – she could handle this alone.

As she arranged her amber collection inside one of the showcases, Estelle cringed mentally. That was what had hurt the most about that night with Liam. A brick had been chucked through the window, yes, but no one had been hurt, and nothing stolen. So why had she succumbed to a panic attack of the screaming habdabs? Why, when everything was going so well, had she collapsed into Liam's arms as if he were a cross between Superman and Flash Gordon? It was pathetic, it was laughable. She was so angry with herself. What had happened to her hard-won independence? What had happened to managing alone? It had all disintegrated into dismal failure, that's what. She had behaved like some Victorian spinster with the vapours.

As for her feelings for Liam – well, for a moment there she had forgotten about Amanda Lake, and it was a good thing the girl herself had put in an appearance after the play, to remind her. They were seeing each other. They were an item. And yet Liam had kissed her. Liam had seemed to still care. Liam . . . For heaven's sake . . .

She closed the case with a satisfying click. Didn't Liam know that Estelle still had her pride at least?

Five minutes later, she peered outside once more, to see that the flapping Lorraine Johnson had been joined by a teenage girl dressed in jeans, a denim jacket and trainers.

Estelle frowned, tried to place her, eventually put mental flowers in her hair and a long grey dress over the jeans and came up with Liam's Juliet.

The body language between the two women (Lorraine's wagging finger, Juliet's hands on hips and everyone can go hang) indicated clearly that they were mother and daughter.

As she watched, Lorraine and Juliet were joined by Stan. 'One day . . .' Lorraine screeched at him. 'One day, you'll expect me to follow you and I won't be around.'

'Promises, promises,' said Stan.

'Don't think I haven't had offers,' Lorraine said darkly. 'Don't think you're the only fish in the sea.'

Stan seemed remarkably unperturbed by this. Probably heard it a hundred times before, Estelle thought.

But wasn't it a small world? She turned her attention to Shelagh Rossi's pearls. She was taking them to auction this afternoon – this was the last time she could finger their voluptuous whiteness, place the globes of cream around her neck and . . . well, pretend.

She recalled the hunted expression on Liam's face as he'd run from the Bear and Bottle all those weeks ago, Lorraine Johnson not far behind. Coincidence? She doubted it very much.

'Real kids versus clones,' Liam muttered to himself as he and Nick Rossi prowled around the clubhouse casting evil looks towards one another and getting their respective groups together for the under-15s tournament. Predictably, Nick's lot were dressed in tennis whites and armed with an expensive array of lightweight rackets and blinding yellow balls. Liam's group were, well, more individual.

He and Nick had finally agreed on playing four boys' singles, two girls' singles, plus one doubles from boys, girls and mixed. It was impossible to tell, Liam thought, who was up for it. Nick's group – from the tennis club itself – looked the part, and of course he'd seen most of them playing here before, but they also looked bored stiff. His lot were dressed in their usual weekend clothes and scuffed trainers, chewing gum, drinking coke, talking or texting on their mobiles. The only encouraging thing was that the clones looked a bit thin on the ground.

Sure enough, when two o'clock came, Nick said that they weren't quite ready, so Liam magnanimously agreed to a fifteen-minute delay, and went to find Erica Raddle. He knew she was around, having heard her megaphone-voice proclaiming the weekend itinerary to someone – probably Deirdre Piston.

He found them both in the common room, a name that so offended Erica's sense of dignity that she insisted on referring to it as the club lounge and was currently campaigning to have the plaque removed from the door.

Liam was unable to stop his body language bordering on

aggressive as soon as he entered the room. Erica, who was also standing, always had this effect on him. She was wearing a white Aertex shirt, as if she'd just walked off a tennis court – though these days she never did – a cream pleated skirt that reached just below the knee and whiter than white old-fashioned tennis shoes.

'Liam.' She acknowledged him, but scowled, baring her teeth in what for her was probably a smile.

Deirdre, wearing her usual nondescript mixture of fawn, beige and tan, was seated at the only table in the room. The rest of the furniture consisted of a couple of settees, several upholstered chairs and (much abhorred by Erica) a table football machine. Deirdre's thin legs were pressed close together, as she made notes in one of her interminable files. What a double act. When, Liam wondered, would CG's enter the new millennium instead of being run like a Women's Institute?

'Could I interrupt for a moment?' he asked with careful politeness. And when Erica seemed to hesitate, 'Only I particularly wanted to know what was decided at that meeting I missed.'

'Meeting?' Erica glanced down at Deirdre as if she were likely to explain what Liam was talking about. 'What meeting?'

'The meeting that coincided with the parents' evening at the school.' Liam tried to remain calm. 'The meeting to discuss the sponsorship of the tournaments and the re-surfacing of certain courts.' Suzi too had been unable to attend, and as for Amanda – well, she had promised to go and then discovered a more pressing engagement (probably supper with Fenella Trenton-Smythe or a missed episode of *Casualty*, Liam thought privately).

'Ah. That meeting.' Erica folded her arms.

'Yes.' Liam wondered if, in a previous lifetime, Erica had been a games mistress at a girls' boarding school. He could see her with a hockey stick chasing girls round the field to punish them for refusing to get in the shower, for not tying their hair back, or just for not being sufficiently sporty perhaps.

'Deirdre can put a copy of the minutes in the post to you.'

'In the post . . .' Deirdre hastily wrote herself a note to this effect.

'Perhaps Deirdre should have already put a copy of the minutes in the post to anyone who was absent from the meeting,' Liam suggested cheerfully. 'I rather thought that was the idea.' He was well aware of how Erica hated to be criticised on matters of form, so couldn't allow himself to miss the opportunity. 'And as I never received one . . .'

'Yes?'

'Perhaps you could you tell me now – what happened about the re-surfacing decision?'

'Re-surfacing decision?'

'Of the courts. *Certain* courts.' He wasn't fooled for a moment by Erica's pretence of ignorance. She knew exactly what she was doing, and if he needed confirmation, he only had to look at the flush staining poor Deirdre's cheeks. Maybe, without Erica's domination, Deirdre might have an opinion of her own, Liam reflected. Maybe, just maybe, she too, wanted CG's to be a tennis club open to all.

'The benefactor increased the gift,' Erica said shortly.

'Increased the gift.' Deirdre looked like one of those nodding dogs people put in their cars.

Erica frowned at her. 'So we decided to have all the hard courts re-surfaced.' She spoke quickly, as if the decision were an unpleasant smell that could be erased if one were quick enough with the fresh-air spray.

'All the courts re-surfaced,' Deirdre confirmed. 'Blue.'

'Excellent.' Liam had hardly dared hope, but he couldn't believe it had been that easy – without Suzi, without Amanda, and without himself of course, to sway the voting. 'Er, so what happened about the purple and green?' he couldn't resist asking.

Erica said nothing.

'It was a close-run thing,' Deirdre began, 'but I believe blue was considered more modern – by some of the committee at least. And by our sponsor too. Excellent under floodlights, I hear.'

'Floodlights?' But they didn't have floodlights. Yet. Liam was beginning to get the picture. 'And all the courts are going to be done?'

'All the courts,' Deirdre said again, looking down at her notes. 'On the understanding that –'

'Quite.' Erica shot her a warning look.

'Yes?' Liam waited.

'Oh, tell him,' Erica said.

'On the understanding that Chestnut Grove Tennis Club remains loyal to its original principles,' Deirdre said, reading from her file.

Bloody hell. Liam was stunned. 'Who is this mysterious benefactor?' he asked.

'Obviously a Socialist,' Erica hissed.

'And the name of the club?' Liam was beginning to enjoy himself. 'Are we losing the Chestnut?'

'No, no.' Deirdre answered for Erica this time. Maybe, Liam thought, the first time ever. 'It was decided – because of our lovely old horse-chestnut trees on the drive – to keep the name as it is.' She glanced at Erica. 'As well as its principles.'

'Can we get on?' Erica was turning purple. All she needed was the green, thought Liam, and she would blend in just perfectly at Wimbledon.

'Most certainly.' Liam was grinning as he left the common room.

So he had an ally – an anonymous ally, but more importantly, a rich ally. Perhaps Chestnut Grove Tennis and Youth Club would survive after all.

In the end, it was the male doubles that decided the competition. The clones had walked away with the four boys' singles, though Tiger Rogers had put up a great show and only lost on a tight tie-break that had had Liam pacing up and down the edge of the court, wondering if just maybe . . .

Jade had walked her singles, doubles and the mixed, while the other girls' singles match had also gone to Liam's team on default, since of the two girls who had turned up for the other side, one left early and the other was the girlfriend of one of the clones (Sebastian) rather than a tennis player in her own right. She had giggled a lot, shrieked, 'help me, Seb!' every time Jade smashed a volley or forehand drive past her, and failed to return most of Jade's first serves.

All in all, a bit of a farce, Liam thought, though he wasn't averse to taking the points. More fool Rossi.

The boys' doubles – Tiger and Gazza versus Sebastian and Oliver, looked as if it was going to be a walkover, until Tiger started getting his serve on target, at which point there was a turnaround in fortunes. Seb and Olly had strolled the first set 6–1, but Tiger and Gazza scraped the second on a flukey tie-break that included no less than two net cords. And now, somehow, they were 5–4 up in the final set, having broken Oliver's serve (thanks to two double faults) and with Gazza to serve.

His first serve was weak and punished by a hot backhand down the line by Sebastian, his second was an ace, and the third led to a breathtaking rally, won with an awkward volley (off the handle of the racket, Liam suspected) from Tiger. Thirty fifteen. Tiger intercepted Olly's forehand return on the next shot and it was forty fifteen.

Nick Rossi put his hand over his eyes.

Liam smiled. He knew how much defeat would hurt Rossi's pride. 'C'mon, lads,' he yelled. The breeze coming in from the sea was picking up – and that had to be to their advantage.

But he had not reckoned on the pride of Sebastian and Oliver. Sebastian took it to forty thirty with a sweeping backhand that took Tiger completely by surprise, and Oliver made it deuce with a whamdinger of a shot that punished a weak serve and that went zinging past Tiger before he'd even got into position.

Once again, Seb and Olly sprinted the entire length of the court in order to touch hands encouragingly in a moment of bonding. Jesus wept . . . Liam had no patience for it. Various bonding sessions had been going on between Nick's players all afternoon. It might signify team spirit, but Liam tended to agree with his lot that it was all a bit too naff for words.

At this point, however, Gazza lost his nerve and double faulted, to make it advantage to the Rossi camp, and Oliver whisked a delicate drop shot over the net that Tiger had no chance of reaching. Game, set and match. And more bonding, of course.

Liam went up to congratulate his team. He was almost glad it had ended that way – he'd hate to have won on default – and at least they'd put up a decent fight.

'Hard luck,' Nick said, holding out his hand. 'Pretty close thing.'

'Winning by default wouldn't feel like winning.' But Liam accepted the handshake.

Nick shrugged. 'Commitment's part of winning,' he said, eyeing Liam's team. 'Dedication, bothering to turn up.'

'Maybe.' And Liam had to admit he was pleased with all of his players. At least they'd all been willing to have a go. And with a bit more practice . . . Who could tell?

'You've proved your point.' Nick, Liam thought, seemed determined to be friendly – now that he'd won.

'My point?' He wasn't sure he'd made one.

'Ordinary kids should be given the chance to play the game.' Nick took off his baseball cap and flicked back his hair in a manner which reminded Liam uncannily of Bradley Jacobs. 'Yeah, why the hell not? What does background have to do with it?'

Hallelujah, Liam thought. But he was surprised. 'I didn't know you felt that way.' He frowned. 'So why did you vote with Erica Raddle at the spring committee meeting?'

'I was being childish.'

Liam would never have imagined seeing Nick Rossi looking shamefaced. He wished he had a camera on him so he could capture it on film.

'I saw you getting it together with Amanda and I saw red.'

'Ah.' Liam considered this. 'But I'm not.'

'Not what?'

'Not getting it together with Amanda. Never was.' It wasn't just a matter of a certain woman he couldn't get out of his head. He liked Amanda, but he'd hate to have to live up to her expectations all the time. Not to mention parties with Fenella, Saffron and the like. God, no.

'Right.' Nick seemed to be subjecting him to a re-appraisal. 'None of my business anyway,' he said at last. 'Amanda's the past now.'

Liam thought of Estelle. 'On to pastures new?' He tried to sound casual, but his voice caught.

Nick, however, didn't seem to notice. 'Yeah. Pastures new.' He clapped Liam on the shoulder. 'See you, then.'

'See you.' He wasn't such a bad bloke, Liam realised, as Nick strolled off to talk to Sebastian, Oliver and the rest of his team. Maybe he'd read him wrong. Maybe he'd even been instrumental in the most recent bout of committee decision-making.

But somehow this thought didn't make Liam feel very much better. Because there was still Estelle. Rossi had snatched her away from under Liam's nose. And so, by God, he still wanted to clock him one.

Chapter 23

When Suzi glanced out of the window of Secrets In The Attic, to see a familiar, battered, white van freckled with rust pulling up outside, she ducked out of sight.

'What's up?' Estelle, wearing a turquoise sarong and matching bandanna around her auburn hair, looked over and then towards the doorway. 'Oh, hi, Josh.' Her gaze travelled back towards Suzi, before drifting heavenwards in despair.

Hell's bells, Suzi thought. But to be fair, how was Estelle supposed to know he was the enemy, since Suzi hadn't actually told her?

He stood in the doorway. Clearly, he had seen her. Suzi came out of squatting position, rubbed her stiff knees, dusted down her jeans, and emerged, cloth in hand, pretending to be engrossed in the lower panels of the grandfather clock. Her heart was thumping so loud in rhythm with the pendulum, she almost expected it to chime spontaneously.

'Hi there. How's things?' Josh strolled in (why did he always take over other people's territory as if he were asserting ownership rights, Suzi wondered) and slumped on to the counter, sitting, lounging, taking up so much more space than necessary.

He was wearing one of those crumpled linen suits that somehow managed to make him look charming, debonair and little boy lost, all at the same time. A model of confusing signals. Little boy lost? Suzi dismissed the thought. That was a joke. Josh Willis was more Big Bad Wolf.

As if to prove her point, he flashed Estelle a particularly wolfish smile and then glanced the question at Suzi.

'Fine.' Suzi shook out the duster and continued. Her teeth were clenched so hard she'd have to be careful she didn't get lockjaw. She decided not to join in the conversation any further. Let Estelle talk to the man.

'They're on their way out,' he said, waving a large hand in the general direction of The Bargain Basement. 'Know where they're off to?'

'I would have thought you'd be able to answer that,' Suzi snapped, forgetting her decision to keep quiet.

'Oh? Why?' His lazy drawl seemed to slide all over her.

Suzi shrugged. She was hardly going to tell him she'd seen him in the pub – plotting their downfall with Stan and Terry, having a good laugh at their expense. But that was one thing. Why had he come in here to gloat?

Estelle eyed Suzi curiously. 'Coffee, Josh?' she asked.

Suzi glared at her.

'Yeah. Great.' He settled in further on the counter (lucky there were no sofas around or he'd be comatose within thirty seconds, Suzi thought) as Estelle disappeared out the back.

Suzi knew he was looking at her, staring at her even. Did she have a smut of dust on her nose? Cobwebs in her hair? She felt hot with embarrassment, her throat harsh as sandpaper. She could hardly ignore him and yet she couldn't for the life of her think of a topic of conversation that was safe.

'You must be pleased,' he said to her, referring, she assumed, to Stan and Terry again.

'S'pose so,' she croaked. Of course she was pleased – if they were really going. She just didn't understand why.

'Though you don't look it.'

Unless it was another wind-up. Judas. Suzi squinted at him, but he met her accusing glare with such a look of innocence, that, having run out of things to dust, she turned her attention to the window display. She moved some moonstone ear-rings to one side, then back again, to the other side, then back again. She might look mad but at least it meant she didn't have to look at him.

'So I guess you'll be pretty pleased that I won't be around either.'

This time she did turn. 'You're going with them?' God, how low had he sunk? Or had he been down there with the scum of the earth all along?

'Give me a break.' Josh stretched out his almost unbearably long legs and Suzi looked away again. 'I'm getting out of antiques.'

'Oh.' No more trips to Germany then. No more reason for Josh Willis to even come into the shop again.

'And out of the area.'

'Oh.' That was that then. She felt an unwilling emptiness – anti-climax maybe. And more fool her for being taken in by him. For thinking, for dreaming . . . Oh, hell. What was the matter with her anyway?

'Don't you want to know where I'm going?' The grey-green eyes were searching.

Suzi took a step towards him and then two steps back.

He sighed.

Yes! she wanted to scream. 'If you like,' she said.

He took a business card – one of *those* cards – from the inside pocket of his jacket and scribbled down an address. He left it on the counter.

Suzi hesitated. Odd, the strange magnetic force that card seemed to have, for an object so small. She moved over to pick it up – slowly, as if it might explode. His handwriting was long and loopy, like on the postcard he'd sent her from Germany. *Farm Cottage*, she read. 'Sounds very rural.'

'It is. I'm selling up and buying a run-down cottage and a few acres of land.'

She was close to him now – she could smell the scent of him, feel his warmth. 'Somerset?' For some reason this word emerged with a phoney West Country accent. Where the cider apples grow, she thought, dealing herself a mental kick in the shins.

'Not very far, really. An hour's drive.' Every word seemed charged, as if he were expecting something from her. But what could he possibly be expecting – after what he'd done?

'I wish things were different,' Suzi blurted. She had so much to say and she didn't know where to start. Her brain and her heart were at cross purposes. She didn't know whether to accelerate or brake, to overtake or stop at the nearest junction.

'Ah.' Josh looked down at his hands. 'Michael?'

That wasn't what she'd meant at all. 'That lot next door,' she began. 'You, and –'

'Coffee up!' Estelle appeared in the doorway, radiant and smiling, and Suzi's words trailed away. Brain and heart seemed to have both kissed the moment goodbye, she thought. But perhaps, after all, it was best to let him go and say nothing. If she confronted him with what she knew, there'd only be another argument. He was leaving – what did it matter?

Estelle picked up the card Suzi had left on the counter. 'What's this, then?'

Suzi switched off as Josh explained, turning her attention to the price list on the far side of the counter. She must ask Michael to move out, she realised. Without delay. It was over between them and this way, they were just prolonging the pain. She was meant to live alone, just her and the animals in the cottage, she'd never find a man she liked enough to share it with her. And bugger it, she was probably better off without one.

'Suzi, you've changed the position of that price list about ten times,' Estelle said. 'I've known you to be more productive.'

'I can't make up my mind.' And that just about summed it up, Suzi thought.

Estelle shrugged and turned her attention back to Josh. 'So you're going organic and living off the land?' She laughed and tucked a stray strand of red hair back into the bandanna. 'And there's an orchard and even a small vineyard? It sounds blissful.' She seemed to lean closer to him, inviting confidences. She looked like an extremely attractive gipsy, Suzi thought, repressing the urge to drag Josh off the counter and away from her.

'I'm after a few more of those open spaces.' Josh looked meaningfully at Suzi but she ignored him.

'So no more trips to Germany then?' Estelle asked him.

''Fraid not.'

'That's a shame,' Estelle waved her hand to take in the contents of the shop. 'Because Suzi and I are desperate to get rid of this furniture.'

'Desperate to get *rid* of it?' he echoed.

Suzi could feel his eyes on her, knew he was laughing at her. Low down rat, she thought. What was it about him anyway? How come he had so much power over her internal organs?

She heard Estelle telling him about their plans (how long before that got back to Terry?) heard him mmming and ohing and ah yessing.

'Sounds a great idea,' he said when she'd finished, as if they needed him to sanction it, for heaven's sake. 'Jewellery, hmm? Good luck with it all.'

Suzi looked across at him just in time to catch the cat's grin – and put the price list back where it had been in the first place. With a bang.

All very well. But it wasn't so easy for her to go back to the beginning, even if she wanted to. And Suzi had the uneasy sensation that nothing would be the same again.

To go or not to go? Liam scowled at his one and only dress suit, that could undeniably use a trip to the dry cleaners. He should support the club – and this was CG's big night. And he'd be there anyway in the afternoon – unless he ducked out of the American tournament as well. But he didn't want his nose rubbed in it.

Estelle and Nick . . . He wasn't sure he could face the sight of them – especially now that Nick seemed an OK sort of a bloke too. All right when he was a poncy git who knew nothing about the real world . . . Liam took a step back to see how far you had to go before the mark didn't show. Jesus . . . He wanted to see her. But could he bear to see her – with another man?

Gloomily, Liam spat on a tissue and rubbed ineffectually at a stain on the collar of the black jacket. Bits of tissue clung stickily to the fabric. Damn it. Why should he bother? This would be an Erica Raddle shindig, and too select for his taste by far. He sighed. Dress suits, indeed . . .

Shit. Liam put the suit back in the wardrobe. It might be the highlight of the club's year, but frankly he'd rather sink his sorrows alone, with a bottle of wine and a take-away. And as for Estelle . . . Well, what was the point in pining for what you knew you couldn't have?

To go or not to go? Michael stared into Hester the goat's pale, uncomprehending eyes. Suzi had invited him to the dance. But should he go? He wasn't sure he felt part of Chestnut Grove Tennis

Club any more. He liked it there – they all did. But when was the last time he'd even played?

Hester said nothing to sway him one way or the other, merely stared back at him, blinking, head drooping slightly as if she'd resume munching Suzi's lawn just as soon as Michael's back was turned.

Michael stroked her coarse white coat. He had forgiven her for the head-butt. She was a goat after all and she'd felt threatened. Maybe in some obscure way it had even been a sign of affection.

It would be easy to duck out of the dance, he realised. He had a gig at the Bear and Bottle tomorrow night. Suzi had suggested he come on later, and of course he could do that – traditionally the dance went on till the early hours. But what was the point?

Hester jerked at her rope in a less than understanding kind of a way.

'Why am I doing it?' Michael asked her. 'Why won't I give up?' Why was he dragging on a relationship that was over, taking advantage of the fact that Suzi couldn't bring herself to end it? And why was he talking to a goat?

'For God's sake look at me,' Michael said to Hester.

At this, Hester, who had clearly had more than enough, bent her head and started chewing.

'And I can't even keep the goat's bloody attention,' Michael muttered.

I really don't understand,' Estelle said to Suzi, 'why you had to be so rude to him.' She looked over to where Suzi was standing by the shop window, looking desolate. 'I thought you liked him.'

'I do. I did. I do.'

Estelle sighed. 'So if you like him –'

'It's not that simple.'

Suzi had on her stubborn face. Jaw clenched, mouth unsmiling and her arms folded in front of her. Just let anyone try to come close . . . Estelle touched her shoulder. 'Michael?' she asked.

Suzi spun round. 'Why does everyone think it's Michael?' Her green eyes were fierce. Clearly, Estelle had touched more than her shoulder – she'd touched a nerve. 'If you really want to know –'

'Yes?'

'If you really want to know . . .' Suzi faltered.

'Hmm?' Estelle was losing patience.

'I saw him in the pub with Stan and Terry.' The words tumbled out. 'I think he was involved in . . . all that nasty stuff that happened.'

'Josh?' Estelle blinked at her. 'You're joking.'

'I wish I was.'

'Y'know, Suzi,' Estelle said later, looking up from the accounts book, 'we've easily got enough to pay the rent this month.'

'That's good,' Suzi said. She wanted to be pleased, but she felt like her face was stuck in a frown. Everything seemed to be spinning out of control. She wasn't sure what she wanted, wasn't sure about anything any more. She only knew that something was horribly wrong.

Thankfully, Estelle continued with enough enthusiasm for them both. 'The jewellery's going well. Really taking off. And if only we could shift some of this –'

She was interrupted by an unexpected sight in the doorway of the shop. Stan and Terry stood there, side by side.

So this is what it had come down to, Suzi thought. A double duel. Their hands hung loose by their belts. Any moment, and they'd go for their guns. Perhaps not, though, because it was hard to say which of them looked the most embarrassed, the most pissed off.

'What the hell do you want?' Suzi snapped. She was tired of not being confrontational. After what these two had done to them, she was *itching* for a fight.

'We've come to buy your stock,' Stan said, not looking at her.

'What?'

'The furniture.' He waved a hand. 'We want to buy the whole blinking lot.'

Not exactly what she'd been expecting . . . Suzi stared at him. Was he winding her up?

'Everything?' Estelle asked.

'Everything.'

'Well, you can stuff it,' Suzi said hotly. 'If you think we'd sell anything to you —'

'Hang on a sec.' Estelle interrupted her. 'All our stock?'

'Yep.' Terry looked dispiritedly around the shop, at the wash-stand, the grandfather clock et al. He looked profoundly depressed.

'But not the jewellery,' Estelle said.

'Not the jewellery.'

'No way!' Suzi glared at Estelle. Where was her pride?

'How much?' asked Estelle.

'Three grand.' Stan pulled out a wad of notes.

'What?' Suzi was gobsmacked. She watched him counting out the money.

'Fifty, one, one fifty, two . . .'

'Four grand,' said Estelle.

'What?' Suzi stared at her. Had she gone mad? Had they all gone mad? And how come her vocabulary had suddenly become so limited?

Estelle narrowed her eyes. She looked, Suzi thought, suitably scary. 'Or no deal,' she said. Not so much Western duel as Mafia entanglement.

Did they all know something she didn't? Suzi continued to look from one to the other of them in bewilderment.

'You drive a hard bargain.' Stan glanced towards Terry. 'Bloody Jules had better come in on this, right?'

'Right,' Terry agreed.

'Is it real?' Suzi said, staring at the pile of cash. She'd never seen so much money before.

Estelle picked up the notes, held the first few up to the light. 'It had better be,' she said.

'We'll have the stuff picked up in the morning,' said Terry as they left the shop.

'The whole damn lot!' Estelle chucked the notes in the air. 'We can pay off the landlord, Suze. We'll even have some left to buy some more jewellery.'

Suzi was glad she was pleased. Hell, she was pleased. Only, 'Why?' she asked. And something else was bothering her. Something Stan had said earlier.

'I'm not sure.' Estelle became thoughtful. She bundled the notes together again. 'But I think I'm beginning to get an idea. And d'you know, Suzi, I really think we can turn things around.'

As they stood there, bemused but undeniably relieved, a little old lady trotted into the shop. She beamed at them. 'Lovely day.'

'Super!' Estelle re-focused and realised it was Mrs Barnaby, whose mood seemed to have vastly improved since her last visit. Estelle tried to calm her excitement, forced herself to be attentive, shovelled the money into the top drawer of the desk. 'Did you enjoy the roadshow?' she asked.

'Oh, yes, my dear.' She winked at Suzi. 'That lovely young man. So helpful, so kind.'

Suzi grunted, Estelle could guess what she was thinking . . . *Lovely young man? She knows nothing.* And even Estelle had to admit that Josh was hardly young – even by Mrs Barnaby's standards.

'I've got a few words I'd like to say to him,' the old lady chortled.

'Haven't we all.' Suzi folded her arms tighter still across her chest. More stressed than a nun in a porn shop, Estelle thought.

'You've just missed him.' Estelle did a double-take as Mrs Barnaby opened her bag and drew out some pearl ear-rings identical to the ones she'd valued some weeks ago. 'But I thought . . .' She frowned as these were joined by a diamond and garnet necklace and an amethyst ring. 'Surely these are the pieces you sold to The Bargain Basement?'

Mrs Barnaby merely fluffed up her grey perm, gave them a knowing look and let them come to their own conclusions.

Suzi came towards the counter and together they fingered the jewellery. 'Aren't they?' Estelle asked again.

'They are indeed,' Mrs Barnaby said at last. 'They returned them to me. And some of the furniture too.'

'Returned them?' Estelle looked at Suzi and Suzi looked out of the open doorway towards the shop next door. What exactly was going on? Estelle had her suspicions but –

'Got my money back and everything.' She nodded serenely. 'But I hope you don't mind, my dears. You see, I've decided to keep everything for now and put that little table I brought to your roadshow into auction instead.'

'Of course we don't mind,' Estelle murmured, her brain working overtime.

'Why would they do that?' Suzi said what they were both thinking.

Mrs Barnaby leaned forwards. 'That young man,' she said.

'Young man?' But Estelle was beginning to understand even more.

'That lovely young man.'

'Josh?' Suzi and Estelle spoke together.

'Mr Willis. That was his name, wasn't it?'

They nodded.

'I thought it was him.' Mrs Barnaby tucked her jewellery back into her bag. 'Excuse my language, but when they said it . . .'

'It?'

'All this is because of that *bloody* Willis.' Mrs Barnaby enunciated the words slowly but clearly and with great relish. She nodded, satisfied. 'That was what the fat man said.'

'When he brought your jewellery back?' Estelle confirmed.

'Exactly.' She closed her bag with a click. 'I'm not a clever woman,' she said. 'But I think one can assume that Mr Willis had a hand in it.'

'I think one can,' Estelle murmured. So that's what Josh had been doing with Stan and Terry in the pub. Sorting it for Mrs Barnaby. Sorting it for them too. She looked at Suzi but Suzi was miles away, fists clenching and unclenching as if she were about to lose it completely.

'The other common denominator,' Suzi said.

'What?'

'Jules Wilson – the landlord. He's the other common denominator. Did you hear what Stan said earlier?'

Estelle frowned, trying to remember. Yes, he had been mentioned, come to think of it. And yes, now she knew what Suzi was gabbling on about. If anyone knew how broke they were it was Jules Wilson – he'd heard enough sob stories as to why they couldn't pay their rent. And it rather sounded as if he was more than just a landlord to Stan and Terry . . . Good grief. The final piece slotted into place.

Suzi grabbed Josh's business card that was still sitting on the counter, and shoved it in the pocket of her jeans. She was looking pretty forceful.

'Suzi?'

'Gotta go.' And she strode out of the door.

Mrs Barnaby smiled at Estelle, as though quite aware of what was going on. 'They're opening a bric-à-brac shop called Cheap and Cheerful,' she said. 'In Brighton, I believe.'

'Good.' Estelle felt the warm flood of relief. For the first time in ages she was calm. 'I'm glad they're not staying in Pridehaven. This town's not big enough for the both of us.' She tried a nervous laugh. It was OK. It was going to be OK. She had no doubts left in her mind. And the furniture? He must have sorted that too – a payment to compensate for those scare tactics and all that harassment. There was more to that man, she realised, than met the eye. Did Suzi realise it too?

Mrs Barnaby was at the door. 'But by all accounts that nice Mr Willis contacted the police as well,' she said darkly. 'So, I don't know about Brighton. They might not be going quite as far as they think . . .'

Chapter 24

He might be an OK sort of a bloke, Liam thought grudgingly, as he and his second partner of the afternoon – Amanda – met up with their opponents – Nick Rossi and Estelle. (Liam couldn't believe it when the names came out of the baseball cap. But in the American tournament, any partnership was possible.) So yes, Nick Rossi was OK, but he was also a prat. For starters, he was wearing wrap-around mirrored blue sunglasses with full tennis whites, though the sun had disappeared behind a cloud half an hour ago, and on top of that, he was now poncing about with the Ralgex spray.

'Problem?' Estelle asked him.

'A touch of tendonitis.'

Liam turned away to hide his impatience. Tendonitis . . . Jesus wept. He bounced a ball against his racket. Estelle, of course, looked great. He sneaked another glance at her. She had this way of throwing things on carelessly – as though she hadn't really made an effort at all – achieving an individual, casual look that he loved. This afternoon she was wearing a figure-hugging white tennis dress, but with crimson shorts just visible underneath (though Liam hardly dared look) and she had tied a crimson and blue strip of silk jauntily around her head to keep the mass of auburn hair out of her eyes.

'Maybe you should strap it up,' she said now to her partner.

Amanda looked at her tiny gold watch and then – like daggers – at Estelle. 'We don't have all day,' she snapped. 'Perhaps you should let us go through on default.'

No way, thought Liam, remembering what he'd said to Nick after the under-15s tournament. 'We'll wait,' he declared.

He surveyed the courts around them, everyone playing mixed doubles. Beryl and Simon were on the adjacent court playing one of Nick's clones from the under-15s tournament, who was partnering Diana. As he watched, the sun emerged from behind a cloud. It was an idyllic scene, the players framed by the view beyond, more people clustered in the conservatory and on the clubhouse patio in front of the honey-stoned building, drinking Deirdre's home-made lemonade or Pimms, eating strawberries, ginger snaps and pavlova. The buzz of conversation filled the air, the thwack of ball on racket could be heard from all directions at once, mixed with the crisper smack of the balls on the hard courts. Laughter, sunshine, tennis. He'd hate to lose all this. And the season wasn't even over, Liam reminded himself.

Nick strapped up his elbow – with some help from Estelle, though Liam tried not to watch – and proceeded to do enough stretching exercises to satisfy a ballet dancer.

Liam and Amanda began warming up, though in truth Liam was warm already from his last match with a girl called Sarah, whose huge blue-veined thighs sprouting from under her white tennis skirt soon alerted him to the fact that she would be unable to run for the ball. He'd ended up taking most of her shots as well as his own. But they had lost and so now he was playing with a winning female – Amanda – because that was the way the tournament operated. Nick, on the other hand, was a winning male, and so he had been put with Estelle, who had suffered defeat in the previous round with Timmy Rogers, acknowledged to be the weakest of the men. The winning players were those with the most wins on their belt at the end; it was at least, Liam thought, a tournament that could be called fair.

Meanwhile, Nick was swinging his arm in preparation for his serve, wincing as he did so. 'I knew I shouldn't have played last night,' he said to Estelle, but loud enough for Liam, who was close to the net, to hear.

Wimp, thought Liam. He'd give him Ralgex spray . . .

This was supposed to be fun, Estelle thought, dodging instinctively as Amanda slammed another forehand volley her way. It was turning into a sweltering day and she wiped the sweat from her brow with her wrist band.

'Sorry!' Amanda called.

Like hell she was. She'd heard of going for the body, but most players varied their shots and tried not to injure their opponent. Estelle tossed a stray ball to Nick, who was serving, making the most of his dodgy elbow (tennis elbow?) for the benefit of Amanda, she was sure. Unlike the weather, the atmosphere was distinctly frosty between them, and as for Amanda's attitude to Estelle . . . She'd be lucky to get off the court alive.

Liam sank Nick's next serve into the net. Estelle noted Amanda's pout of irritation and smiled to herself. The girl liked to win. Liam was not going to be flavour of the month if he carried on like this.

'Who are you bringing to the dance tonight?' she asked Nick as they sent the balls up the other end of the court for Liam's service game.

'Mother.' He sounded a little embarrassed. 'She's got it into her head to come, so I thought . . .' He glanced across at the immaculate Amanda. 'Why not?'

'You care about Amanda, don't you?' Estelle knew it was probably the wrong moment to bring the subject up, but what the heck. Liam and Amanda were involved in some sort of tactical discussion (at least she supposed it was that) at the far end of the court – what a pair, Amanda in a pure white tennis dress, Liam in a T-shirt that declared that GANDALF RULED OK with a picture of the wizard underneath, and red and white seaside shorts patterned with ice cream cornets and images of Punch and Judy. Heavens. She remembered those shorts and she was sure Liam had sworn never to wear them again after that holiday in Penzance . . .

'Is it that obvious?' Nick looked so desolate – at least what she could see of him that wasn't covered up by the blue wrap-around mirrored shades looked desolate – that she put a comforting hand on his shoulder.

'Ready?' Liam yelled.

Estelle jumped. 'Hang on.' She got into position to receive.

Liam – who was by now sweating heavily – hit a wild serve that didn't even make the tram lines.

The next one was in, but weak, and Estelle swept her forehand across court. Amanda – still looking cool as ice – intercepted it, whacking it back at her with considerable force, but Estelle managed to swerve to one side and hook it back, determined to give as good as she got, and not to die in the process.

'Yours, darling!' Amanda called to Liam.

Darling ran, but didn't make it. He began to sweat even more. Love fifteen.

Estelle smiled as Liam growled, 'shot', followed by 'fuck it', followed by the banging of his racket on the net tape. There was nothing like a good loser. And Liam was nothing like one either, she thought.

As Liam served to Nick, Estelle found her mind wandering from the game. If Nick still cared about Amanda, then where did that leave Liam? Did *he* care for her too? She scrutinised him as he tossed the ball too high and too far forward and had to catch it again. She couldn't tell. He just looked bad-tempered, sweaty and sweet.

'Fuck it,' he said again as he smashed the serve into the net. Sweet? Who was she kidding?

As the game went on, and Liam became more and more uptight, so Estelle was able to relax and enjoy herself, playing with the strongest guy on the circuit. What she liked about Nick was that he didn't spend too much time congratulating her on a shot well played or apologising for his own mistakes. Not that there were too many of those. He didn't encroach on her side of the net either, basically just got on with it. She felt better too about the shop, now that she was free of Stan and Terry. Somehow, she thought, driving the winning backhand down the line to leave Amanda stranded, somehow, even without Liam, she would move on.

'Played.' Estelle couldn't help noticing how forcefully Amanda shook hands with them both, how they all avoided eye contact. She sensed Liam lingering behind as Amanda strode over to collect her bag and decided to linger too.

But Nick had other ideas. 'What a fabulous partner!' He grabbed her and kissed her on both cheeks and then, much to her surprise, firmly on the mouth.

Estelle was so taken aback that it was a moment before she reacted. She pushed him off with a laugh and a 'hey!'

But by that time, both Amanda and Liam were walking off the court and towards the honey-coloured clubhouse. Thanks, Nick, Estelle thought. If he imagined that the way to get Amanda Lake back into his life was to go around snogging other women, the poor deluded man should think again. A change of tactics was called for.

Liam joined the players and spectators for the prize-giving ceremony held on the patio. It was late afternoon, very warm and hazy. Chairs and tables had been moved aside, while certificates, a silver-plated rose bowl, two bottles of champagne and two bouquets of flowers laid out on a white cloth on one of the clubhouse tables, were presided over by Erica Raddle. Erica Raddle – self-important and yet still making some concession to sportiness in her white suit with navy trim. Beside her was a microphone on a stand.

'Ladies and gentlemen . . .' Her bosom swelled. 'The American tournament has been a *tremendous* success. Thank you, everyone, for making it so.' There followed a round of polite, disinterested applause.

Automatically, Liam looked amongst the small crowd for Estelle. She wasn't with Rossi. She was standing, alone, towards the back. There were a lot of people between them, but he had a clear view of her pale face, surrounded by the halo of auburn hair, free now of the bandanna that had been holding it in place. As he watched her, she half-turned and caught his glance. Liam didn't look away. For about ten seconds they seemed to absorb one another's gaze. Ten seconds could be an awfully long time . . .

And then someone spoke to her – a woman standing nearby, and Estelle's attention was distracted, she blinked, looked away, replied to the woman.

Liam re-focused his attention on Erica, who was still sounding off.

'But I mustn't waffle on . . .' She paused, but no one disputed this. 'You'll all be wanting to go home or into the changing rooms to get ready for tonight's dance.' She rubbed her hands together with glee. 'Our big night. I know you'll all be offering your support.' At this, her brow furrowed and her gaze scanned the players and spectators in front of her. Yes, Liam thought, she was old-fashioned teacher material. She reminded Liam of his old nightmare, Miss Dithercott. She would stride the corridors in her black and dusty flowing gown like a vampire bat on the prowl. And when she found a transgressor, she would fix him or her with a steely grey eye behind round metal-framed spectacles, and pounce . . . with a detention.

'And I'm proud to announce . . .' Erica turned a little pink. 'That one of our special benefactors will be here to grace the occasion. Henry Lake himself.' She beamed at Amanda, who was standing near the front, arms folded, looking bored. At Erica's words, she unfolded her arms, smiled briefly and insincerely and then resumed her pose.

'So, to the winners.' Impatiently, Erica beckoned Deirdre Piston forwards. 'Deirdre has done her sums . . .'

Deirdre nodded. 'Done my sums,' she confirmed.

Erica frowned. 'And the winners are . . .' she beamed once more, flashing horsy teeth to all and sundry, 'our own dear Amanda Lake, and Nick Rossi.'

Bloody typical, Liam thought. The guy who had everything, and who now had Estelle. He watched their body language as Nick and Amanda went to the table to collect their prizes. They stood carefully a few feet away from each other, eye contact still not an option apparently.

'A few words?' Erica suggested.

Amanda flicked her hair from her shoulders. She held her flowers cradled in the crook of one arm with casual grace – a girl clearly used to receiving such gifts. 'Thanks,' she said briefly, merely leaning slightly towards the microphone. 'And apologies to everyone I bullied when I played with them.' She shot a special smile towards Liam, who shrugged and laughed.

'And Nick?' Erica said.

Nick took a deep breath. He didn't look quite so comfortable with the flowers and placed them gingerly back on the table while he spoke. 'I'd like to say that Chestnut Grove is a great club,' he said. 'That's the tennis club and the youth club.' He too seemed to be addressing Liam, unless Liam was getting a power complex all of a sudden. 'I know some of you aren't too sure about the bright blue acrylic all-weather courts, but I'm confident they'll be popular with our younger element. We may be a club steeped in tradition, but we still like to move with the times.' He smiled. 'After the re-surfacing, Chestnut Grove may be an even sunnier place than it is today.'

People began to clap – Liam included. But Nick hadn't finished yet. He held up a hand. 'And it's important that we keep the original ethos of Chestnut Grove in mind.'

'Yes, yes, absolutely.' Erica tried to grab the microphone from him, but he shrugged her away.

'We should ensure that the tennis facilities are available for everyone,' he said, nodding at Liam. 'The youth club, people who can't afford to pay costly annual fees – in fact everyone who wants to play the game of tennis. And I'm sure you'll all have lots of fund-raising ideas, to help make it happen.' He shook the bottle of champagne and opened it with a flourish. 'Here's to taking the snobbery out of the game,' he said as the liquid shot out in a spray.

'Hear hear!' Despite everything, despite that kiss, Liam had to admire the bloke for speaking his mind, for defying Erica. And he had to admit that a few words from someone like Nick Rossi – who, some might argue, belonged to the privileged classes – had a lot more clout than what Liam – avowed Socialist – might have to say.

Erica didn't look quite so happy. 'You'll have to share the cup,' she told Nick and Amanda. 'We only have one. Or –?'

If she had been about to make some coy assumption about whether Nick and Amanda might be sharing the same trophy cabinet at some time in the foreseeable future, she didn't get the chance. Amanda shoved the cup towards Nick with a hissed, 'You can have it for the first six months, lover-boy.'

At which point Erica made frantic signs to Deirdre to switch off the microphone, Nick merely looked hurt, and Amanda stalked off, flowers in one hand, champagne held loosely by the neck of the bottle in the other. She brushed past Liam.

'Congratulations,' he said.

She raised her eyebrows. 'You'd think they could have run to a magnum,' she said.

It was some time before the rest of the people started drifting away, and by the time Liam escaped from Amanda and got to where Estelle had been standing, she had gone.

So he was left in the same quandary as before. To go or not to go, that was the question.

Chapter 25

Estelle was propping up the bar of Chestnut Grove clubhouse, waiting for Suzi to get the drinks. The band, a throwback to the 60s or 70s – they didn't seem to have made up their minds – hadn't yet begun to play, though they'd got to the stage of plugging in, tuning instruments, and all the hoo hah that preceded sound. But Chestnut Grove's clubhouse and conservatory were already full and fit to bursting.

The place had been festooned with silver banners and balloons, and by the doorway floated an enormous silver helium butterfly, whose purpose Estelle couldn't begin to imagine. The tables had been cleared to the sides of the clubhouse to create a dance floor, and were decorated with lacy cloths and white daisies in tiny glass vases. The conservatory looked much as it always did – a haven.

Women of all ages – sometimes hard to recognise out of tennis gear, it had to be said – were dressed in all their finery and men were in dinner jackets and dress shirts, sporting wing collars and bright bow ties. She saw a lot of people she recognised. But there was no Liam.

Estelle shifted her weight and smiled at Nick, over on the other side of the room. He was looking, she had to admit, very debonair in his black baggy dress suit, waistcoat and black bow tie. Very debonair, but still not Liam.

At this point Suzi returned with their white wine. And Suzi had really made an effort. Estelle felt ridiculously proud of her. For once, she had thrown aside her usual blue jeans, and was wearing instead a jade green chiffony creation that matched her eyes and whose soft lines certainly gave her a new femininity. Or at least, Estelle assumed it was the dress . . .

'Where the bloody hell is Liam?' Suzi handed Estelle her glass.

OK, Estelle amended, a new and fierce femininity. 'Maybe he won't bother to come,' she said, looking around vaguely as though she'd only just realised he wasn't there.

'He'd better,' Suzi ground out. 'I've got something I need to tell him.' And from the look of her, that wasn't the only item on her agenda.

Estelle shrugged. 'Where'd you get that dress, Suze?' She admired the drape of the sleeves, the slashed neckline that . . . hang on, she bent closer, that didn't quite look as if it had been slashed all its life.

'C.S.' Suzi joined in the applause as the band struck up the first notes. 'About time,' she added.

'C.S?'

'Charity shop.' Suzi hissed. 'And why not? I'll never wear it again, for heaven's sake.'

Estelle suppressed a giggle. Talk about living up to the ethos of CG's.

Suzi grabbed her arm. 'Estelle, I've got something I really need to talk to you about —'

'And to take us away into the first dance . . .' The lead singer — who was wearing 60s flares, a 70s collar and had a pudding-basin haircut — smiled encouragingly at Nick, who remained where he was, lounging on the far side of the clubhouse. 'May I ask our two glamorous winners . . .' he tried again, 'to take to the floor?' There was an expectant hush. Neither Nick nor Amanda moved a muscle.

'Please?' the lead singer added valiantly.

Nick put down his drink and advanced towards Amanda, a tightness to his mouth and a certain menace in his eyes.

Wicked. What now? Surely they'd have to look at one another at some point? 'Tell me later,' Estelle whispered to Suzi. She wanted to watch this.

Nick reached Amanda, who was standing near the bar, and held out an ironic hand to her. Estelle wasn't sure how a hand could be ironic, but Nick seemed to manage it. 'Shall we?' he muttered.

'If we must.' Amanda smiled sweetly and placed her hand in his.

There was no denying that she looked fabulous, Estelle thought. She was wearing a silver, black and gold beaded creation which had a high cut-away neckline, three narrow back-shoulder straps on each side and a scooped low line at the back. No bra, Estelle thought dismally, admiring the fact that Amanda could get away with it.

The band began in earnest and predictably, with 'Congratulations', which neither Nick nor Amanda seemed to have any idea how to dance to. Amanda sashayed gracefully from side to side, arms akimbo, but Nick was having none of that. His footwork wasn't bad and as his confidence increased, he took her hand and led Amanda into a twirl and then a spin. It was impressive, though obvious to Estelle that Amanda didn't want to go there. Maybe it was the length of her dress. It was full at the back where it fell to the floor and rustled provocatively as she moved, but it might not have the give required for this kind of dancing, Estelle guessed.

Nick seemed to have no idea of any of this. He spun her again, pulled her back into a semi-lift, plainly enjoying himself now.

Amanda struggled to get her balance, dragged herself upright, adjusted the dress, glared at him.

'Oh dear.' Estelle grinned at Suzi.

'What a lovely couple they make.' Erica's tones boomed even over the big band sound. She was standing on the other side of Estelle and addressing Amanda's father, Henry Lake.

'Charming.' But Estelle could see that Henry was distracted, more interested in who was coming through the door by the silver butterfly than in Erica or his daughter and her dancing partner. Who was he waiting for? She was intrigued.

Erica turned to her husband. 'Pull in your stomach, William,' she whispered loudly. 'Don't breathe.'

Estelle and Suzi exchanged a glance, Suzi got a fit of the giggles and at that point Nick steered Amanda purposefully towards the doorway and the silver floating butterfly.

He turned her into another lift (this time supported on his knee); there was the ominous sound of tearing fabric; wide-eyed the two dancing partners stared into one another's faces, and everyone – or so it seemed to Estelle – held their collective breath.

Michael grinned at his audience. They were listening, really listening, and some of them – like that guy in the denim jacket over there in the corner, for example – had been here last month. Maybe they'd come back specially to see him, Michael. Bloody great.

He ripped open his shirt so that the buttons flew in all directions, laughed at himself, strutted a bit (eat your heart out, Rod Stewart) grabbed the mic, stuck it in the bent wire coathanger and put that round his neck so he could move around more freely, encouraged the audience to laugh too.

His act had changed a lot in the past weeks. It had evolved, by accident mostly, and now included all sorts of touches – like that wire coathanger he'd bent to create a mic-holder, like chucking

273

his guitar to the landlord waiting by the bar, so he could do an impromptu somersault or two. That worked well (though not the time he'd tried to chuck it while inadvertently standing on the lead). He'd even incorporated a short impression of Dylan – thanks to Blondie and 'Lay Lady Lay' – of Elvis, and a jokey version of 'House Of The Rising Sun'.

Yeah, he was enjoying himself tonight – there was a kind of freedom in singing and playing when Suzi wasn't here to watch him. No hassles. No worrying what she was thinking about the new part of his act – the strutting, the semi-strip, the falling off the stage stuff. No looking over at her every ten seconds, trying to read every expression on her face.

He tripped over the wire, whispered, 'fuck it', soulfully into the mic like it was a sweet nothing and grinned himself into their good books. Michael had come to a decision. He was going to the dance tonight – after the gig – and he was going to tell Suzi the score. Things weren't standing still. He was moving on. He'd got a room here above the pub which would do him until he found something better. And in return he was going to help out in the bar a couple of nights a week. Sorted.

He felt even more cheerful as he dropped into 'My Girl' without thinking of Suzi and more cheerful still when the blonde (he'd almost started thinking of her as his blonde) waltzed through the door, wearing her usual black mini skirt with a skimpy, clingy, violet-coloured top. Sexy. She smiled at him, clocked his bare chest, pouted, waved, but, ah shit, she had a guy with her. First time ever.

What the hell. Michael played on. 'Last one before the break,' he murmured into the microphone. 'Dedicated to an ex of mine.' And he launched into 'Someone else not you'.

Just before he closed his eyes, he caught the look that Blondie shot him, the ironic lift of the eyebrows, the sexy full-lipped smile.

The kind of girl he'd always dreamed of having. And it's never too late, he thought.

'Idiot,' Amanda hissed, just as the band stopped playing. 'How could you be so bloody careless?'

Estelle – and quite a few of the other guests – peered closer, trying to see which part of Amanda's dress had finally given in to the pressure. But with the unquestionable grace of one born to be admired at all times – including times of adversity, no doubt – Amanda merely swept the torn skirt over one arm – thus creating a look not only dramatic, but revealing in the leg department – and made for the door.

'It was an accident,' Nick protested, following her.

'I don't care.' She turned on her heels, probably not realising he was so close behind her.

Estelle gave her the benefit of the doubt. Because Nick tripped over the silver-sandalled foot, and went down with a crash.

He landed awkwardly on his right arm and shoulder. Several people moved forwards to help. But Amanda was there first.

'Darling, darling, I'm so sorry.' She knelt down beside him, all contrition. 'Are you hurt, my darling?'

Nick's face was white. 'My bad arm,' he muttered. And then, 'Hang on a sec. Did you just call me your darling?'

At the end of the number, Michael went to get a pint, observing the body language of Blondie (how the hell was it that he still didn't know her name?) and the guy she was with. He was short, stocky, didn't look her type, and, to Michael's relief, there was no touchy-feely, lovey-dovey stuff, just some pretty intent talking and the odd burst of laughter. Her brother maybe?

She saw him looking, said a few words to her companion and

made her way over. Lovely legs, Michael thought, watching appreciatively.

'Let me get that for you,' she purred. 'Can we have a chat?'

Michael shrugged. 'Why not?' He followed her over to the table, wondering what was coming, and why he'd ever thought her predatory. She was just sexy and sure enough of herself not to be afraid to come on to a guy. Anyway, she could hunt him down anytime.

'This is Chris Baker.' She introduced them. 'He's an old colleague of mine. From when I was working in London.'

Michael nodded to the guy, but he was more interested in his blonde. 'What did you do in London?' Modelling, maybe, with those legs.

'I was a P.A.'

'Oh yeah? Who to?' And brains, Michael thought. A P.A? His life could do with some organising and assisting of the personal variety.

'A guy who handled Public Relations internally for the company.'

Public relations. 'Right.' Michael thought about making a joke about private relations, but decided that now was not the time. He'd always had a habit of cracking jokes when he was a bit nervous and Suzi for one had never appreciated them. Why should this woman be any different? Perhaps jokes were a lad thing. Sure, women sometimes seemed to find them funny, but were they pretending, as if they thought a guy had to be flattered before he'd take any notice of them? Michael took a gulp of his beer. He might be forty but sometimes he thought he was doing more learning now than he'd done in his whole life before. 'So why did you leave London?' he asked her.

She smiled. Great teeth, Michael thought. In fact great all over.

'Looking for the rural idyll. Me and my ex thought we'd put down roots, have kids, start a business.'

Her companion grinned. 'It's a dream most of us Londoners have from time to time. Sounds great, doesn't it?'

'Until you wake up,' she agreed.

Michael wasn't sure where all this was leading. And he couldn't think how the hell to find out what she called herself. How could you ask someone you seemed to have known for ages, someone you'd chatted to so often, 'oh, by the way, what *is* your name?'

'So you woke up?' he asked instead, wanting her to go on. There were things he wanted to know. Like, what had happened to the ex, for example?

'With a jolt.' She sipped her wine. 'We never got as far as the kids. Steve missed London . . .'

Great, Michael thought. He knew the name of her old colleague and now the name of her ex-lover. But not hers, damn it.

'He couldn't wait to get back there,' she went on. She hooked a strand of blonde hair behind one ear.

Out of a bottle and who the hell cared, Michael thought. 'How about you?'

'I didn't.' She shrugged. 'Didn't miss it, didn't want to go back.'

'Sandy did start her own business, though,' the guy called Chris said.

Sandy. One problem solved, Michael thought. 'Doing?' He watched the way her fingers played with the stem of her wine glass. Not nerves, but a kind of restlessness he could empathize with.

'I set up an independent travel agency.' She glanced at her watch. 'But listen, I didn't drag you over to hear all this stuff. Chris was down for the weekend and so I got him to come along and have a listen.'

'Yeah, great.' Michael picked up his glass and got up. It was time for the next part of the set. 'Nice meeting you, Chris, but I've gotta –'

'He likes the song.' She seemed to be waiting for something.

Michael had no idea what. 'Song?'

'"Someone else not you".'

'Oh, great. So –' He began to move away from the table.

'Michael – Chris works for Echo.'

'Echo.' Michael's brain finally lumbered into gear. 'Echo, the record company?'

She nodded. 'That's where I used to work too. They handle all their PR internally.'

'Sit down, Michael,' said Chris.

Michael sat.

Chapter 26

'I think I owe you an apology.'

Estelle blinked at Amanda in surprise. She seemed to have recovered her poise. Now, she was looking positively dewy-eyed and smiling. 'An apology?'

'I was a little um . . . forceful. In the match today.'

She wasn't kidding. 'Ah.' It didn't take much imagination to work out what had brought this on. Estelle was still standing close to Henry Lake and the Raddles, who had now been joined by Nick and his mother. And Amanda of course. A glowing Amanda. And from the way she and Nick were looking at each other, Nick's fall (from which, Estelle noted, he appeared to have completely recovered) had been a productive one.

'I haven't behaved well,' Amanda admitted. 'Daddy says I'm too used to getting my own way, and I suppose he's right. You can't always expect people to fall into line. And of course some things have to be worked for.' She smiled. 'All that jazz.'

Estelle thought of Secrets. 'Very true.' And she supposed she shouldn't be surprised about Henry Lake's work ethic. Someone had told her once he hadn't always had money. And it was his father who had founded Chestnut Grove in the first place.

'But you see,' Amanda went on. 'I thought you'd taken something rather special away from me.'

Estelle shrugged. 'Nick and I were never involved.' She had never, she knew, felt free enough of Liam to be involved with anyone else. Would she ever be? She looked around the crowded room. Couples were dancing, chatting, drinking, eating. Even Deirdre Piston had a man in tow. Right now they were attempting a version of the twist to 'Sugar and Spice' – not an easy task for anyone, Estelle reflected, and Deirdre had never seemed the twisting type. But there was no Liam. She had to face it. If he'd wanted to see her, he'd be here.

'Nick told me that already,' Amanda said. 'And in case you're interested – neither were me and Liam, not really. I just did it to make Nick jealous. To make him, oh, I don't know . . .' she batted her eyelashes. 'To make him do something about us.'

Estelle looked into the baby-blue eyes and sighed. How could Liam have ever been interested in anyone as shallow as Amanda? Playing games with people's loves, lives and emotions. She had no idea why Nick hadn't made a move on Amanda before. And she didn't much care. It was all very well for them. But what about Estelle? What about Liam? Maybe right now he was drowning his sorrows all alone in his garret flat. Maybe he simply couldn't face seeing Amanda with another man.

'And it worked.' Shelagh Rossi came over and linked arms with them both. 'My Nick has been hell to live with, I can tell you.'

Amanda leaned closer to the older woman. 'And have you told him our plans?' she whispered.

'Plans?' Nick had come up behind Amanda, put his hands round her waist. Estelle thought she'd probably throw up soon if she had to watch much more of this soppy stuff. And yet – despite the fact that Liam wasn't here, she felt strangely at peace.

Ten minutes ago, as they'd stood chatting at the bar, Suzi had dropped a bit of a bombshell, but it wasn't, now she came to think about it, a destructive one. It presented, actually, a way to go.

'I wasn't aware you two even knew each other,' Nick went on.

'You don't know everything,' Shelagh teased him. 'Amanda invited me over for lunch.'

At this point Estelle managed to extricate herself from Shelagh's grasp. She might go home, she decided, if Suzi didn't mind. She wasn't in the mood for drinking and she wasn't in the mood for dancing. Thinking was more what she was after right now. And planning the way ahead. But Shelagh was still talking.

'The three of us had a lovely chat . . .' She exchanged a meaningful look with Henry Lake, who took a step closer.

'We certainly did,' he agreed. 'It was most enlightening. And rewarding.'

Erica Raddle's head shot up to attention. All eyes were on Henry and Shelagh. That was some look. And some sub-text. Goodness, Estelle thought, as she headed for the ladies loo. Whatever next?

Michael couldn't think of anything to say. It was so far from what he'd been expecting . . . He waited.

'It's a good song.' Chris pulled a business card out of the inside pocket of his jacket and handed it to Michael. It was simple, understated, just the name, Chris Baker, with phone number and the usual email and website stuff.

'Why don't you give me a call?' Chris suggested. 'We could have a chat about it.'

Michael stared at him vacantly. Nobody had mentioned the words recording deal or contract. It was nothing like the way he'd dreamed it – no drama, no effusiveness, no promises, no cash. No, *hey, kid I can really do something with you. I'm gonna give you a new name, new clothes, new image.* Nothing like that. Just, *give me a call sometime.* 'OK,' Michael said.

'We've got to go.' Sandy's smile was apologetic. 'Chris has got an early start in the morning.' They both got to their feet and Michael followed suit.

'It was good to meet you.' Chris shook his hand (Michael hadn't imagined a handshake either – it seemed far too bloke-ish and ordinary).

Sandy kissed his cheek – one each side and then one more, continental style. He smelt the sharp insinuation of her perfume, though he had no idea what it was, and saw her faint smile. 'See you,' she said, like it was a promise.

And as they left the pub Michael knew his grin went from ear to ear. 'Yes,' he said. 'See you very soon.'

'I'm opening the house up to the public,' Shelagh told them all.

It seemed to be, Estelle reflected, a night for revelations.

'Hallelujah,' Nick said. 'Though really, Mother, you should –'

'Not sell.' Amanda looked very firm, and Estelle had a glimpse of who would be in charge between the two of them.

'Definitely not sell,' Henry agreed. 'Your mother loves the place and we should respect that.'

We? Estelle saw Nick open his mouth, look at Amanda, shut it again.

Amanda took his arm. 'Daddy thinks your mother could manage if she opened it up to the public. In fact he thinks she could do well. In fact,' she smiled, 'he's going to make an investment in the scheme.'

Shelagh nodded. 'We might open a tea-room,' she said.

Estelle glanced towards Erica Raddle, whose mouth gaped slightly as she absorbed all this information.

'Or a sushi restaurant,' Amanda added, also casting a wicked glance towards Erica.

Estelle giggled. She'd long suspected Henry to be CG's secret sponsor and Erica's horrified expression seemed to confirm this. But no doubt Henry would have enough funds left over to support CG's – especially if it was to remain a club for the people as Liam and now Nick intended.

'So you knew about this?' Nick asked Amanda. But he was smiling too.

'Amanda's in charge of the entire project,' Shelagh replied. 'She understands that the house is all I have left of your father.' She squeezed his arm. 'Apart from you, darling, of course.'

'And your mother understands,' said Amanda, 'that she can't go on like this. She needs to face up to the practicalities of her situation and use them to her advantage. She needs to move on.' She shot him an understanding look. 'And neither can she expect you to go on pouring money down a drain.'

Estelle couldn't help smiling. Amanda had certainly made the most of her lunch with Shelagh Rossi. It struck her that Amanda might be shallow, but she was clever too. She had probably put her finger on the main reason why Nick Rossi had not formalised an arrangement of a romantic kind with her before now. Amanda was a girl who was used to money.

'Though I'd still adore him if he didn't have a bean,' Amanda assured Shelagh, re-draping her designer dress over her arm.

'So you're taking care of the whole thing?' Nick's expression as he gazed at Amanda was one of total admiration, Estelle observed. With only the faintest touch of astonishment thrown in.

'I told you ages ago I was looking for a new career path.' Amanda's dress rustled as she moved closer to Nick, the beads catching the light. 'This is exactly my kind of thing.'

A little bit of sparkle, Estelle thought, that's what she would call it.

Michael saw her as soon as he walked into the conservatory. She looked like she'd never looked before, in a green floaty number that almost took his breath away. And yet . . . And yet . . .

'Hi.' She came towards him. 'I thought you weren't coming.'

And yet his feelings for her seemed to have drifted away, Michael thought. What a pity. He sighed. What a pity they couldn't have just been friends. 'You look beautiful,' he said.

'Thanks.' Suzi smiled and a slow flush spread across her neck and up to her face. 'Michael, there's something –'

'I can't go on like –'

They both stopped.

'You first,' said Suzi.

'No, you,' he told her.

She took a deep breath. 'I'm so sorry, Michael. But it hasn't worked out between us,' she said.

'I know.'

'So . . .' she paused. 'You know?'

'I was going to say the same thing to you.' He took her hand and led her into a dance. 'So let's cut the crap and just say, sorry it's over, ta ta, have a nice life.'

'Oh.'

He could feel her tense shoulders under his palms. 'Don't worry, Suze,' he said.

She looked up at him, wide-eyed. 'I'm moving out of the cottage,' she told him. 'Maybe for good.'

He was surprised. 'What about Hester?'

'Hester?' At last she laughed, as if this had been held inside for a very long time. 'Hester? I was more worried about you.'

'I've got somewhere.' He told her about the room above the

pub, but not about the song, not about what had happened tonight. For one thing he didn't want to tempt fate – and he had to face it, nothing had happened – yet. And for another, he wanted to hold the thought of it to himself, for a while longer at least.

'So you're not angry?' Suzi asked him. 'Or upset?' She was clearly relieved. She looked as though the worries of the world had been lifted from her narrow shoulders.

'Not a bit.' Michael wanted her to feel as good as he felt. He had, after all, a lot to thank her for. Without Suzi, he would never have written that song.

Estelle swept out of the revolving doors of the clubhouse in much the same way as she had swept out of it once before and bumped into Nick Rossi. Only this time she bumped into a different someone. 'Oh,' she said. 'It's you.'

'You're not going already?'

Liam looked gorgeous. Estelle drank in the sight of him. He was wearing his dress suit with a red cravat she'd not seen before. His dark hair curled over the wing-collar – unruly, thick, fat curls she'd like to slip her fingers through.

She shrugged. 'It's not so hot in there. And I've got things on my mind.'

'Things?'

She wondered if Suzi had told him. Probably not, that would be why she had wanted him to be here tonight. It looked as if Suzi was doing all her telling in one go. 'Suzi's giving up the shop,' she said. 'She's becoming what you might call a sleeping partner.'

'Really?' But Liam didn't seem all that surprised. And he kept looking towards the doorway of the clubhouse as if he couldn't wait to get in there.

'Amanda's inside,' Estelle told him. It wasn't cold, but all of a sudden her fingers felt icy. She shivered.

'Oh.'

'With Nick Rossi.' Well, she couldn't have him going in there and making a fool of himself, now could she?

'Good,' said Liam. 'Don't you think he'd make an excellent chairman for the club? I mean, Erica's bound to resign now, don't you think?'

Good? Chairman for the club? 'Good?' She moved her black clutch bag from one arm to the other. Wished she'd brought a warm fleece instead of this ridiculous crocheted cardi thing. 'Wouldn't you want to be chairman?'

'Not really.' Liam looked decidedly shifty. 'I wouldn't have the time, would I? I've got far too much on.'

Something about his expression reminded Estelle of when he'd been haring out of the pub and she'd seen him from across the road. 'What happened between you and Lorraine?' she asked.

Liam shuddered. 'She scared me to death.'

Estelle smiled. Now that she could believe. She looked at him, all dressed up, and thought of how he'd appeared on the tennis court this afternoon in those crazy shorts and T-shirt. Probably the only items in his wardrobe that hadn't needed washing. And the way he'd been – all hot and bothered and stressed out. Gorgeous.

'Y'know, Estelle.' Liam took a step closer. 'If you ever thought that there was ever any chance, you know, ever, for me and you . . .' He faltered. 'I know there isn't and I've blown it but if there ever was . . .'

'Yes?'

'I'd leave Pridehaven like a shot,' he said.

'You would?' It was funny, Estelle reflected, that she had always thought Liam and Suzi so rooted here. Always resented the fact that he'd never leave.

He nodded. 'Like a shit, I mean, like a shot.'

They both smiled.

'I'm not leaving,' Estelle told him. 'I'm taking over the business. Paying only one salary will help out. But I'm branching away from antiques and into jewellery. No more Secrets . . . Now it's A Little Bit of Sparkle.'

'Does you good.'

'I hope so.' All the signs were that she could make a success of it this time around. She could only do her best.

Liam still looked shifty. 'You're not going to like this,' he began.

'What?' In that case, she wasn't sure she wanted to hear it.

'But I still want to do all the things with you that I've always wanted to do with you.'

She let out her breath. 'What sort of things?'

'Oh you know, get married, have kids maybe. Those sort of things.'

Estelle had thought she'd never hear that from him again. And the timing seemed particularly ironic, after the decision she'd just made to be a full-time businesswoman.

'We could choose a house together this time,' Liam said. 'I could see you as one of those women.' His eyes were dreamy, his smile for her alone.

'What women?'

'Oh, you know, juggling home and career, husband and children, nannies and cleaning ladies.' He grinned. 'I wonder if our kid would be good at tennis? Might be the next British Wimbledon champion, what d'you reckon?'

That it was never too late to feel safe enough, Estelle thought. Never too late. 'I've always fancied a house-husband myself,' she said, moving in closer. 'Especially one that's good with children. Like an ex-teacher maybe.' She could picture Liam in the role, and yes, it was a pretty appealing picture. Why shouldn't she feel safe at last? He was who he was, and she certainly wasn't her mother. 'So you certainly wouldn't have time for too many chairperson activities. Not for a while anyway.'

He stared at her. 'Is that a yes?'

'I think . . .' she smiled, 'it might well be.'

Suzi ran past Liam and Estelle, who were so wrapped up in each other on the steps that they didn't even see her. Geronimo! Success at last! She must remember, she thought, as she yanked open the door of the battered white van, to tell Michael that the flat above the shop was likely to be vacant in the very near future.

'You took your time,' said Josh Willis. But he looked at her frock in a way that told her he might want to take it off later.

'I always do,' she said, fastening her seat belt with a smart click.

'That's a fact.' Josh grinned his cat's grin. 'You've kept me waiting a lot longer than any other woman I've known.'

Suzi found herself for practically the first time in her life wanting to tease. 'How long would you have waited?' she asked him.

'Oh, maybe a year or two.'

'That all?' Suzi shifted over so she was nearer to him. She tucked her arm under his and snuggled into his shoulder. It felt like the right place to be. 'So are you pleased that I phoned to apologise for my terribly suspicious nature?' she murmured. It had been a rather revealing phone call after all. And it had led to something rather unexpected.

'Ecstatic.' He turned the key in the ignition and the van spurted unconvincingly into life. Suzi wondered if it would make it to Somerset. 'But then I knew you were trouble the first time I laid eyes on you,' he said.

'Yeah?' She leaned back just enough so that he could drive without obstruction, though she would far rather be on the other side of the handbrake.

'Yeah.' He accelerated and the van rumbled away from Chestnut Grove Tennis Club. Down the drive lined with the old horse-chestnut trees. Into the road beyond.

Suzi would miss it, but she knew it was in safe hands. And she'd come back to visit – to play tennis again, to sip a G & T in the tranquil conservatory overlooking Pridehaven.

'But I've always liked a challenge,' Josh said.

A challenge, hmm? 'You've asked me to move in with you,' Suzi said, wondering if he'd been joking when he'd said this. 'Without so much as an interview.'

'Yep.'

'Did you mean it?'

He didn't reply – just gave her a long look from those grey-green eyes. And the look seemed to say it all.

'It's a bit of a risk,' she said.

'Hmm.'

'A big step to take.'

'Hmm.'

She hesitated. 'But I s'pose we could see how it goes. This weekend. I mean.'

'We could, yeah.' He cast her another sidelong glance. But his hands stayed on the steering wheel.

'Organic farming certainly sounds like my kind of thing.' Suzi scrutinised him carefully with a sidelong glance whilst pretending to be checking the fuel gauge. 'I wanted a career change, so I appreciate you offering me the position.'

'My pleasure,' he said.

'I rather fancy working in the open air. And I've always wanted a bit more land to play with.' Or on, she thought.

'Mmm. I do love those wide open spaces,' he said, face deadpan. 'Don't you?'

'Mmm. Only thing is,' Suzi continued.

'Yeah?' He frowned.

'I think I should point out that you haven't even kissed me yet.'

'Haven't I?' He indicated and turned to the right, heading out of Pridehaven.

'Not properly. And I feel it's the sort of thing that will probably come with the job.'

'I won't argue with that.' He brought the van to a screeching halt half up on the pavement, and took her in his arms. 'No sooner said than done.'

Ten minutes later, Suzi emerged, out of breath and with a grin in her heart that didn't seem to want to go away.

Wow. It's never too late for a girl to find love, she thought. It was even kind of spooky, the way it lurked round the corner and jumped out at you when you were least expecting it. Maybe she was mad to be giving up her life in Pridehaven. But every instinct was urging her to jump. She'd been dithering on the romantic sidelines for far too long. But, 'Just one more thing . . .'

'Another?' He groaned.

'Do you like goats?'

And that was the kind of man he was. He didn't bat an eyelid. 'Love 'em to bits,' he said.